FOCUS ON MURDER

The diary read, "It is settled. I am going to kill him." And with those words begins as unusual and spectacular a mystery as anyone could ask for. Johnny Kendall, a photographer whose job has been squeezed out in a merger, sets up shop in a small state capital as a commercial photographer. He lands the job of taking pictures of corpses for the sheriff's office, and that is how he manages to be in on the ground floor of the attempted ax murder of Dr. Harry Rigmire in his weekend fishing lodge. Kendall's busy camera catches all the evidence both in the unsuccessful attempted murder and in the successful one which follows. Peopled with characters spicy and salty by turn, displaying real novelty in both plot and method of detection, *Focus on Murder* is equally interesting in human terms.

FOCUS
ON MURDER

By Dale Clark

WILDSIDE PRESS

Focus on Murder

Published by Wildside Press LLC
www.wildsidepress.com

FOCUS ON MURDER

DEATHDEALER'S DIARY

Friday, Oct. 17, '41

It's settled. I am going to kill him.
—Why set this down, in ribbon-inked
tracks across a white page, this
confession that <u>might</u> be found, that
might lead to arrest, trial, conviction,
and the sentence of death?
q Why?

I am trying to help the detective on
the case, that's it. The <u>great</u> detective,
the <u>only</u> one in possession of all the
clues, who <u>alone</u> can expose my hand in
the cutting of this night's piece of
cloth. I mean, of course, that detective
who will accompany me to the scene and
oversee Dr. Harry Rigmire's violent end.
q I mean myself, or my counter-self.
q For, if anyone will stop and think of

7

it, clearly, every adventurer outside the
Law must be, in his or her one person,
both the criminal and the policeman. The
criminal is the creator: all fire,
imagination, invention, audacity. The
criminal conceives the deed, perfects the
conception with patient artistry, and
provides the high energy requisite to its
accomplishment. <u>He</u> is the composer,
and the conductor. The policeman-within
is not even a collaborator; he is merely
the critic. And, like a good critic,
he must restrain his enthusiasm—he
will not applaud until the curtain is rung
down. He is ice, practicality, common
sense, and caution.

q "Fingerprints," he warns.

   "Elementary, my dear Holmes. I shall
wear gloves."

q "Then I've got you," says he. "Impressions of glove fabrics can be taken, you
know."

   "The gardener's gloves. Those rubber-
coated, black ones with the big cuffs."

q It is a game of chess we play.   Move
and move again, move and check—and
if _he_, with all the clues on his side,
can't mate me . . . then, who can?

But I must admit my sympathies are
against the fellow.   If I were prepon-
derantly a creature of ice, practicality,
common sense, and caution, it is obvious
that Dr. Rigmire might live to be a
hundred!   Which only means, naturally,
I have got to ensure the policeman-self
rather better than an even break.

I don't want him to overlook something,
some trifle that could be of significance
to a professional investigator later on.
q "That stupid sheriff?" I think.

"Don't fool yourself," says my detective.   "There'll be a damned good private
investigation.   You can count on the
family to see to it!"
q But his is the answering, the second
thought.

It always is.   Which is why I mustn't
hurry him, precisely because he _is_ slow.

(I encourage a methodical deliberation on
his part, in fact.)

q So I write this down.

   Not that I (the composer-conductor-
self) need guidance in my performance.
But simply to give the policeman-within
the opportunity to do his critical,
painstaking, laborious work.

I

It was Saturday night in Altamont, and on a downtown street corner Blind Bert was crying the bull-dog edition of the *Sunday Blade.* "Sunny poipee!" shouted the blind newsboy. "Getcha Sunny poipee!" People were leaving the big movie houses, the *Fox* and *Orpheum* and *Plaza,* and walking slowly past the big plate glass windows of the downtown department stores, *Stanley's* and the *Will Company* and *Rogers Bean.*

It was ten o'clock, and for the majority of the movie-goers Saturday night was just about over.

But on The Hill, where the great white floodlights bathed the dome of the State Capitol, Saturday night had not yet begun. In the right wing, angry grey-faced men bargained bitterly over the county relief bill; the legislative clock had been stopped, and for them it was still one minute before Friday's midnight.

In the left wing, in the offices of the Attorney-General, a Mr. Edward Thatcher sat before a desk littered with encyclopedias, history volumes, and American biographies. Mr. Thatcher was a small, se-cretive, studious clerk currently concerned with win-ning $25,000.00 in a patriotic cartoon contest. For him, the time lacked exactly two hours of that midnight before which his entry must be postmarked in the mails. Hearing footsteps in the corridor, the clerk hastily slid his cartoon booklet into a desk drawer. He picked up a letter instead.

A thick blue pencil line had been looped around the sendee's address, 12 Sussex Place, and around the signature, Jos. E. Hanlon.

"E.T.," the Attorney-General's secretary had jotted, "ans. this for W.W. per self."

To settle a bet, Jos. E. Hanlon wrote, please advise when Eastern, Pacific, etc., Times officially adopted.

The letter was Edward Thatcher's excuse for being in the office at this hour; Edward Thatcher did not have the necessary reference volumes in his own home; nor had he the authority to use freely the office library and the office light. Edward Thatcher was an underling, one whose days were spent in unearthing various odd, sundry and dusty fragments of fact and law for the more important underlings who briefed the Attorney-General's opinions.

He smiled secretively as he studied this letter; it was too transparent; he recognized the hand of a rival contestant. For the answer was the answer to cartoon 23 in the series of 50.

"Lazy dog," murmured Edward Thatcher. "And that's one of the easy ones—I wonder how he's making out with 49?"

At 12 Sussex Place, Mr. Jos. E. Hanlon was not making out with the 49th cartoon; "Cousin Joe," as they called him in the Rigmire household, had given up that contest at the halfway mark. Cousin Joe's progress through life had been a succession of abandoned contests; of shipwrecked financial ventures, of patentless and unpatentable inventions, of inconclusive amorous affairs. He had reduced himself to subsisting on the bounty of his relatives; to an existence devoted to solitaire games that never came out, crossword puzzles that never got finished, and small bets on horses that never, or almost never, won.

He was a handsome man. He had a handsome talent for borrowing money on his prospects, which prospects had recently been extinguished by his Uncle Walter's will. Cousin Joe bore his uncle's memory a grudge in consequence. And he had a talent for bearing grudges of a small, mean, vindictive nature. His quarrels, like all else in his life, were never finished.

Cousin Joe, at ten o'clock of this Saturday night, was concluding a game of Klondike.

"Five, ten, fifteen, twenty dollars," he counted his winnings. But the deck had cost fifty-two. He was out thirty, and a total of one hundred twelve for the evening.

He shuffled the cards.

Downstairs, Miss Madeleine Rigmire was speaking into the telephone.

"Yes," she said. "Right away. I'll get Dr. Sawyer and start right away. You'll stay there until we come, Dr. Dwyer?"

She looked frightened.

She replaced the phone in its cradle, then lifted it, and dialed hurriedly.

"Hello," she said. "Dr. Earl Sawyer, please." There was a pause. "He isn't?" Madeleine Rigmire said. "He didn't say?"

She put the phone down. She smoothed her hands along the sides of her hips. A clouding of disappointment was added to her frightened expression.

She thought of something.

She hurried from the entrance hallway to her father's study. There was another phone on Dr. Harry Rigmire's study desk, and beside it, a shiny black-bound book. She flicked at its pages with a wetted thumb.

She dialed with the finger of her right hand, with the finger of the left pressed down onto the page:

Carr, Geneva BL-2203

That phone rang and rang and rang. While she listened to its futile sound, Madeleine moved her right forefinger to a push button on the desk.

A servant appeared in the study doorway.

Madeleine Rigmire said, "Henry, tell Cousin Joe to come downstairs. Tell him to come right away. I'm going out, and I've got to see him, and I haven't a single instant to spare."

She gave up waiting for BL-2203 to answer. She ran out of the study, across the hall, into another room. She returned wearing a light grey coat over her tailored tweed ensemble, with a large natural-colored handbag

tucked under her arm. When Cousin Joe came down
the stairs, she was speaking into the hall telephone.

"I want to leave a message for Dr. Sawyer," she was
saying. "Tell him I've gone to Crestpeak. . . ."

It was Saturday night in Crestpeak; a bunch of the
farm boys were whooping it up in Mike Salol's saloon
at the lower end of Main Street. At the upper end, in
the American Legion hall, the Mountain Music Swing
Band dispensed intoxication of another sort. It was
10 P.M., and in the County Jail Sheriff Frank Ellsworth
was extinguishing all lights save the thirty watt bulbs
in the hallways.

A fitful sobbing reached the sheriff's ears; the voice
was that of old Hazy, christened Theodore Hazelle,
the town drunkard; Ellsworth was used to the sound,
and used to locking up old Hazy on Saturday nights.

The lights still burned brightly in the stores along
Main Street; gaunt-fingered women hesitated over the
percales, calicoes, muslins, and rayons; girls behind the
counter listened to their customers with one ear, and
with the other, to the Mountain Music Swing Band. The
drugstore soda fountains drove a thriving, sticky trade;
three men cobbled furiously in the basement shop under the Commercial Hotel; on the hotel steps Ed Hor-
ton, the Socialist carpenter, held forth on the subject
of international finance. Five blocks away, at an upstairs window, Wesley Clement—cashier of the Crestpeak State Bank—sat with a pair of opera glasses in
hand and waited for Miss Babette Hazelle to remove

her brassiere. Mr. Clement was disappointed. The glimpse of golden, nubile femininity vanished as Babette only proceeded to pull a dance frock down over her head. At arm's length, she carried a wisp of discarded dress out of her bedroom and out of the glasses' range.

She was going to the Legion Hall, the cashier knew. He would have liked to go himself. But he couldn't, of course. Not without his wife.

And anyway, he couldn't have been seen dancing with Babette Hazelle. No businessman in Crestpeak would even think of asking that Hazelle girl. . . .

Unless it was that new fellow, Kendall.

In the Photo Studio, Johnny Kendall was totaling the week's receipts. "$14.40," his pencil noted; from Miss James, the high school teacher who wrote "pieces" for the county paper.

Johnny Kendall was new in Crestpeak. His appearance proclaimed his newness; the mark of the metropolis was on him. His black, Indian-straight hair had been trimmed last by Joe, of the third chair in the St. Regis, in Altamont. It was a casual haircut, unlike the painful local barbering. Johnny Kendall's pale rose, cream figured shirt had not yet visited the Crestpeak Home Laundry; hence the collar, unlike every other soft collar on Main Street, was not the victim of excessive starch. His grey flannels had the look of being both expensive and informal; whereas the businessmen of Crestpeak, when they paid eighty-five dollars for a suit of clothes, did not seek an appearance which

would be inappropriate to Sunday morning services.
The flannels were, in fact, downright sporty.

Johnny Kendall was further marked by a certain
crispness of manner, a forward-forging air born of an
existence among traffic semaphores, crowded passenger
elevators, noon hour rushes in cafeterias, ninth inning
departures from baseball parks; the minute-by-minute
hurry to beat the light, catch the elevator, get to the
head of the line.

Johnny Kendall said, "$74.60, Pop. Of course, I'm not
going to get an order from Miss James every week, but
still things are picking up—picking up—"

Pop Capp denied this. "Things never pick up," Pop
Capp said. "They get picked up. To understand that,
my boy, is to understand the difference between success
and failure."

Pop Capp winked at the dog as he said this. Pop
was *not* new in Crestpeak; his appearance proclaimed
it; the mark of the village was on him. He had the
Saturday night look common to the Main Street businessman; even as the cashier and the sheriff, he had
been close-shaved for the occasion; the cashier, the
sheriff, Pop Capp, and all of the rest of them exuded
the same Saturday night aroma of lilac talc and bay
rum.

Pop was white-haired; he wore an improbable celluloid collar; his black suit was suitable for successive
service as Sunday-best, everyday-business, odd-jobs, and
finally as a duck-shooting costume. But the clue to his
personality was at his fingertips. His fingertips were

yellow. They testified to an old-fashioned faith in pyro developing solutions; they established him as one contemptuous of non-toxic, non-staining, fine-grain in-novations; they were fingers that had never toyed with candid cameras, ultra-rapid emulsions, nor scientifically calibrated instruments for the determination of light measurement.

Pop Capp was a Photographer of the Old School. And Johnny Kendall had known it from his first glance at Pop's fingertips.

Johnny Kendall said, "I don't know about being a success. But I think I can pick up enough here to beat the newspaper racket all hollow."

Miss James would have been shocked. But Johnny Kendall knew the newspaper racket, and not from pursuing a correspondence course in journalism. He had, as recently as a fortnight ago, been employed as a photographer on the *Altamont Herald*. It had been a good job, a suitable outlet for his energies, demanding both shrewdness and the use of his elbows. But the *Herald* had been absorbed by the *Blade,* and Johnny Kendall had not been absorbed with it.

He was the victim of a trend in journalism, the decay of the racket. The question of professional proficiency did not enter into it. Johnny Kendall was in fact a pretty fair camera; the *Blade* simply did not need his services, nor the services of a majority 'of the leg-men, rewrite men, ad solicitors, linotypers and pressmen from the *Herald*. The economy of amalgamation consisted, in large part, of terminating the *Herald* staff's connection with the payroll.

Johnny Kendall had not sought employment on another Altamont newspaper; there was no other; Altamont had become a one-paper town. Johnny had not sought employment elsewhere, either; he reasoned correctly that newspapers elsewhere were already overwhelmed with applications from discharged photographers, reporters, and rewrite men off other, foundered publications. That section of *Time* devoted to "Press" was, he observed, becoming a regular obituary column. There were simply too darned many papers folding, into the grave or into the arms of their rivals. He moved the purchase of a ship's bell to be installed in the Altamont Press Club. Like the one at Lloyd's. *Bong,* for the *Herald. Bong,* for the *San Diego Sun,* old Scripps' pet. *Bong,* for the *Minneapolis Journal* and *Bong* for the Chicago *Herald-Examiner. Bong, Bong, Bong.*

"I move," said one of those present, "we appoint Kendall custodian of the bell."

"No. Somebody else will have to do the rites by our knell," said Johnny Kendall. "The fact is, I've got my eye on a little business proposition upstate—"

The fact was, he had seen Pop Capp's portrait and photo-finishing business advertised for sale. He had driven up to Crestpeak to investigate the proposition. It proved to require only a modest outlay in cash; for Pop wanted to go on living in the rooms above the shop, and wanted to go on using the downstairs darkroom for purposes of his own, personal and non-commercial photography. In his own words, he "aimed to be underfoot a lot," and was willing to cut his price accordingly.

This, then, was the situation in Kendall's Photo Studio on Saturday night at 10 p.m.

"I don't know about success, either," said Pop Capp. "I'm speaking of a failure. I never picked up a thing in my life. Never wasted my time."

Johnny Kendall began toting up the bank deposit slip for Monday morning. "Don't you fall in that cracker barrel," he said, grinning.

"You know," said Pop placidly, "I ran this shop twenty-nine years, and I never added up at the end of the week. Or never went out after the business, either. I left the door open, and enough blew in."

He gestured with a pyro-stained hand:

"You know how I figure it, Johnny? People get married, and they come in for a wedding picture. Married people get kids, and they bring the kids in for baby pictures. The kids grow up, and you take the graduation picture. Then they get married, and so it goes. Until one day you look in the ground-glass and see the coffin *and* floral displays."

"Yeah. Biology. I got a book from the library once."

"I'm speaking of the business angle," Pop Capp said. "Some people you don't do business with at all, and some never pay you. But then, there's others that'll buy a dozen up to two dozen pictures on every one of those occasions. By and large, take it on the average, I figure a human being is worth just about twenty dollars to a photographer, from the cradle to the grave. Crestpeak's got four thousand population, and that's eighty thousand dollars."

"Spread out," Johnny Kendall said, "over a lifetime."

"Well, you can't hurry those things. Folks only move along so fast. They won't die any faster because you offer special rates on funerals," Pop Capp said. "A man can make a good, comfortable failure on eighty thousand dollars in a lifetime. Seems to me."

Johnny Kendall said, "You've got something on your mind. What is it?"

"Nothing much," Pop Capp said. "I guess maybe I'm bothered by that $74.60. Doesn't look to me like it can keep up. I'm trying to convey the idea that it isn't so important, Johnny."

Johnny Kendall said, "Well, I—" and stopped; the phone was ringing. He lifted the receiver. "Hello?" he said. "Yeah? Right away. You bet." He replaced the receiver and grinned at Pop Capp:

"Business is doing all right," he said. "That was the sheriff."

"Ellsworth? What does he want?"

"I asked him for a crack at the county business," Johnny Kendall said.

"At what?"

"Legal photography," Johnny Kendall said. "I offered to work with him. Go out on his cases, take pictures of the evidence—you know. Then, if the county wants to introduce the photographs in court, they buy them from me. I've an idea it might work up into a nice sideline for me."

Pop Capp sighed.

"What's the matter?" Johnny Kendall said.

Pop Capp said, "It's your business. It's your sideline. But I don't know if I like the sound of this."

The *Herald's* ex-photographer picked up his Speed Graphic case, lifted the plushlined lid, and checked his unexposed film holders. "Why not?"

"I think I'd let Frank Ellsworth attend to his own sheriffing," Pop said. "If he wants to take pictures, I'd do his developing for him. I don't think I'd carry it any farther than that."

"*Why* wouldn't you?"

"I don't know," Pop Capp said.

Johnny Kendall said, "You must have some reason. You think it'll make people sore at me? My pictures being used against them in court?"

"Not to amount to much. That class of people."

"Well, then?"

"I don't know," the old man said. "I just have a feeling you're making a mistake."

Johnny Kendall laughed. "You're old-fashioned. You have a feeling that any change is a mistake. You don't realize that this business can be bigger than family portraits, nickel postcard views, and Brownie snapshots."

An automobile horn sounded in the street. Johnny

Kendall picked up his camera case and ran to the door.

Pop Capp said, "I still think you're making a mistake," and worried a pyro-yellowed forefinger around the rim of his celluloid collar.

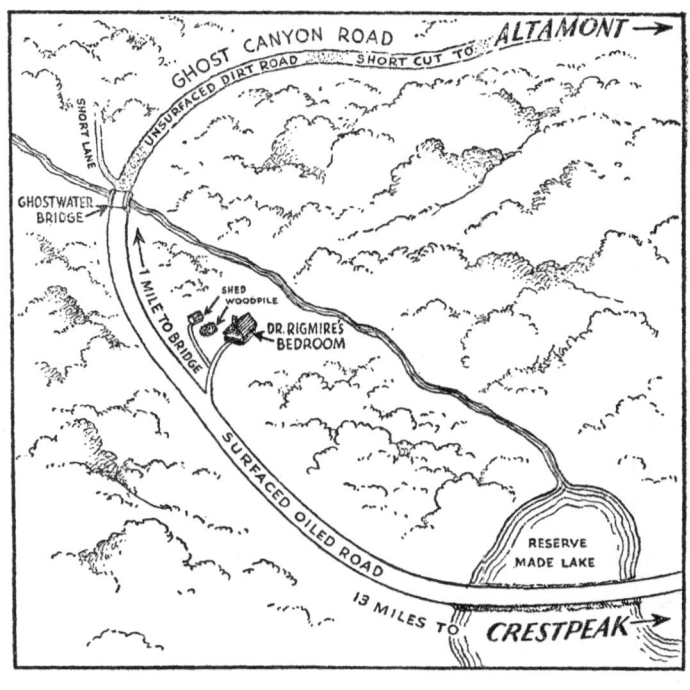

DEATHDEALER'S DIARY

Saturday a. m. Oct. 18, '41

The detective-mind has a fondness for
maps, plans, diagrams, sketches, and
enlarged photographs. One wonders why?
Owing perhaps to a lack of imagination?

At any rate, I don't propose to handicap my policeman-within in this respect.
He shan't be deprived of the tools of
his profession through any fault of mine.

And if he can solve this problem by
poring over its stage setting; why, then,
to it. . . .

The lodge (it is really a remodeled
farmhouse) stands at a quarter-mile
from the surfaced highway. (But it isn't
really a highway, either.) I have
heard this graded, country road was
oiled on the motion of a county commis-

sioner who had an interest in a projected
resort inn.   The surfacing extends only
to the Ghost Canyon bridge, a mile
beyond the Rigmire property.   (This was
to be the site of the inn, only that
project fell through for lack of financial
backing.)   By crossing the bridge and
following the extremely bad Ghost Canyon
road, one can eventually reach Stokesville.   But no one ever does so, certainly not at night.   I should say that
traffic passing the Rigmire lodge is
practically non-existent once the trout
season has closed.

Besides, a passing machine won't matter
in the least.   I am merely calling attention to the isolation of the scene.   I
have called the lodge a remodeled farmhouse, but of course it has been
years since anyone has attempted to **wring**
a livelihood from those abrupt and
flinty acres.   The nearest cultivated
field is a good three miles down the valley.   The upper valley is timber and

brush, rock and red soil; picturesque
enough, but scarcely fit to be grazed.
Or at least, not worth the fencing.
A few cattle do find pasturage there.
Somebody in Crestpeak—I don't know who
—has placed a colony of beehives along
the stream, to the annoyance of the
fishermen. But he visits the hives only
once a month, if that often. And the
cattle receive rather less attention
than that.

It would be God-forsaken but for the
summer cabin folk.

There are a dozen or fifteen cabins in
the upper valley, when before the road
got improved there were none. The mountain nights are bracingly cool; and the
very things which make the locale
unattractive to the natives—the stubborn
timber, the steep and boulder-strewn
slopes, and the solitude—are highly
prized by the city week-ender. The
week-ender gets the illusion of "roughing
it," of "getting away from it all."

It was the trout stream, though, which induced Dr. Harry Rigmire to fix on this retreat for <u>his</u> week-ends. Not that our medical friend really enjoys fishing! What he cares about, of course, is the affectation of hearty and bluff masculinity. He has his "masculine manner" just as he has a bedside one—and for identical, professional reasons. He wants to be thought a thoroughly rugged, gruff, plain-speaking, two-fisted fellow.

He isn't, at all.

He is a timid, vacuous, vacillating old maid. His professional position he owes to personal charm plus a fortunate marriage. He is a family doctor —to the best families. If the diagnosis suggests any difficulty in the treatment, the good doctor loses no time in referring his patient to a specialist. (He probably splits many a fat fee, does Dr. Harry Rigmire.)

Besides, he has a competent assistant in his employ.

How does he get away with it?

He has made a career of getting away
with it, is how. His patients, being
wealthy, have pecuniary standards; and
our medical friend flaunts the pecuniary
evidences of success. He lives in a
mansion (his wife's) and entertains
royally therein. When entertained elsewhere, he arrives in a Packard (not a
little Packard.) His office resembles
a movie set; its reception chamber
bristles with antique "pieces," and the
examining rooms with modernistic scientific apparatus which he would probably
be hard pressed even to name. He has
the leisure to cultivate the acquaintance
of his fellow medicos, and thereby
secure his election to posts of honor
in their various professional organizations. He lends his name to the
letterhead of charitable endeavors. His
professional fees are terrific.

He makes it easy for his patients to
forget that either there was never

anything seriously wrong with them, or
else that he did not treat the ailment.

But the great thing is his manner.
And I do not mean his bedside manner—
for of what use is that, until you have
got yourself summoned to the victim's
bedside?

I mean his every-day manner; the solid
masculinity he assumes, to conceal his
secret timidity and want of confidence.
The blunt old sinner! he wants you to
think. The old-fashioned medico—plainly
capable of traveling horseback through
forty miles of blizzard to yank an
appendix by kerosene lamplight on a
kitchen table! The iron Doc!

Hence, his mighty slaughter of wild
duck and trout.

Hence the mountain cabin, remodeled
—he will give you to understand—
mostly with his own hands.

Hence, the week-ends. When, between
the wholesome intervals of wood-chopping

and dish-washing, he toils over his
memoirs. . . .

Those famous week-ends!

They are more than a pose, of course.
He doesn't play out the uncomfortable
pose merely to impress his audience.
An equal virtue of these week-ends is
that they permit him to shift the burden
of his practice onto his assistant's
shoulders—without giving up the senior's
financial reward.

Our medico is a lazy man. And worse,
a cowardly one. Every moment he can take
from the practice reduces by so much
the possibility that Dr. Harry Rigmire
might, in an emergency, have to make a
decision. . . .

How he hates responsibility! How he
loves to consult—and the more consultees,
the better, in relieving him of the
necessity of deciding!

There's the trouble.

For frankly, if he were only a lazy,
incompetent, pretentious fraud—why, I

shouldn't mind. It is his damnable trick
of <u>consulting,</u> of running to authority
with his problems. He can't keep his
mouth shut, that's it. He's dangerous,
not because of his strength—he hasn't
any—but through his weakness.

His fatal weakness, in fact.

He compels me to take heroic measures.
If he were only a <u>man</u>—if he only had
the courage and integrity to respect
his own judgment—! But, no, he's not
that sort. He's the sort who can be
dealt with in only the one, firm,
final way.

"Don't you agree?" say I.

It is beyond the policeman-within's
sphere, this question. He is neither
judge nor advocate, but detective; and
it is not in the detective's province
to determine whether or no the deed
be <u>justified.</u> My question poses problems of law, of ethics, of morality.
He is concerned only with the fact, and
whether the fact can be apprehended.

If the fact can be gotten at, detective
intelligence has done its job; the
question of <u>justification</u> is up to the jury.

I withdraw the question; I don't want
to confuse the policeman-within, distract
him from the facts.

"Never mind," say I. "I'll get on
with it."

II

Johnny Kendall's thought—less a thought than
a familiar sensation—was, *like old times,* as he sprang
from the curb into the rear seat of the sheriff's Buick
sedan.

Not that his newspaper career had been a succession
of breathless adventures. The succession had run to
routine assignments, indeed. But the routine was subject to interruption. You never knew—the next hour
might bring wreck or riot or some other form of violent catastrophe.

Like old times, he sensed, thrusting his camera case
into the corner of the seat and wedging an elbow
against it as Deputy Ed Bundy shot the car ahead.

"What gives?" he asked.

He did not know—Frank Ellsworth had not said on
the phone—what violence or catastrophe was in store
now.

The sheriff, beside his deputy, braced himself as Ed
Bundy whirled the car around the corner at the foot of
Main Street. He said, "Dang it, Ed, you'll put us in
the ditch."

And then he turned his head to explain:

"Doc Dwyer called me. Some woman was out to

Rigmire's place, and took an axe to Rigmire. So Doc says."

"*Killed* him?"

"I don't know. I don't know if he'll live or not," Ellsworth said. "He's cut pretty bad. I couldn't say just how bad."

The Buick rushed past the last scattering houses. Its headbeam raked the oiled, country road. Sheriff Ellsworth and his deputy were large silhouettes between Johnny Kendall and the windshield.

Frank Ellsworth made the larger silhouette. The sheriff was, in fact, an impressively big man. He was even an impressive man.

The bulk of him moved with a slowness that seemed less ponderous than deliberate; his bulk conveyed the suggestion of enormous reserves of physical strength.

Johnny Kendall asked, "Who's the woman?"

The sheriff said, "I don't know. She got away before Dwyer got out there."

He paused.

"She's gone, so it's hard to tell who she was," he said.

There was another, longer pause. The car increased its speed.

Frank Ellsworth said, "Maybe you know Rigmire. He's from Altamont. He's a doctor there, from what I hear."

Johnny Kendall said, "I know of a Dr. Rigmire in Altamont. Dr. Harry Rigmire."

Ed Bundy said, "That's the guy. He comes out from the city every so-often. He's quite a fisherman."

Johnny Kendall puckered his lips, whistled.

"What a story!" he said. The whistle paid a news-paperman's tribute to the event. He estimated the proportions of the story professionally, and said, "This is front page. Dr. Harry Rigmire's a pretty prominent guy—Betterment League President—things like that."

The sheriff considered this.

"No wonder Doc Dwyer got excited," he said. "Dwyer would probably know who he was, all right. They both being doctors."

The car swept around a curve. The headlights showed the clumped grey-green rushes and the dark glimmer of Game Reserve water.

Frank Ellsworth clung to the door handle.

"Yi, damn it, Ed," he said, "you better watch your driving here."

Ed Bundy drove at exactly the same reckless pace as before.

"You don't need to kill us," the sheriff said. "Maybe it's a false alarm. Maybe Doc Dwyer kind of exaggerated. Being excited."

"Maybe he was thinking about the bill he's going to send in," Ed Bundy said, laughing.

"No. Doctors don't charge each other."

Ellsworth reflected.

"Dwyer wouldn't send another doctor a bill," he said. This time with increased emphasis. "It's just because Rigmire's a doctor, too—made him excited—so he'd make it out worse than it probably is."

You said that before, Johnny Kendall thought. The

sheriff was a repetitious man; he wondered why. That trick of saying everything twice, and saying it louder the second time, jarred upon Johnny Kendall.

"He sounds," Johnny thought, "as if he's afraid no one listened to him the first time."

He was a practical psychologist—in the sense that a newspaper photographer *must* be a psychologist. He had learned, for professional purposes, to "size up" a stranger at a glance, a greeting, a gesture.

Johnny Kendall had to be able to do this; every press photographer has to do it. For of course not every person wishes to be the subject of a newspaper half-tone.

Johnny Kendall knew when to say, "Please, this is my job. Give me a break, won't you?" and he knew when to say, "Listen, your mug's going in the paper whether *you* like it or not. You can have a lousy candid pix, or you can give yourself a break and pose pretty." He had a dozen different approaches; it all depended on the individual, and how he "sized up" the individual on the spur of the moment.

He was sizing up the sheriff now.

"He sounds," Johnny Kendall thought, "like an inferiority complex walking around behind a badge."

Which was a snap judgment. It might explain Frank Ellsworth, or it might be extremely unfair to him.

While he wondered, the Buick had raced across the causeway dividing the Game Reserve. The road now climbed sharply upward. Patches of timber alternated with boulder-strewn, bare slopes. The mailboxes became fewer along the shoulder of the highway.

At length Ed Bundy braked the machine into a sharp turn off the road. The Buick bounced into a drop which lifted the three men from the seat cushions; and began climbing again—this time up a quarter-mile stretch of bare, red earth lane.

The house in front of which they stopped was, to external appearances, the ordinary oblong box of white painted, frame farmhouse.

Johnny Kendall stared at another machine parked on the other side of the yard.

"That's Doc Dwyer's Chevvie," Ed Bundy said.

"I wonder why he left it there," Johnny Kendall said. For the Chevrolet stood thirty or forty yards from the house.

The sheriff said, "It's just Doc's car," and went up the porch steps. Now—as Doc Dwyer opened the door —Johnny Kendall gained a sharply different impression of the place.

Its interior was that of a luxuriously "primitive" resort cabin. It had the pegged plank floor, the knotted pine paneled walls, and the native stone fireplace; the Navajo floor coverings, rustic chairs, and sporting prints; the deer's head, the preserved pike, and the stuffed pheasant. It looked like a movie set.

Frank Ellsworth asked, "Well, Doc?" in a constrained, sickroom voice.

The physician who faced them was a thin, grey complexioned, grey moustached country practitioner.

His suit, too, was grey; and his person smelled of disinfectant, of cigars, of lilac talc and bay rum.

He said, "Oh, it's under control now," but his voice wasn't. His voice had an uncertain note. Dr. Dwyer looked uncertain, and apprehensive.

"You understand," Dr. Dwyer said, "things aren't too favorable. He's suffering from shock and loss of blood. I want to make it as easy for him as I can."

This was not the brisk and dapper Dwyer who proceeded, at nine in the morning, from the postoffice past Johnny Kendall's Photo Studio to his office in the State Bank building.

"I can give you the general picture," said the anxious physician. "So you can cut it short when you talk to Dr. Rigmire."

"Yi, dang it, I don't want to make it any harder for him," the sheriff said. He looked around for a chair; his deputy sat down, too; Johnny Kendall moved over and braced a shoulder against the stone mantel.

Dwyer chafed the palms of his thin, grey hands. "The first *I* knew of it was when the woman phoned me."

"Yeah. What'd she say?"

"She said there'd been an accident here, that Dr. Rigmire was bleeding to death, and for me to hurry. Those weren't her exact words. I wouldn't be able to quote her word for word," the Crestpeak physician said. "I was interested in the gist of it, not the identical words she used."

Frank Ellsworth nodded, and Dwyer said:

"I did what any physician would have done under the circumstances. That is, I tried to tell her how to stop the bleeding. *She* said she couldn't, she'd strangle him."

"On account of it being his head," the sheriff said. "She couldn't put a tourniquet around his neck."

"She wouldn't have to. I tried to question her about the wound—the bleeding could be checked by pressing the fingers to the proper arteries—but I was wasting my time, talking. According to her description, Rigmire's entire face and head was flowing blood."

Ellsworth said, "Women are scary that way. A lot of women."

"Yes," Dr. Dwyer said. "She was obviously too frightened to take the proper steps. There was nothing I could do except get out here myself, and as quickly as possible. I timed it—from my front door into the yard here, in eleven minutes on the dot."

"You drove like a bat out of hell," Ed Bundy said.

"Well," the physician nudged his moustache with a bent forefinger, "I did. I always have claimed they ought to teach auto racing in medical schools. Fellow that can't drive a mile a minute over mountain roads shouldn't be licensed for a country practice."

"You done better than a mile a minute. Fourteen miles in eleven minutes," Ed Bundy said.

"Thirteen miles. It's fourteen to the bridge. I remember when they let the contract to oil this road."

The deputy observed that was driving, anyway.

There was a pause. Johnny Kendall turned and

looked at the titles along the bookshelves flanking the fireplace. The selection ran wholly to medical tomes and outdoor books. Tunhill on *Cardiac Diagnosis* rubbed shoulders with an ancient *Nautical Almanac;* Gregg's *Spine* neighbored *Twenty Years Among the Trout.*

"I'm a hard driver," Dwyer said. "You know, I've put thirty-three thousand miles on that Chevvie this year?"

Johnny Kendall took two steps to the rustic table; peered down at the typewriter and book there. The typewriter was a Royal portable; the book, Larue's *Diseases of the Skin,* revised. A slip of brown paper showed cornerwise among its pages. Johnny opened the volume. The brown slip said:

TO THE LITERARY EDITOR:

This book will be published

Oct 27 1941

Reviews should not appear before.

A clipping is requested.

Price: $7.50

THE GARANT PRESS
New York

The sheet of white paper in the portable said:

"This is the standard treatise on the subject, brought up to date, and copiously illustrated with color photographs which supplant the earlier and less faithful plates. Dr. Larue's revised edition will be welcomed by the profession. . . ."

Dwyer's voice resumed, "Well, anyway, it was just a quarter past nine when I started," and Johnny Kendall swung around. "When I got here," the physician continued, "the house was dark. The only light in the place was out in the yard. It looked like somebody standing there, pointing a flashlight at the ground. Then, when I jumped out of the car, I saw different. The flashlight was stuck into the woodpile, aimed so it threw the light onto Dr. Rigmire. He was lying on the ground there."

"Yi, now, he was?"

Dwyer said, "Lying there alone, for the woman had disappeared completely. But she'd propped his head on a chunk of wood, and she'd dragged a Navajo rug —really a blanket—from the lodge and covered him with that."

"She did that, huh?"

"I made an immediate examination," Dwyer said. "The axe was dropped right there on the ground beside him. He'd been struck on the left side of the head, above the ear—and down—through the ear itself, just about cutting half of the ear off. Dr. Rigmire was coming around, that is, regaining consciousness. He mumbled something about his arm. I threw off the Indian blanket, and I found then his right hand was deeply cut across the base of the thumb. The woman tried to apply a tourniquet to his wrist; she found some cord in the lodge, I suppose, and tied that onto his wrist." He shook his head. "Cord, you know, was the worst thing she could have used."

"His *right* hand and his *left* ear," Frank Ellsworth said. "That's a hell of a combination, ain't it?"

"No," Dwyer said, "it's natural. It's the way a man would try to save himself. Suppose that *you* have an axe in your hands, and that you step up to me—what'd I do? I'd throw up my arms to save myself. Like this—"

Dr. Dwyer ducked his head away from the sheriff, brought up both arms; his left elbow now pointed at Ellsworth, with his left hand in front of his face; the right arm crossed the left, so that the doctor's head was almost hidden in the crook of the right elbow. The right hand, palm outward, did in fact shield his left ear.

He said, "You see, Frank. I'd dodge like this; just what he did. And a good thing. He maybe saved his life, blocking the blow partly with his hand."

"You ain't worried about his life, then?" the sheriff asked. "You figure he'll pull through?"

"Well, it's a little early to tell . . ."

"Dang it, you mean you can't tell whether he's dying or not?" Ellsworth asked.

Dwyer's thin face flushed.

"I've seen worse," he said. "Dr. Rigmire was able to get into the house with my assistance. I've seen a farmer kicked in the head by a horse, lying unconscious in the field for half a day, and that man got well. But still, a head injury like this *might* result *very* seriously. It's too early to tell the extent of the complications that might set in."

He moistened his lips.

"What I did, Frank, I notified the family, long-distance. His wife wasn't home, but I spoke to his daughter. From the way she talked, I expect she'll be out here tonight with a whole flock of specialists."

An inflection in the physician's voice brought a sharpened glance from Johnny Kendall. It was at this moment that he surmised the nature of Doc Dwyer's anxiety.

"And of course, that's right. Dr. Rigmire is entitled to the best," said the Crestpeak practitioner quickly. "That's why I want to keep him quiet until the family arrives. Until the specialists have a look at him and decide whether they want to move him to the hospital here—or take him to the city—or what. . . ."

Yes, thought Johnny Kendall, it explained Dwyer's apprehension. *His* handling of the patient was bound to be reviewed by the city specialists. That circumstance gnawed in Doc Dwyer's mind. The country doctor felt himself, in a professional way, on trial before his superiors.

Doc Dwyer said, "The woman's identity and her motive for the attack are a complete mystery to Dr. Rigmire. It preys on his mind. I don't like to have a lot of questions asked—it'll only excite him, Frank, and not do any good."

The sheriff said, "Huh." Then he said, "Hah, hum." Finally he said, "I guess I better take his statement. Just to make it official. It'd be more legal if I heard it from him, I guess."

Dr. Dwyer led the way, reluctantly.

DEATHDEALER'S DIARY

The policeman-within has an idea.

"There's no alibi," says he.

Alibi?

"Yes," says he. "Where were you on the night of the crime?"

On the night of the crime, obviously, at the scene of my crime.

"You can't admit that," says he. "You ought to think of something to tell the police—"

I object to this on principle. . . .

"That," I say, "would be playing the game according to your rules. It's your gambit, my dear fellow, and I refuse it."

The policeman-within expresses his disappointment. And very rightly, too.

For an alibi (no matter if it is a sound one, which mine couldn't possibly be) offers the police investigator something

into which he may sink his teeth. It
gives him occupation, persons to inter-
view, time-tables to check, facts to worry
and nag into some sort of perspective.
What perspective doesn't matter. The
point, that he is getting nowhere, means
absolutely nothing to a cop. He is happy
to be just sniffing over the trail, any
trail. If you will provide him with
alibis enough, and an occasional false
clue, the fellow will go on sniffing for
months.

What kind of crime do the authorities
detest? The "mystery" replete with
contradictory evidence, the comings and
goings of a dozen suspects, the bric-
a-brac and claptrap of the fiction tale?

By no means!

The police adore that sort of thing! In
the first place, being essentially animal-
istic and muscular types, they delight in
incessant activity. They want "action."
How important they feel, hurtling from
scene to scene in their siren-screaming

official car! How masterful, dragging
this and that poor devil to Headquarters
for questioning!

Besides, they love publicity. Whoever
heard of policedom abandoning a case so
long as they could dredge from it some
preposterous tidbit for the press?

And the press loves mystery, too. Let
the supply of tidbits be forthcoming, and
the newspapers will headline the affair
until the public is worked up into a
lathering hysteria. Honest men become
self-appointed sleuths, not to speak of
the unfailing cranks. The authorities are
deluged with "tips" which must, of course,
be run to earth.

Hence, fresh detectives and investiga-
tors and deputies are assigned to the
hunt. The district attorney takes notice,
and sends his staff to the chase. Now it
is the turn of the so-called public
spirited busy-bodies to post a reward. It
becomes a high carnival of cops, reward-

hunting private sleuths, headline hungry
reporters, and sniveling stool pigeons.
If an arrest is made, that only encourages
shystering, publicity-seeking attorneys
to leap bellowing into the fray. Every
angle must be sifted, aired, pawed by
a dozen hands. The end result being, no
least detail of the victim's affairs
escapes scrutiny.

That is what you get for killing a man
"cleverly."

But what of ordinary, run of the mill,
"stupid" murder? The sort of crime which
hardly rates a paragraph in a first class
metropolitan daily? A citizen, for example, is found in an alley, done to death
with a brick prized from the alley paving.
His pockets are turned inside out, his
watch and wallet lifted. What happens in
such a case?

As for mystery, there is none. The
victim had been about to open his garage
door, let us say. Well, then, it is
obviously the work of a garage bandit.

(Confronted with dual crimes—theft and
murder, sexual assault and murder—police
mentality invariably attributes the
greater to the less. The citizen resisted, and the thug struck too hard, is
all.)

There is a routine, vain effort to
obtain fingerprints from the brick. That
failing, the officers content themselves
with the hope that the criminal will seek
to pawn his loot. Or that some tramp,
vagrant, or footpad, eventually picked up
and subjected to a third degree beating,
will blurt out a confession. For the
rest, nothing is done. There is nothing
to do. And policemen are quickly bored by
staring at blank walls.

I don't say that such cases are never
solved—when the criminal is fool enough
to put the stolen watch in pawn, or
drunkenly brags of his exploit within
hearing of an informer.

I wonder, though, how many dozens of

such "stupid" affairs remain unsolved on the police blotters of the land?

Among which, surely, a few weren't stupid at all!

I ask myself, why should an intelligent mind go to the lengths of fabricating an elaborate and precarious alibi? Why adventure a forged note in order to construct the semblance of suicide? Or stage implausible accidents in bathtubs and at traffic intersections?

The answer is, intelligent minds don't.

Nor do they devise infernal machines, distill subtle poisons, obtain firearms through false addresses, pose problems of locked chambers, and generally attempt the novel and unheard-of.

Much less will an intelligent mind waste energy with butchering, burning, burying, and otherwise conjuring away the physical being of its attentions.

I am aware that some of the most famous Murderers have resorted to one and another of these stratagems. But does not their

fame (since they were found out and <u>known</u>)
prove them men of minor talent? And
minor talent is always rococo and decadent
—little men love decoration and elabora-
tion, since they lack the bold flight of
fancy to envision pure and sweeping forms.

Murder, I say, is a Fine Art. And at
its Finest, is classic in its simplicity.

III

Dr. Harry Rigmire's head wore a turban of white bandage. The turban slanted rakishly, covering the left ear and the left eye. It gave him a falsely jovial look; in fact, the man was in obvious pain.

Dr. Rigmire's hand wore a white bandage, too. The remainder of his person made a large mound under the bed covers. He was at a disadvantage seen thus; he lay there like a fallen oak, cut down in the prime of life. But the prime of life varies among men, being one thing with respect to pugilists and baseball players, and another with judges and college presidents. Dr. Rigmire's was the prime of professional life; the prime of a vigorous, well-fleshed, self-assured fifty.

Dwyer said, "Doctor, this is our county sheriff."

Dr. Harry Rigmire opened his right, blue eye at the company. "Which one of them?" he asked.

"Me," said Frank Ellsworth.

"If you'll tell him in a few, brief words what happened," Dwyer said.

Dr. Rigmire ignored the suggestion. "Any luck, sheriff?" he asked.

"Well," said Ellsworth.

Dr. Rigmire lifted his bandaged right hand, grimaced, and made the gesture with his left hand instead. . . .

"I want that woman found," he said. "You've notified the Highway Patrol, have you?"

The sheriff said, "They'd have to have some description of her to go on. What kind of car she's driving. I was hoping you could help us out a little there."

Dr. Rigmire breathed heavily. The mound of bed cover lifted and sank.

"Great God, sheriff!" he said. "I can't describe her. She jumped at me out of the dark, from behind the woodpile."

"You saw her do that," the sheriff said. "You can describe her that much."

"Yes," said Dr. Rigmire, "I can tell you that she wore a dress. It might have been a black dress, or a red one, or blue. It was of some dark color, not white or light."

"Bareheaded? Wearing a hat?"

The Altamont physician drew down his right eyebrow.

"I'm not sure," he said. "She had either dark hair, or a beret, or a hood of some sort. You understand the whole thing happened in an instant, and when it happened, so far as I consciously watched anything I watched the axe."

"Would you know her face, if you saw it again?"

Dr. Rigmire said, "I didn't see her face. I was looking for the axe at the time. I heard the rustle of her dress. If I hadn't heard that, she'd have caught me from behind."

His left hand gestured:

"I turned, partly. In time to catch a glimpse of her, swinging that axe. I have the impression, now that you ask, that her arms were swung up in such a way as to hide her face. You understand, I didn't have the flashlight pointed at her at all. I threw up my hands to break the blow, and that was the end of it. Until I found Dr. Dwyer working over me."

Dr. Rigmire's lips worked.

"I can't account for it," he said. "I know of no one who bears a grudge against me. Certainly no one who'd try to brain me with an axe."

Frank Ellsworth said, "It's a thing. It sure as hell is."

"You've heard his statement, Frank," said Dr. Dwyer. "There isn't anything else you need to ask him, is there?"

"I guess not. I guess not."

Dr. Harry Rigmire said, "I don't want you to leave any stone unturned, sheriff."

"A couple of things occur to me," Johnny Kendall said. "I don't know if they amount to much."

Dwyer's hand fell on Johnny Kendall's sleeve. "We mustn't excite him," he said. "Later. Tomorrow, maybe."

Dr. Rigmire stirred; the bed sighed. "No. No, let's get to the bottom of it."

"I wondered," Johnny said, "what time you went out to the woodpile."

"It was after nine. Five or ten minutes after, possibly."

"And did you turn out the lights when you left the house?"

A look of surprise tightened upon Dr. Rigmire's pale face.

"No," he said. "I didn't. I wonder why *she* did that."

Doc Dwyer said, "You mustn't worry about it. That's the sheriff's job. Your job is to rest and recover from this experience."

He shoo'ed Johnny Kendall, Bundy, and Ellsworth from the room.

"I want him to rest," Dwyer said firmly. "He shouldn't be bothered with details like that."

"Yeah," said the sheriff. "Well, we'll go take a look around the woodpile. I don't see what else we can do. Just look around."

They crossed the yard, the sheriff pausing to get a flashlight from the Buick.

Johnny Kendall removed his camera from its case. A flashbulb winked as he snapped a picture of the Navajo blanket. He used several bulbs, photographing the blanket from different angles.

"He sure lost plenty of blood," said Ed Bundy.

Frank Ellsworth did not seem particularly interested in the bloodstained blanket, axe, and chips carpeting the ground around the woodpile. He trudged about the yard, playing the flashbeam over the dry, bare earth.

"Damn it all, a woman behind the woodpile," said the sheriff. "Who ever heard the like?"

He wandered to the door of a shed, opened the door, played the flashlight over the tan sedan inside. He came back, searching the bare, grassless yard.

"Look here, Ed," he said. "You too, Kendall. Maybe you could get a picture of this."

The sheriff squatted, pointing.

Ed Bundy and Johnny Kendall came over.

"I don't know," Johnny said. "It'd be hard to get much of a picture of oil against the ground. No contrast."

"Well, we saw it. We can remember that," Frank Ellsworth said. "There was a car standing right here tonight. Not so very long ago. Or that oil'd've soaked into the ground."

"I'll take a crack at it," Johnny Kendall said. He stepped to his camera case and returned with a small metal tripod. "I'll make it a double-extension close-up," he said.

Ed Bundy said, "How'd you figure, Frank?"

"To tell you the truth," the sheriff said, "I was only hoping I'd run onto some tire tracks that his car or Dwyer's didn't make. I like this better. It looks pretty positive to me."

Johnny Kendall ran out the legs of the tripod. The sheriff said, "How the hell could that woman drive up here in a car, and Rigmire not hear her?"

"If he was writing a book review," Johnny Kendall said, "he might have been absorbed in that."

"I don't think so. And anyway, dang it! How could he come out here with a flashlight and not see a car standing here, forty feet from the woodpile?"

"You think," Ed Bundy ventured, "he knew she was here?"

"Hell, yes, he knew it. He just ain't telling. Boys, you both know she couldn't come chugging in here with a car and park it under his nose, and Rigmire not know something about it."

There was a silence.

"Hell," the sheriff said, "of course he ain't telling. He's a married man. He's got a family. He isn't going to admit he had a woman calling on him here tonight. He has to say he didn't know she was here."

Johnny Kendall made adjustments of his camera. "Put your flashlight there. I want to focus on it."

Ellsworth complied. "I don't figure he went out after wood at all. He followed this woman out to the car—if he'd tell the truth about it. There was some trouble or other, and she grabbed the axe. I don't put any stock in that woodpile story, boys."

He shook his head.

"I don't know," he said, "and Rigmire ain't telling. It looks to me as if he maybe made a grab for her. She had something he wanted, and she wasn't going to give it up without a fight. I expect they got to chasing around the woodpile, and she grabbed the axe—the first thing she could lay her hands on."

"Take it away," Johnny Kendall said.

The sheriff sighed, "He won't admit it. But that

woman was right in the house with him tonight. Why, of course she was."

The flashbulb winked. Johnny Kendall replaced the slide.

"She was in the house long enough to phone and to turn out the lights," he said. "She might have left fingerprints."

Frank Ellsworth said, "Well, yes. Only I ain't equipped to do fingerprint work. I'd have to hire a man out from Altamont to do that kind of a job. I don't know if I should spend the county's money, not if Rigmire isn't interested in prosecuting the case."

Then he said:

"I'd be wasting the county's money, looks like. Fingerprints aren't conclusive evidence, anyway. They'd show maybe she was here sometime in the last two, three days. But they wouldn't stand up, not against Rigmire's word. If he wants to stick to that story he's telling, and I guess he does. Being a married man, I guess he'll stick to it until hell freezes over."

Johnny Kendall looked at the sheriff. "What are you going to do about it?"

"I don't think Doc Rigmire wants me to do much. Not that I can see."

"But," said Johnny Kendall, "it's a crime against the State, isn't it? Assault with a deadly weapon?"

The sheriff said:

"Well, sure. Look at it like that. Only the State wasn't here, and Rigmire was. Suppose I had this woman in court, whoever she is? He'd just get up and swear I got the wrong one—that the real one was older and fatter or different in some damned way."

He sighed.

"Yi, dang it," he said, "you can't get a conviction out of a case where your only witness is bound and determined to shield the guilty party."

Johnny Kendall agreed he saw the point. He said, "If Rigmire is lying, and if her car dripped this oil."

"Sure it was her car. How else did she get here, and get away?" the sheriff asked. "God Almighty, you don't stand there and say you believe that story about a woman behind the woodpile? If she didn't drive here, she must have sneaked here on foot. And where does that get you? If you figure that way, you've got to figure she came here on purpose to use the axe on him. That don't make sense to me. A woman doesn't come sneaking around, hitting a man a lick with an axe, and then go running to call him a doctor, does she?"

He said this over again. He said:

"Why would a woman hide behind the woodpile? Why would she jump out behind him with an axe? You believe that, and you've got to figure she meant to kill him. But she didn't. She ran and called a doctor instead. God Almighty, no, I can't see the sense to it."

Johnny Kendall said it didn't make sense to him, either.

"Still, if I were you, I'd take that axe along. You could mail it to the Identification Bureau lab in Altamont. In case her prints are on it."

"Well, yes," the sheriff assented, "you better put the axe in the car, Ed. We'll send it in and see. But Doc Rigmire knows who that woman is. Sure, he does."

And Frank Ellsworth shook his head.

"We won't get anywhere with this kind of a deal," he said. "Unless something turns up, we won't."

"Want the blanket in the car, too?" asked Bundy.

"No. There couldn't be any fingerprints on a thing like that. Damn it all, let it lay."

DEATHDEALER'S DIARY

Saturday, p.m., Oct. 18, '41

Take the case of this blustering medico.
Consider the handsome economy of my moves:
First, the needful supplies. A flashlight, thick woolen socks, the gardener's
gloves—already at hand. The one
purchase, the lady's raincape—a hooded
cape of a material resembling oil-silk.
Nothing more suspicious than that!
Second, the plan.
I turn off the highway at the Ghost
Canyon bridge, into a little lane that is
used only by fishermen in season and by
the keeper of the bees. Here, at a dozen
paces from the road, a sufficiency of
shrubbery shields my machine from the view
of any passerby . . . even though it is
a moral certainty none will pass by.

(Thus I avoid telltale tire impressions
along the dirt road to the cabin. It will
be easy enough to eradicate tire traces
from this lane, once I have returned and
backed the car onto the highway. Nor will
I leave an identifiable footprint, since
I intend drawing on the socks over my
shoes before quitting the car.)

I proceed directly to the cabin, using
the flashlight when it is necessary to
find a way through the undergrowth. (No
snagged clothing, no threads left on a
thorn!)

Our medical friend is within, and alone.
(He wouldn't be roughing it if he had a
servant in attendance! And his wife is at
home—rather, at the Capitol in the interest of sweet charity.) But to make
sure he is alone, I make the circuit of
the cabin windows.

It only remains to don the raincape and
the gloves, and to repair briefly to his
woodpile.

When I leave, a few minutes later, I

have with me his wallet, watch, rings.

Whether it will be necessary to rinse
the raincape in the stream, I am uncertain; but if there are any stains, they
will be upon the gloves and the cape, not
upon my person. At any rate, the stream
is there, if rinsing be needful. I have
only to make these articles, the socks,
and the abstracted articles into a bundle.
Their final disposition is easy enough.
I shall chuck the lot from the causeway
into the Game Reserve waters on the way
to Crestpeak.

—"There," say I, "you've got it. And
what can you make of it?"

The policeman-within racks his wits.
The total lack of clues, the lack of a
foothold anywhere, leaves him baffled.

It is a stalemate, and therefore a
victory for me.

He expresses the attitude of all policedom in the presence of blank walls.

"Well, something unexpected may turn
up," he says.

Exactly. Maybe something will turn up—until and unless it does, they can only shrug their shoulders. All of them.

"All right," I say. "Now let's really get on with it."

IV

THE INSISTENT RINGING OF THE TELEPHONE WAKENED Johnny Kendall.

He sat up, switched on the bed lamp, and crossed the hotel room to the instrument, which was attached to the wall.

"Yeah?" he mumbled. "Hello?"

He heard the voice of the Commercial House night clerk.

"There's a lady to see you," the night clerk said. "A Miss Rigmire."

"Who? Oh-h. Well, I'll come down to the lobby."

He trudged back to the bed, lifted the pillow, and stared sleepily at his strapwatch. It was twelve minutes past two o'clock.

"My God," said Johnny Kendall, rubbing his eyes.

He hastily put on shirt, trousers, shoes, and coat. He didn't bother with socks, necktie, or undergarments. He buttoned the shirt as he walked along the green carpeted corridor toward the stairs.

The three-story Commercial House did not have an elevator. The water which trickled from its hot water faucets was either lukewarm or scalding, and at either temperature was discolored with rusty sediment. The sheets were patched, and the towels frayed. And even

65

on a monthly rate basis, lodgings here cost Johnny Kendall a good deal more than rooming house accommodations. But it permitted him a greater degree of personal liberty, too. It was okay to play poker in your room, for instance. The Commercial House wasn't modern, but its management was broadminded.

A young, unescorted woman in the lobby was a rarity, particularly after midnight.

The night clerk frankly stared at this one. She got up from the depths of a leather chair as Johnny Kendall came down the stairs.

At first glance, he thought that she was theatrically pretty. Then he saw that she wasn't, at all. She had a well-formed, youthful, engaging face. But too much expert, professional care had been lavished upon her blonde hair, eyebrows, and complexion. No girl of her age really needed to be so evidently a product of the beauty salon. She wore only a minimum of make-up, skilfully applied, however, to create the illusion of interesting hollows and shadows.

The effect was to add five years to her twenty-one-or-two.

"Mr. Kendall?" she asked.

He admitted it.

"I'm Madeleine Rigmire," she said. Her voice was a nicely cultivated, Junior League drawl. Her accent was one that girls acquire in expensive finishing schools. "Dr. Rigmire's daughter, y' know."

Johnny Kendall wished he had taken the extra moment to put on a necktie. His feet felt extremely naked inside his shoes.

He said uncomfortably, "If there's anything I can do—"

She gestured. "Suppose we sit down."

She walked to a leather divan, selecting one near the front of the lobby, and therefore beyond earshot of the night clerk.

"I understand you took some pictures at the lodge tonight."

Johnny Kendall nodded.

"Well, I want to buy your pictures," Madeleine Rigmire said.

Johnny Kendall looked at her. "That's fine," he said. "If the sheriff hasn't any objections, I'd be glad to sell you a set of the prints."

"I've just talked to your sheriff." She smoothed the skirt of her tweed ensemble. She said abruptly, "I'm not satisfied with him. He hasn't gotten anywhere with this affair, hasn't even made a start, and I don't believe he will. Why, he didn't so much as notify the Highway Patrol to be on the watch for that woman."

"He didn't have her description," Johnny Kendall said fairly.

"But she put a tourniquet on father's wrist. Surely her dress must have been bloodstained. I should think that'd be description enough."

Johnny Kendall said:

"Your father brought up the Highway Patrol idea, too. You have to realize that Sheriff Ellsworth wasn't notified until ten o'clock. By that time, the woman had three-quarters of an hour head start, more or less. She could have driven forty, fifty miles in any direction."

He shook his head. "Miss Rigmire, Ellsworth didn't even know what kind of a car she was driving. He couldn't broadcast a request for the Patrol to stop every vehicle within a hundred mile circle, on a search of that kind.

"You wouldn't stand for it yourself," Johnny Kendall said, "having your car stopped at night. The Patrol cops ordering you out of the car, so they could examine your garments for bloodstains."

Dr. Rigmire's daughter opened her handbag. She drew from it an Oriental, lacquered wood case.

"Perhaps you're right," she said. "Smoke? They're Turkish."

"No, thanks," Johnny Kendall said. He held a light for the girl.

She exhaled a jet of thickly scented smoke. "It's just a detail, anyway," she said. "The woman got away, out of this county, and out of Mr. Ellsworth's jurisdiction. So it doesn't matter how good an officer he may be. *He's* not going to Altamont to press this investigation."

"You think that's where the woman went?"

"I think that's where the solution is," Madeleine Rigmire said. "Not here. Why, I don't suppose father knows a dozen people here in Crestpeak, even to speak to. He uses the lodge to get away from the people he already knows, not to become involved with more of them."

She paused thoughtfully.

"Surely no one of your local people would have the motive for an attack on his life," the girl argued. "His life is in Altamont. He practices in Altamont. His professional and social and personal contacts are all in the city. So I'm sure that's where the answer must be. And anyway . . ."

She turned the cigarette between her thumb and forefinger.

"—anyway, this isn't the first time!"

Johnny Kendall asked, "There've been other attempts on his life?"

She said, *"He* didn't think so. But I can see now, that's what it was. Although then I wasn't sure that I hadn't imagined the whole thing."

"Imagined what?"

"Well," Madeleine Rigmire said, "it was Monday night. I'd been writing some letters, and I hadn't any stamps, and I went down to the study to look for some there. And just then Cousin Joe turned his car into the driveway, and that's how I happened to see it. There was someone in the shrubbery beside the driveway."

"A woman?"

"I don't know. Whoever it was stayed crouched down, almost on all fours."

"Well," said Johnny Kendall, "what then?"

"Nothing very much," said the girl reluctantly. "I

called from the window, and Cousin Joe stopped. Mother was with him, and she asked me whatever was wrong. I told her we had a prowler, and I ran back to the desk and looked for my father's gun. He heard the shouting and went outside and helped Cousin Joe look around, but the prowler was gone.

"*They* thought I imagined it—" she shook her head "—but of course there was somebody. Waiting for my father, you see, but instead it was Joe Hanlon's car and that spoiled the plot."

"Unless," Johnny Kendall said, "it was a prowler, after all."

"It wasn't tonight," she pointed out. "I found over a hundred dollars in his wallet, so the motive wasn't robbery. That's another example of Mr. Ellsworth's efficiency—he didn't check up to see whether anything had been taken from the lodge."

Johnny Kendall said, "Let's be fair to the sheriff. After all, Dwyer didn't encourage him to ask the patient a lot of questions."

"It isn't important. He's not in a position to follow up this case, anyway."

She tapped her forefinger on the cigarette. It was an impatient movement.

"The evidence will be of no particular value in Sheriff Ellsworth's hands," she said. "And I don't suppose the Altamont police will be interested in anything outside their jurisdiction. I imagine we'll just have to turn the whole affair over to a good private detective, and that's why I want to buy your negatives."

Johnny Kendall opened his eyes. "I thought you were talking about a set of prints."

"No. The negatives."

He said, "Well."

"They're yours to sell, aren't they?" Madeleine Rigmire asked. "You're not employed by the county, as I understand it. You simply take such pictures on speculation, on the chance that the county authorities may want to buy them."

"Who told you all that?"

"Ellsworth."

"And did he say it'd be all right for me to sell you the negatives?"

She leaned forward to drop her cigarette into a push-button, pedestal ash tray.

"I didn't think of buying them, then," Madeleine Rigmire asserted. "He said I could get copies of the pictures from you. I got to wondering about that later. I suppose you'd also be willing to sell copies of the pictures to anyone else, provided the sheriff didn't object."

"I suppose so, yes."

Her lips tightened. She shook her blonde head stubbornly.

"That's no good. You might sell the pictures to a newspaper. Or to one of those filthy true crime magazines. Mr. Kendall, we are a respectable family. We're entitled to a reasonable amount of privacy."

Johnny Kendall smiled patiently. "I meant that anyone who could show a reasonable, legitimate interest could buy copies of those pictures."

"Who could that be?"

"The attorney for the defense would have a legitimate interest. If the case comes to trial. Or an insurance company might, if a claim for insurance arose out of this thing." He smiled again. "I didn't volunteer to do this work so I'd be in a position to cash in on the general sale of confidential, official photos."

Madeleine Rigmire stared at him.

"You *say* that. But I'd prefer to have something better than just the word of a perfect stranger."

The warmth of a flush began to burn in Johnny Kendall's cheeks.

"I'll tell you what I'll do," he said. "There are five negatives, and for twenty-five dollars I'll turn them over to the county attorney, to be kept in his files, as county property. In other words, you can buy the negatives for the county if you wish."

The girl drew a deep breath. She said, "I'll give you twenty-five dollars *apiece*. And keep them myself."

Johnny thought fast.

"Sight unseen? Without even knowing what's in them?"

She said, "I don't *care* what's in them. I don't know anything about clues. I'm buying them for a private detective to use, and it's up to him to decide how useful they will be."

She gave Johnny Kendall no time to reply. "The pictures won't be worth anything to either the sheriff or the county attorney, because they're in no position to go ahead with this investigation. It's an investigation into my father's personal and professional affairs, and we're going to have to pay for it ourselves, and what we pay for, we're entitled to have."

Johnny Kendall went on thinking. "What about Ellsworth?" he asked.

"Can't you—can't you just say the pictures didn't turn out?"

Johnny grinned. "He'd hardly take that, coming from a professional. Of course, I *could* say that my flash equipment was out of order—that the bulbs flashed a fraction of a second before or after the shutter movement—if I wanted to. . . ."

Madeleine Rigmire looked relieved.

"If I wanted to," Johnny Kendall repeated.

She said, "I'll make it—two hundred dollars for the lot."

"Cash? Tonight?"

"Cash," she said briefly.

"They're in the shop." Johnny Kendall stood up. "Come on."

Main Street was deserted except for a yellow cabriolet at the hotel curb. The only lights were on the street corners, in the Commercial House lobby, and in the jail across the square. Miss Rigmire's heels racketed noisily along the sidewalk.

"You haven't made any pictures from them, have you?" she asked suspiciously.

"No. I developed the negatives and left them in the

dryer, so I could run through some prints first thing in the morning."

He stopped, fumbling with his keys. A dog began to bark inside the frame, two-story building.

"Shut up, Butch," Johnny Kendall said. He explained to the girl, "It's the former owner's dog. He doesn't know me very well yet."

A window sash banged up, overhead. Pop Capp, in his nightshirt, leaned out.

"Hey, you, down there," Pop said.

"It's all right, Pop," Johnny said. "Go back to bed." He twisted the key, turned the doorknob. "Hi, fella," he said to Pop's spaniel.

Butch sniffed Johnny Kendall's hand. Then he sniffed in the girl's direction.

"Wait here," Johnny said, snapping on a light back of the counter. He stepped through a curtained doorway into the studio. He didn't go into the darkroom at all, but lifted his voice and said:

"They're still damp. I'll turn up the juice in the dryer, if you can spare five minutes more."

"All right," Madeleine Rigmire said.

Johnny Kendall stepped back into the front of the shop, lifted his Speed Graphic from under the counter, and said, "It'll take a bit of adjusting. I'll put it out of synchronization, and then get Pop to fix it in the morning. That way we'll have a witness that it *was* out of order—"

The bulb blazed whitely.

Madeleine Rigmire's slender figure sprang back.

"Why—why—" she gasped— "you took my picture!"

Johnny Kendall laughed.

"Why not?" he asked. "You haven't given me any proof that you're really Rigmire's daughter. You might be anybody. You might even be the woman who was at the lodge tonight."

She stammered in wordless surprise. Her voice formed inarticulate sounds, but not words.

"You could be a reporter hunting for an exclusive angle, though God knows that's not likely," Johnny Kendall said. "You might be a private detective agency operative, or you could be working some sort of blackmail racket of your own. Under a set-up like that, do you suppose I'd be fool enough to sell you those negatives?"

Madeleine Rigmire said falteringly, "I can show you my driver's license. . . ."

"Never mind," Johnny Kendall said. "I know you're none of those things. You're too green to be a professional. You're a simon-pure amateur, and you shouldn't try to cheat at the other man's game."

Her eyes were wide and injured.

"For example," Johnny Kendall said, "I wouldn't have needed five minutes back there. It would have taken me only a few moments to put those negatives into the printer with some copy film. In that way, I could have taken your two hundred dollars and still I'd have had the negatives, too."

The girl moistened her lips. "You're making a complete fool of me, aren't you?" she asked unsteadily.

Johnny said, "No. I've kept you from making a complete fool of yourself. Next time you'll know better—and never, never, offer anyone a fancy price for a photographic negative. Negatives can be duplicated by contact printing, just exactly as paper prints are. They can be made by photographing positives, if there's even one single positive print to be had. The possession of a negative isn't any protection at all, because there may be one, two, or twenty duplicates in existence. Remember that in case anybody ever tries to blackmail you, because the blackmailer isn't going to overlook it."

He shook his head.

"It's like everything else," he said. "You can't beat the game without knowing all the rules. You'll only burn your fingers trying. You might just as well lay your cards on the table right now."

The girl looked extremely unhappy and unconfident about the whole thing now.

"Well?" Johnny Kendall asked. "Why do you really want the negatives?"

"I told you. I feel this is our own, family affair—"

She stopped short.

"Oh, what's the use?" she asked. "You won't sell them to me, anyway. No matter what I say. Will you?"

"No," he admitted.

She turned abruptly.

Johnny Kendall said, "But you can buy a set of the prints, if it's okay with the sheriff."

She went out, pulling the door noisily shut. Johnny Kendall heard her heels tapping swiftly up Main Street.

"I didn't make a hit with her, Butch," he said to the spaniel.

He pulled the cut film holder from his Graphic and walked back through the studio to the darkroom. He walked through the double, light-trapped doors and touched a switch.

The smile faded from his lips. He stared at the open door of the drying cabinet.

"Good God!" he said.

The negatives weren't there.

V

"Damn it, Pop," Johnny Kendall said, "the back door isn't locked."

Pop Capp came down the stairs, barefooted, in a white nightshirt reaching to his knees. Pop, seen thus, did not cut a comic figure. Rather he acquired from this voluminous garment a somewhat toga-esque, Roman dignity.

The back door was Pop's responsibility. It provided him with an entrance-way through which he could go in and out without intruding upon a sitting in the studio. It opened into a small rear hallway, whence painted pine steps led to the living quarters on the upper floor. Under the steps was a closet space, shelved, and opening into the darkroom; the closet served to store paper and film apart from the chemical fumes in the darkroom. At the inner end of the hallway, a second door gave into the studio—"the gallery," in Pop's phrase. This was a middle chamber, provided with the necessary lights, standards, reflectors, background screens, chairs, and "Hollywood coffin" for portraiture work. The studio had one large, north window; which —Johnny Kendall had ascertained—was locked. It had three doorways: first, the curtained one into the front shop; second, the hallway door; third, the light-trapped

darkroom entrance. This trap was in fact a double
one; it consisted of a tiny vestibule; you turned, right,
into the film darkroom, or—left—into the printing
and enlarging room.

Obviously, anyone finding the back door unlocked
could have passed through the hallway into the studio
and thence into the darkroom.

Pop Capp tried the back door; a very ordinary, pine
door equipped with a spring lock. It was unlocked,
certainly. Pop peered out, into an unlighted rear area-
way heaped with pasteboard packing boxes. A brick
walk ran to the paved alley, past the shed where Pop
kept his ancient Dodge, and Johnny Kendall his Ford
coupé.

"It beats hell," Pop Capp said. "I'd just about swear
to it, this door was locked."

He shook his head. He knelt down, fumbled under
the outer sill, and said, "No, it's here, all right."

"What's there?" Johnny Kendall asked.

Pop Capp opened his hand and said, "Why, I always
kept a spare key hid here." He showed Johnny Kendall the key. "For years," he said. "You know,
Johnny, I always used this back door on Sundays. A
man has to make little concessions like that, like not
going in and out of the shop, on Sundays. If I didn't,
if I used the front door at all, I'd pretty soon have a
bunch of loafers tagging me in off the street. Fellows
all dressed up and no place to go, looking for a warm
stove to sit around and chew the fat. If I allowed that
on Sundays, it'd pretty soon be the same every day in

the week. I'd be running a hangout like the poolhall
and barbershops and livery stable used to be. I wouldn't
have any business left, because the ladies give those
hangouts a pretty wide berth. Or they used to."

Pop Capp sighed.

"So I went in and out the back way, Sundays," he
said. "Only a time or so I forgot, and didn't change
my keys to my Sunday clothes; then I had to fetch a
ladder up to the window; that's why I hid a spare key
down under the sill. But I didn't think there was a
living soul knew about it. Not that would come in
here and steal anything."

Johnny Kendall listened impatiently.

"But are you *sure* the door was locked at all?" he
asked.

"Well," said Pop Capp, "I am, and I ain't. I remember I looked at it before I went up to bed. I shook it a
little. To go upstairs at all, I have to go past this door;
it's always been my habit to make sure it was locked,
last thing at night."

Johnny Kendall stared. "What do you mean, you
ain't? If you remember doing it?"

Pop smiled. "Johnny," he asked, "didn't you ever
forget to pull a slide?"

Johnny Kendall said, "Sure." He drew a deep
breath. "Look, Pop, I'm not *blaming* you. I'm trying
to figure out what happened here. If the door was
locked, and the thief knew where to look for a key,
that's one thing. If the door wasn't locked, that's a

different thing entirely. The difference is important. Hell, don't take this personally."

"That isn't the point," Pop Capp said. "The point is, you've forgotten to pull slides. So have I. So has everybody in the business. Why, I remember reading in a book, somewhere, about Jerome Zerbe spending one whole night at the World's Fair shooting on just one plate.* Of course, it's an exaggeration and misstatement. I said to myself when I read it, Zerbe probably never took a picture on a *plate* in his life; that's why I remember it. The point is, Johnny, that there isn't a professional photographer in the world who hasn't forgotten to pull out slides, or made double exposures, or failed to wind a shutter. And yet it's our business to do those things; we do 'em every day of our lives, every time we take a picture; they're habitual with us. And yet, once in a while, we all slip. But if we were asked, at the time, we'd swear we'd hadn't made any such a mistake. So far as remembering goes, we don't remember. If we remembered, why, we wouldn't spoil good film that way. It's only when we come to develop a blank film, or a double exposure, that we catch the mistake."

Pop Capp paused.

"I don't know, Johnny," he said. "According to my memory and according to my lifelong habits, the door was locked. It's just that I've been a photographer too

---

* *People on Parade,* a collection of photographs by Jerome Zerbe; David Kemp, New York, 1934. From the Introduction by Lucius Beebe.

Actually, Mr. Zerbe uses fast press film in packs.

long to trust either memory or habit beyond a certain point. I know my limitations, humanly speaking."

"Mistakes like that don't happen very often," Johnny Kendall said. "Not once in a thousand times."

Pop Capp admitted this. "Still, it's funny how the spoiled picture is the very one you want, more'n nine hundred and ninety-nine others."

He shuffled his bare feet.

"You, Butch," he said. "You son of a gun, you tickle."

"There's another screwy point," Johnny Kendall said. "How anybody could sneak in here, and the dog not bark."

Pop Capp said, "Butch isn't any watch dog, Johnny. He's never been kept on a chain. He's just a smalltown dog that's had the run of the town since he was a pup. Why, I expect Butch has got more friends along Main Street than I have. He ought to. He has more time to make friends—and he doesn't have to worry about them borrowing money from him, either."

Pop laughed.

"No," he said, "the gallery wouldn't half hold the men who could come in here, and Butch not let out a yip."

"He barked at me," Johnny Kendall said.

"Sure. You're on the jump. You don't take the time to scratch him back of his ears. That's what he likes," Pop Capp said. "I never could put any stock in that dog-knowing-human-nature theory. Especially when I take notice of the type of men you see making friends with somebody else's dog. You pay a little attention to that sometime, Johnny. Notice in front of Salol's, or over at the filling station, the guys that pay attention when somebody else's dog comes along. I'll be danged if they're not the biggest do-nothings, good-for-nothings in town. You take old Hazy; why, Hazy has more friendships among the canine population than any other three men in Crestpeak; that's the dog's eye view on the human race—the best ear-scratcher wins, every time."

Johnny Kendall had stopped listening to Pop Capp moments ago.

"Okay," he said. "Okay. Butch barks at strangers, anyway. It was someone *he* knew. And that door was locked—almost certainly. It was someone who knew where the key was hidden. It all adds up. It all points one way. The answer is right here in Crestpeak."

Johnny Kendall rubbed his hands together.

"Pop," he said, "you get Frank Ellsworth on the phone. Get him over here. Tell him this is the break. If he's willing to spend a little money on a fingerprint expert, he'll probably find his answer right on our film dryer door. Tell him that I've gone out to the Rigmire place. I'm going to shoot those pictures over again, just as fast as I can get there."

"Wait a minute," Pop Capp said. "You're going alone? Wait a minute first."

"I want to pick up a substantial tripod this time," Johnny Kendall said. "Filters and a wide-angle lens, and a lot more bulbs."

When he lugged these things into the back hallway, Pop Capp was waiting there; rather a ridiculous figure, now, with his night shirt tucked inside his trousers.

"Maybe you better take this," said Pop, and pushed a big, blued, Frontier six-shooter Colt at Johnny Kendall. "Be careful with it," Pop said. "That's a filed gun, Johnny. It goes off easy, too blamed easy. That Forty-four won't stand for any scratching behind its ears, Johnny."

VI

Johnny Kendall's strapwatch said 2:51, flat, in front of the Commercial House in Crestpeak. When he looked at the watch again, it was after braking in the yard between the remodeled farmhouse and the woodpile. The hands now pointed to 3:05, and the second-hand, to 47 seconds. "Fifteen minutes, practically." And he had not spared the horsepower. As a matter of fact, he had overtaken and passed Madeleine Rigmire's yellow cabriolet, several miles back.

"Dwyer could give Barney Oldfield pointers," he thought.

He didn't believe it. The difference, four minutes, nearly a third cut from his own time, simply passed all credence.

"Damned blowhard," Johnny Kendall thought. He unlatched the Ford's door, slid out from under the wheel, and reached for the tripod on the shelf back of the seat.

He heard a scream.

Johnny Kendall's fingers slid over the polished hard-wood legs of the tripod, and closed on the checked black rubber stocks of the Frontier six-shooter. It was a very big gun; its peculiar, low-cut grip was over-large in his hand. It was a very heavy gun; it weighed around forty ounces. Johnny Kendall got no confidence at all from the feel of the gun in his palm; he felt afraid of it, in fact.

He would have felt more afraid without it, though; with that hoarse, wild, terrifying scream echoing in his brain.

Grasping the Forty-four gingerly, his forefinger curled outside the trigger guard, Johnny Kendall loped toward the house.

The scream was not repeated. There was no sound at all—no indication of anything wrong—his eyes were glued to the dimly lighted, curtained windows.

Johnny Kendall had parked the Ford close to the woodpile, facing the woodpile; had thought to use his headlights for illumination as he set up his equipment. He was nearly across the yard, within fifty feet of the porch, when the front door swung open.

He saw a woman in the lighted doorway.

Her back was toward Johnny Kendall. She was looking into the front room—was backing out of the doorway, he thought.

He caught only the one glimpse of *her*.

In the next instant, a man came racing past the corner of the porch. He was running very fast, and silently, on tiptoe; with his body gathered down, doubled at the hips, and his head turned—turned away from Johnny Kendall, and toward the woman in the doorway.

Johnny Kendall shouted:

"Stop—hands up!"

The first thing that flashed into his mind. Ten paces away, the running man jerked his head—and swerved, drove straight toward Johnny Kendall. The ex-*Herald* photographer tried to do two things at once; tried to sidestep, and tried to bring up Pop Capp's Colt. The gun was no help at all. The gun was a nuisance, diverting his attention with its bulk and unfamiliar balance.

The runner left his feet. He hurled himself projectile-fashion in a long, flying, low-to-earth dive. He crashed across Johnny Kendall's knees.

Johnny's feet flew out from under him. He had the sensation of rising and turning in mid-air. It seemed a long while before he came down, onto the palms of his hands, then his head, shoulders, and hips. Somewhere in this aerial somersault, he had dropped Pop's gun.

The other man rolled over, leaped to his feet, and ran.

Johnny Kendall heard the woman exclaim, "Earl! Earl!"

Her voice sounded far-off, thinned by remote and whirling distances. Johnny Kendall was a little dizzy, and knocked breathless. He had been hit hard, shaken up, bruised. He was not unconscious—he was able to separate a number of tingling impressions; his palms smarted stingingly, one wrist throbbed sharply, his head ached, and his back felt as if elephants had walked upon it.

He flopped over, onto his hands and knees. He was

in the condition of a pugilist who has been knocked down, but not out; who can hear the roar of the crowd, and the voice of the referee tolling the count; who knows that he can get up before he is counted out.

Johnny Kendall shook his head, just as a pugilist would.

"Earl!" the woman wailed, sounding much closer now.

Johnny Kendall saw Pop Capp's Forty-four, a dull blued glimmer on the earth in front of him. He grabbed the gun. He straightened on one knee.

He said, "Stop—in the name of the Law!"

The running figure, nearly to the car shed now, was blurring into invisibility.

The Frontier six-shooter went off with a startling roar. Johnny Kendall had not been aiming at anything. His forefinger had been merely exploring, searching for the trigger. His finger had barely grazed the trigger, in fact.

A pair of arms closed strongly around the photographer. They dragged him backward. He caught a whiff of perfume. "Help!" the woman panted. She didn't sound frightened, only breathless with struggle and exertion.

"Earl—hurry—help!" She threw herself across Johnny Kendall's prostrate figure. She fought like a cat—she was *like* a cat, quick and supple and light.

Johnny Kendall struggled up, sat up. The woman was sprawled across his knees and thighs, hanging onto his right wrist with both hands.

She squirmed. She wasn't trying to get away from him. She tried to bite his right hand, the hand with the gun.

Johnny Kendall said, "She-devil!" He used his other hand to grasp a fistful of soft, silky hair.

Dimly, in the darkness, he saw the woman's shining eyes and bared teeth.

"You bastard!" she panted.

A man came running across the yard.

"Get his gun!" the woman said.

The man bent down and twisted the Colt from Johnny Kendall's fingers. The gun clicked, cocked.

Johnny Kendall said in alarm, "Be careful! That goes off easy!"

Headlamps of a car turning from the lane flooded the scene. The car stopped. Madeleine Rigmire ran up to the three.

"Dr. Sawyer!" Madeleine Rigmire exclaimed. "Miss Carr? Why—it's Mr. Kendall! What in the world—?"

"Yes," Dr. Earl Sawyer said. "What happened, Gene?"

Miss Carr said:

"Why, I don't know. There were two of them out here, fighting. The other one ran away, and this one started shooting. I was afraid he'd shoot you, Dr. Sawyer—he was shooting in that direction—"

Earl Sawyer said, "But the scream? Who screamed?"

"It was in the house," Johnny Kendall said.

Madeleine Rigmire wailed, "Father!" She ran up the steps, across the porch, into the open doorway.

"Cousin Joe!" she choked.

Johnny Kendall stopped in the doorway, and stared at Cousin Joe on the floor.

His throat thickened, his knees gave weakly. It was always the same, and he never got hardened to it. He had seen firemen bring bodies out of burned buildings, ambulance crews pick up the victims of motor accidents, river boatmen recover suicides with their grappling hooks. It was always the same, and he always felt the need for a drink as now.

Madeleine Rigmire stumbled in a little circle wide of Cousin Joe's body, to the bedroom door. It was ajar. She pushed it open.

Johnny Kendall followed her. He stared at the large bulk of Dr. Rigmire's body, the lift and fall of the large chest.

Madeleine's breath slid away in a long sigh of sound. "It's all right, he's just asleep," she said. Her voice had a ragged edge. "Dr. Dwyer gave him morphine. He'd have been *killed* like that—drugged—helpless—if it wasn't for Cousin Joe—"

She began to cry.

"Where's the phone?" Johnny Kendall asked.

"The kitchen," said Dr. Earl Sawyer, on one knee beside Cousin Joe.

Johnny Kendall cranked the old-fashioned party line wall phone. "Operator," he said, "ring the sheriff for me."

VII

Frank Ellsworth said, "A man this time. A woman the first time. I don't make sense of it."

The sheriff rubbed his chin. He closed his eyes and shook his head.

He said, "A woman the first time. Doc Rigmire saw her. It was a woman that talked to Doc Dwyer on the phone."

He peered at Johnny Kendall.

"You didn't get a good look at him, at all?" the sheriff asked.

"Not his face," Johnny Kendall said. "He was a man—a hell of a good man. He hit me like a ton of bricks. He was probably as big as I am, maybe bigger. A hard, fast baby."

"A young guy," Ellsworth said.

Johnny Kendall said, "I think he must have played football. That was a football block he threw into me."

The sheriff said, "A young guy, as big as you—five-ten, a hundred seventy or eighty pounds, maybe bigger. I wish to God you got a look at his face, though."

Johnny Kendall said he wished so, too.

"He was coming fast, and I was looking at the door —at Miss Carr in the doorway."

The sheriff stared at the floor. Dr. Earl Sawyer had drawn a sheet over Cousin Joe's body.

The hatchet still lay on the floor, between the body and the fireplace.

There was blood on the hatchet, and hair; it had been used to split open Cousin Joe's skull. A blanket and a rumpled pillow on the divan indicated that Cousin Joe had been napping there when the murderer came in. He had leaped up, perhaps only half-awake, to be struck down under the furious blow.

"A woman," Frank Ellsworth said. "A man. A hell of a funny deal."

He mused another moment.

"Well, folks," he said, "I guess Ed here had better take down your names and addresses. Sort of take down your statements, officially."

Dr. Earl Sawyer said, "Earl H. Sawyer, the Wellington Hotel, Altamont."

"One *e* or two?" Ed Bundy asked.

"One."

Ed Bundy wrote it in a red leather-bound notebook. "Where is that?" he asked.

"It's a residential hotel up near the Capitol, on Eleventh just off Capitol Plaza," Earl Sawyer said.

"Occupation, doctor, I suppose," the sheriff said.

A nod. "I am Dr. Rigmire's assistant. I've been with him the past two years. Before that, I acted as resident physician at Clay General Hospital."

"And before then?"

Dr. Earl Sawyer colored. "State Medical," he confessed.

He was a strongly built young man, thirtyish, or not quite thirty. He hid his youth behind a moustache, a conservative single-breasted grey suit, and an aloofly dignified, professional manner.

"How old?" the sheriff asked.

"Twenty-nine," said Dr. Sawyer, without enthusiasm.

Frank Ellsworth peered at Miss Carr.

"Amy Geneva Carr, but I don't use the Amy. My address is 1234 Buxton Street, Apartment 3, Altamont."

"Hold it," Ed Bundy said. "Spell the name."

Geneva Carr spelled it.

She was an attractive young woman—red-haired and green-eyed.

She still reminded Johnny Kendall of a cat.

"I'm a trained nurse," she said. "I've been in Dr. Rigmire's office five years. Before that, I took private cases, in homes."

"How old?"

"Twenty—" she hesitated—"seven."

Frank Ellsworth looked around, to Madeleine Rigmire, huddled in a chair pulled close to the bedroom door.

The girl started under his glance. "You *know* who I am," she said.

Frank Ellsworth nodded. "Well, yes, but I guess Ed ought to get it down, officially."

Ed got it down:

Madeleine Helen Rigmire, 20, 12 Sussex Place, Alta-mont; occupation, none.

The sheriff said, "Well, okay, that identifies every-body. So we can go ahead with it. Now we're all iden-tified officially."

He frowned. "I guess we'd better start at the begin-ning," he said. "Start with you, Miss Rigmire."

"But you know about me."

"I want you to make a statement," the sheriff said. "Ed will write down what you say, and afterward you can initial it. A man has been killed here, and we have to do things in a legal, official way."

Madeleine Rigmire made a tired gesture, shook her blonde head a little.

"I don't want a lot of details," the sheriff said en-couragingly. "Just the main facts. You can cut it short, just so long as you don't leave out any of the facts."

Madeleine Rigmire said, "I've told you all this before. I was at home tonight. Dr. Dwyer telephoned a few minutes after ten. I took the call because my mother wasn't in. Mother belongs to the Betterment League, on a committee, working for the passage of the relief bill. She was at the Capitol, lobbying for that. I didn't know just where to reach her. I called Dr. Sawyer's hotel immediately, and left a message." Her blonde brows met.

"No," she said, "I left a message the second time I called. In between, I tried to reach Miss Carr—I thought she might know where Earl was—but she wasn't in, either. So I—"

Geneva Carr stirred felinely.

"Wait a minute," the red-haired nurse said. "I was at home at ten o'clock. All evening, in fact. My phone didn't ring at all."

Madeleine Rigmire said, "Why, it rang and rang."

"Then you must have dialed a wrong number," Geneva Carr said.

"I looked up the number."

The nurse smiled. "Very well, dear, but you still must have made a mistake dialing. I assure you, my phone did *not* ring."

Frank Ellsworth lifted both hands, dropped them, and said, "Don't argue. You're not getting any place. Either of you. It can't be proved now, and anyway, it's just a detail."

Geneva Carr said, "I'm not arguing. It probably isn't important, but I want my statement in the record along with hers."

"Put it in for her, Ed," the sheriff said. He peered at Madeleine Rigmire.

The girl brushed a hand over her blonde hair. "I left a message for Dr. Sawyer," she said. "That my father had been hurt, that I was going up to the lodge here, and for him to follow. Oh, and I sent upstairs for Cousin Joe."

"Hanlon, here?"

She said, "Yes. I wanted to ask for his car. I haven't one of my own. I use mother's car, usually, but she had taken it tonight. I thought Cousin Joe would let me take the cabriolet. He offered to drive me. He wanted to come along, himself. It was his car, and his privilege, and so we both came. If I'd known—"

"Madeleine, this wasn't your fault," Earl Sawyer said quickly. "You musn't blame yourself."

Johnny Kendall said, "How long'd it take you to drive out from Altamont?"

"About an hour and a half," Madeleine Rigmire said. "Dr. Dwyer was still here. There was a kind of a mix-up about that. I'd told him, on the phone, I was bringing Dr. Sawyer. He'd thought I meant Dr. Hugo Sawyer, the brain specialist. He thought Cousin Joe was that Dr. Sawyer, when we first came in. Of course, I went right in to see my father. He was upset about it all, and he didn't think it was a local matter which Mr. Ellsworth would ever get to the bottom of—I told you all this in town, sheriff."

She hesitated, drew in her breath.

"Dr. Dwyer gave father the morphine injection, and left, and I left just after he did. I wanted to talk to you, Mr. Ellsworth, and I could have telephoned—but I wasn't sure about using a party line. People listen in, and repeat things, and sometimes they don't get it straight, either. All this was personal, or it might relate to my father's practice—"

She was stressing this heavily, Johnny Kendall thought. She had to. She could not very well explain the impossibility of buying photographic negatives by telephone, he thought.

"That's all," the girl said. "I left here about twelve-thirty, drove to Crestpeak, and talked to you, Mr. Ellsworth, and I also talked to Mr. Kendall at the hotel about buying his pictures in case we hired a private detective—and last of all, I telephoned my mother."

"I don't think that's quite all," Johnny Kendall said.

The girl looked up at him quickly. "Mr. Ellsworth doesn't want every little detail," she said. "I've explained that I went into town, and didn't get back until all this other had happened. You know. You passed me on the road, two miles below here. I'm only trying to make it clear how it was—Cousin Joe being here with father, while I went into Crestpeak." She moistened her lips. "That's what you wanted, isn't it, sheriff?"

"Okay," Johnny Kendall said. "I'm like Miss Carr. I just want it in the record, along with your statement."

Ed Bundy grunted. "You want *what* in the record?"

"That she left out some details," Johnny said.

There was a pause.

Dr. Earl Sawyer broke it.

"I think I'm next," he said. "I didn't get Madeleine's message until, oh, about one o'clock. I'd been out to a movie—a double feature—and then I stopped for a sandwich. The clerk handed me the message when I came in."

The sheriff sighed.

"I've been wondering about that," he said. "A doctor going out, and not leaving word where he can be reached. I don't know, in Altamont. But here in the country, I'd wonder about that."

Dr. Earl Sawyer smiled broadly.

"We are not country doctors, engaged in general

practice," he said tolerantly. "Dr. Rigmire is a specialist, a diagnostician. Neither of us is on call, outside of
office hours."

Frank Ellsworth said, "Well, then, never mind the
details. I don't mean, leave out anything important.
What we want now is a general picture. We'll go back
and fit in the details, later on. You got the message at
one o'clock. Okay, so then?"

Dr. Sawyer said:

"I put through a long-distance call. I talked to Hanlon, to Cousin Joe. He told me that Dwyer had left,
that Madeleine had driven into town, and that Dr. Rigmire was sleeping—was sleeping it off, he said."

The broad smile came again.

"Unfortunately," he said, "I didn't know how much
trust to put in Cousin Joe. It is a curious fact, and a fact
that we encounter frequently in our profession, that
some people refuse to admit that any illness or injury
is a serious one—when the injury or illness involves
some member of the family. I should say that is a pe-
culiarity of more or less irresponsible personalities.
Some individuals won't face the facts—I daresay they
don't want to be burdened with the responsibility and
worry arising out of unpleasantly serious fact."

Ed Bundy said, "My God. You want all that in here,
Frank?"

The sheriff made a throat-clearing sound.

"I'm sorry," Dr. Earl Sawyer said. "I wasn't so sure
Dr. Rigmire would 'sleep it off.' I thought it might be
a good idea to have a nurse up here with him. I called

Miss Carr and asked whether she wanted to go, or whether I should get someone from the hospital."

"I was glad to go," Geneva Carr said. "I threw some things into a suitcase right away."

Dr. Sawyer said, "We started about one-twenty or thirty."

Geneva Carr said, "Dr. Sawyer put his car into the shed, beside Dr. Rigmire's machine. He drives a coupé, and my suitcase was in the back, in the rear deck. He had to get that out, and get his own bag, and I didn't wait. I started toward the house, and I was almost there when I heard the scream."

Johnny Kendall stared at the red-haired nurse. "You were what?" he demanded.

"I was almost there, almost to the porch."

Johnny Kendall said, "You didn't do the screaming?"

Miss Carr looked at him.

"What makes you think I screamed?" she asked.

"I don't know," Johnny said. "It was a shrill scream."

"Did you ever hear one that wasn't?"

"Well—"

Miss Carr said, "I'd like to know what makes you think that."

"It was just an idea," Johnny Kendall said. "I had an idea that maybe you opened the door, and screamed when you saw the body, and then the murderer ran out the back way, through the kitchen."

The nurse fixed her green eyes on Johnny Kendall.

"It was Mr. Hanlon who screamed," she said. "I suppose when he saw that man with the hatchet. The man struck him down, and then heard me on the porch, and so ran out the back way."

Johnny Kendall opened and closed his mouth. Miss Carr removed her green glance from him, after a long moment.

"I was startled," she said to the sheriff. "I thought Dr. Rigmire had fallen out of bed. That very often happens with sick persons, especially with head injuries, and it was always the dread of my existence— when I took private cases. I dashed up to the porch, but it took me awhile there, fumbling to find the doorknob. Then, just as I pushed the door open, I heard something *outside*—a man running—and the next moment there were those two men fighting in the darkness."

Her curved bosom lifted. Her eyes gleamed. Her voice took an edge.

"Heavens!" she said. "I didn't know! One of them might be Earl—Dr. Sawyer. I called to him. One of the two broke away, ran away, and the other started shooting. You have to realize I didn't know who *he* was—the one with the gun. He might have been the one who ran out of the house, for all I could tell."

She leaned toward the sheriff.

"He was shooting," she said. "He might have killed Dr. Sawyer, or me, or both of us. I tried to stop him. I tried to get the gun away, and I called for Dr. Sawyer to help me. I realize *now* I made a mistake—but at the time, it seemed the right thing to do."

Ed Bundy admired the red-haired nurse. "It took guts," the deputy said.

"She didn't have long to think it over," Johnny Kendall said. He looked at the nurse. "How long, would you say, from the time you heard the scream until you opened the door?"

"I'm not sure . . . I was startled. And then, I couldn't find the doorknob. I suppose it was a minute."

Johnny Kendall said:

"The scream came at 3:06. I'd just looked at my watch, checking the time it took me to drive from town. I fumbled for a second or so, finding the gun on the shelf back of the seat. I grabbed the gun, and ran a hundred feet—that part of it all happened inside of ten seconds."

"Well! Well-l-l," said the sheriff softly.

Johnny Kendall said, "Yeah. If Hanlon screamed, the murderer killed him and ran out of the house, all in ten seconds. If you can believe that."

"Yi, if."

"I don't think so, either," Johnny Kendall said.

Geneva Carr looked from one to the other, looked at Johnny Kendall longest.

"You're wrong," she said. "You didn't grab that gun as quickly as you think. It was at least *half* a minute."

The sheriff said, "One against the other. What do you say, Doc?"

Dr. Earl Sawyer said, "I honestly don't know. I didn't hear the scream."

"How could you help hearing it?" Johnny Kendall asked.

"I was in the shed. I was getting the suitcase out of the rumble. The first thing *I* heard was the shot."

Johnny Kendall said, "Okay, we'll get at it this way. You saw my lights when I drove into the yard, didn't you?"

"Yes."

"And how long after that did you hear the shot?"

"It might have been a minute," Dr. Earl Sawyer said. "I didn't time you, and I realize that impressions can be wrong, but it seems to me a minute or so later that I heard the shot."

"Two," the sheriff said. "Two to one. I don't know, but it sounds more reasonable. A minute does." He sighed. "Ten seconds is cutting it fine."

Johnny Kendall shrugged.

"There's another angle," he said. "How fast'd you drive out from town, Miss Rigmire?"

"Forty," Madeleine Rigmire said. "On that kind of a road."

"And I passed her two miles back," Johnny Kendall said to the sheriff. "How much time do you think I could gain on her, in two miles? She was right behind me, probably not more than a minute behind me, and by the time she drove into the yard, the shooting and everything else was all over."

The girl nodded her blonde head.

"He wasn't a mile ahead," she said. "I saw his lights in the lane, from down the road."

The sheriff thought, and gnawed his underlip, and

said, "Two-to-two. A tie. Yi dammy, I don't know which to think now."

Johnny Kendall frowned over Madeleine Rigmire's last words.

"That's something else," he said. "Miss Carr didn't wait, she says. She went straight to the house, and that puts them here just ahead of me. But I didn't see their lights from the road."

"Were you looking?" Geneva Carr asked.

"Yes, I was looking. I was watching for the house lights, because I didn't know the road too well—didn't know where the lane was."

"Well, we saw *your* lights," the red-haired nurse said sharply. "From the shed. I told Dr. Sawyer someone was turning into the lane, and he said it was probably Madeleine returning from town. We'd just driven into the shed, oh, moments before. It took me a few seconds to get out of the car. Dr. Sawyer said he'd get my suitcase out of the back, and I told him not to bother, that I wouldn't wait. He was fumbling in the glove compartment for a flashlight. He didn't find it, and I said never mind, I didn't need one."

She smiled at Frank Ellsworth.

"I didn't know you wanted every little detail," she said. "Dr. Sawyer and I arrived here maybe a minute or two minutes before Mr. Kendall. We had that little bit of conversation in the shed, while he hunted for the flashlight, and I'd have put it in in the first place, but you said you wanted the general picture."

VIII

"JOHNNY," SAID POP CAPP, "YOU BETTER COME UPSTAIRS and have some breakfast with me."

"I could use a cup of coffee."

"A man generally can," said Pop, "when he's been up all night."

Johnny Kendall came out of the darkroom. It had been quite a session, he admitted. "Ellsworth and Ed Bundy didn't get out there until about a quarter of four this morning. They had Doc Dwyer out there—I didn't know it, but he's county coroner. Then after that, Jim Wallach showed up." Jim Wallach was the county attorney.

"I didn't get finished shooting pictures until daylight," Johnny Kendall said, "and I thought I might as well put the film through the soup before I went to bed."

Pop Capp's upstairs apartment was bright with sunshine, and cheerful with aromas of coffee and bacon. A table, fresh with white linen, stood by the window; Pop never ate from an unclothed table; he never let himself slip into what he called "just baching it."

There were a good many photographs around the walls—glass-framed ones—small, literal, exact prints. Photographically, Pop Capp derived straight out of the great tradition of David Hill, Matthew Brady, and Eadweard Muybridge. Of course, Pop *did* touch up his commercial work—had to—but his heart wasn't in it. Anybody could tell that, looking around at these framed prints. Pop's photography was as vigorous as his old-fashioned pyro developing solutions.

His coffee was vigorous, too. Johnny Kendall put down his cup after a long, appreciative interval. He lighted a cigarette and inhaled gratefully.

"It's the damnedest mixed up mess I ever ran into," he said.

He braced an elbow on the table, puffed at the cigarette again, and stared through the exhaled smoke at Pop Capp.

"Frank Ellsworth has a nice, slick, smooth theory," Johnny Kendall said. "A woman visits Dr. Rigmire last night. They quarrel. Rigmire follows her to the car, her car, the one that dripped the oil. She snatches up the axe, more or less in self-defense. Then she's terrified by what's she's done. She runs to call Dwyer. She puts a tourniquet on Rigmire's wrist. She runs off, runs home, to keep her name out of the scandal.

"You see how that works out, Pop," Johnny Kendall said. "When she gets home, she tells this man— her husband, brother, sweetheart, whoever he is. He takes up the quarrel. It's logical, it's just what plenty of men *would* do. She'd have told him only her side of the story, naturally. And the man takes her word for it.

"He goes to see Rigmire, sneaks up to the house

there under cover of darkness, but he stops first at the car shed. He looks for a weapon of some sort, a hammer or something, and he picks up the hatchet from among the tools in the shed. He slips into the house, but then Cousin Joe Hanlon wakes up and screams. The man strikes him, kills him—has to, if he intends to kill Dr. Rigmire. He can't leave a witness alive, that's obvious.

"The nurse, Miss Carr, runs up onto the porch. The murderer hears her there, fumbling to find the door-knob. He takes to his heels, dashes out through the kitchen and the back door, and so runs into me.

"That's just about the way Ellsworth sizes it up."

Johnny Kendall sighed.

"That's one theory," he said. "It covers the ground pretty well, if you're willing to admit the murder could have happened that fast. If ten seconds was time enough for the murderer to hit Cousin Joe three licks with the hatchet and then escape from the house. It doesn't explain why the killer dropped the hatchet, though. You'd think he'd take it with him; he might need it; if anyone tried to stop him outside, as actually did happen."

Pop Capp said, "What's the rest of it?"

Johnny Kendall told him the rest of it.

Pop Capp got up, opened a humidor at the other side of the room, and took out his Sunday morning cigar. He pinched the cigar between his pyro-stained fingers. He said, "I don't know, Johnny. That theory bears pretty hard on Dr. Rigmire himself, seems to me."

"Well—"

"If you figure it that way, you have to figure your Dr. Rigmire is plain lying when he says he doesn't know who the woman was. That's a pretty serious charge, all-fired serious, considering a member of his family is dead as a result of all this. If he knows, you'd think he'd tell."

"Yes," Johnny Kendall said, "the man must have been gunning for Rigmire. He couldn't have gone there to kill Cousin Joe Hanlon. Hanlon's being there at all was happenstance; nobody knew he'd be there; except Madeleine and Sawyer—Dr. Sawyer having talked to him on the phone. Cousin Joe's life was sacrificed to save Rigmire's, and it's true, that would put Dr. Rigmire in a bad light. If he really does know."

Johnny Kendall rubbed out his cigarette.

"It's Ellsworth's theory, not mine," he said. "He figured on that basis from the start."

Pop Capp drew at his cigar reflectively.

Johnny Kendall said, "You warned me last night." He half-closed his eyes. "You said you'd let Frank Ellsworth do his own sheriffing. Why?"

"I had a feeling," Pop Capp admitted. "A feeling you two wouldn't pull in a double harness."

"But, *why*?"

Pop Capp said, "You're high-strung, Johnny. You've got city ideas. You've got that newspaper bug in you.

You're just a little bit too fast on your feet for this town."

Pop laid his cigar carefully in his saucer.

"I'm not saying anything against Frank, either. He gets along all right. He's a pretty good sheriff. Only he works at it on the dog-fight theory." Pop Capp smiled. "Let me tell you, hardly anything can beat a first class dog-fight, for kicking up noise and excitement. While it lasts. 'Course, it doesn't last long. It blows over and settles down, and it's all forgotten half an hour later."

Johnny Kendall said, "Never mind the sermon, Pop. Just shoot me the text."

Pop spied a crumb on the tablecloth. He retrieved it. He said, "It's different in Altamont. Different in the newspaper business. Dog bites dog, that isn't news. In a city, a certain number of big things are bound to happen. You're used to the big things, used to the news happening around you, and Frank isn't. A lot of noise and excitement here in Crestpeak, generally speaking, means just another dog-fight. That's not your experience, but it's been Frank Ellsworth's."

Johnny Kendall said, "Murder is murder, anywhere."

Pop Capp said, "But Frank had his mind made up from the start."

Johnny Kendall thought and said, "Yes, he did. Yes, you're right about him. He figured it was a dog-fight —Dr. Rigmire and some woman having a quarrel— and he made up his mind Rigmire didn't really want it investigated."

"That's your text," Pop Capp asserted. "Most people don't thank a sheriff for nosing around in their personal affairs, and he knows it."

"So he said. That Dr. Rigmire wouldn't prosecute, wouldn't appear in court, even if the woman was found."

Johnny Kendall fumbled for another cigarette.

"If he's wrong about that," Johnny Kendall said, "his whole theory is wrong. It's just as possible that Dr. Rigmire is telling the truth, that he doesn't know, and wants to find out. It looks that way, from what I can make of Madeleine. It's clear now that she wasn't acting on her own responsibility last night.

"Madeleine talked to her father last night. He sent her in to town, that's certain. Her ideas—about the sheriff's inefficiency, the notion of hiring a private detective, the notion that all this has its roots in Altamont—she got those ideas from him. It's hard to imagine him dragging his own daughter into it, unless he intends to go ahead with an investigation."

Johnny Kendall shook his head.

"Rigmire's a clumsy liar, if he's lying at all," he said. "The way to protect the woman, if he wanted to shield her, was to say he saw her clearly—and then give Ellsworth a completely false description."

"It's as likely he's telling the truth," said Pop Capp. "Until it's proved otherwise, anyway."

"But that brings us back to the same old stickler," Johnny Kendall said, frowning. "Why didn't the woman kill him, then? Instead of phoning for a doctor?"

Pop Capp said, "You better have another cup of coffee on it."

He poured the coffee.

"Johnny," he said, "Rigmire was knocked senseless, wasn't he? Maybe she didn't know the difference."

Johnny Kendall stared at the old man.

"My God!" Johnny Kendall said. "Maybe that's it!"

He wetted his lips.

"My God, she might not have known! Pop, that's an idea. That may be it," Johnny Kendall said warmly. *"She thought he was dead!* So of course she'd call a doctor. She couldn't lose. If she was traced—if she was ever arrested—"

He pushed back his chair, stood up, struck his fist into his palm.

"Now we're getting places," Johnny Kendall said. "She phoned Dwyer. She even put a tourniquet on the victim's wrist. So she could claim she never meant to kill him at all. It was self-defense, that's her story. She fled for fear of scandal—she was afraid Rigmire would do her bodily injury when he came to his senses —it's a *good* story."

Pop Capp said, "You better sit down and drink your coffee, Johnny." He sighed. "It was just an idea of mine."

Standing, Johnny Kendall took a hasty swallow of the coffee. He rattled the cup into its saucer. He said, "All right, let's keep on with that idea. . . . She left

Dr. Rigmire for *dead*. Then she found out, later, he wasn't dead. So she came back—brought a man along with her the next time—"

"Not mentioning any names, of course," said Pop Capp.

"You mean Geneva Carr," Johnny Kendall said. "I don't know. She might have been in the house. Both of them might have been in the house—and then I drove up—but, no, that won't work either."

He sat down. He rubbed a hand slowly over his face.

"There was no blood on either of them," Johnny Kendall said. "Doc Dwyer says blood must have literally sprayed over whoever swung that hatchet. It's all possible—she could have been in the house, and Sawyer could have been the guy who ran into me—but the bloodstains let them both out."

He drank the coffee. He picked up the cigarette.

"Besides," he said, "neither Geneva Carr nor Dr. Sawyer would have known where to look for our back door key. Even if the door wasn't locked, neither of them could have come into the shop without Butch raising hell. So that's out. You've got half of the solution, Pop, but not all of it."

Pop Capp said, "I'm no detective. It was just a half-baked idea I threw out there."

Johnny Kendall said he thought Pop was close to it. He said he'd like to see that idea fully baked.

He said, "You don't know who to believe. That's the trouble. Maybe Rigmire is leveling; maybe he isn't; you can't tell. My God, Pop, you can't even take the word of absolutely disinterested witnesses. There's Dwyer—county coroner, at that—and *his* word just isn't worth a damn. Driving out there in eleven minutes!"

"He might have looked at his watch wrong," Pop Capp said. "Make him five minutes off. Make him drive it just about your speed, wouldn't it?"

"It isn't just the time that's wrong with Dwyer," Johnny Kendall said gloomily. "His testimony doesn't amount to a damn anywhere along the line. *He* doesn't know what the woman said to him over the phone— he can't quote her word for word, and he admits it. Not only that, but he got his phone conversation with Madeleine Rigmire all screwed up. He'd have sworn in court that she was bringing a brain specialist, Hugo Sawyer, out here. You just can't believe a word Doc Dwyer tells you; he gets it all wrong, balled up, foxed."

Pop Capp said, "He's a pretty fair doctor, though. Good as any. Better than most."

"I'd hate to have him take out my appendix," Johnny Kendall declared. "I'd be afraid of waking up with an arm amputated instead."

"Now, Johnny, you're away off base," Pop Capp said. "You've got to realize human beings are a good deal like cameras. You focus a camera on something six feet away, and you get a good sharp picture of what you're focused on. But something else, something twenty feet away, isn't clear at all. And the better the camera, the more critical the lens, the more true that is. You can't have a critical focus on one thing, and expect the whole background to come out just as clear and distinct, can you?"

"Well—no—"

Pop Capp said, "Doc Dwyer's a good man; good sharp brain; smarter than you or me, probably. He just wasn't *focused* on remembering what words the woman used; he was focused on making her understand how to give first-aid, as I understand the story. He didn't any more than barely glance at his watch when he drove into the yard there—he was concentrating on his patient—and suppose he didn't get his conversation with the Rigmire girl straight? His mind was in the other room while he was talking. Don't worry," Pop Capp said gently, "about Doc Dwyer cutting off your arm instead of your appendix. When he's focused on your appendix, he wouldn't even know you had an arm."

Johnny Kendall said, "Well, yes. I shouldn't have made that crack. He's a good doctor, but outside of that, I still say his testimony doesn't amount to a damn."

Johnny Kendall frowned. He nicked his nether lip against his teeth.

"My God, Pop," he said, "according to your theory, nobody's testimony really amounts to a damn. All of these people were going about their own business. All of them were *focused* on their own affairs. If you could get a photograph of what's inside our heads, you'd have just a lot of background fuzz, distorted, underexposed in the first place, and then overdeveloped by thinking about it. Nobody has a clear picture of what happened last night."

Johnny Kendall drew a deep breath.

"Nobody except the murderer," he said.

DEATHDEALER'S DIARY

Sunday a.m., Oct. 19, '41

"There's a divinity that shapes our
ends, rough-hew them how we will—" should
have been written, _fine_-hew them how we
will. No man ever shapes his ends,
except in fine and in detail.

What is life but Destiny, luck, fate,
call it what you will?

What is history but a succession of improbable accidents?

—The Washington who led Braddock into
the wilderness would never have returned
to become the Father of His Country—
had the bullet passed through the man instead of the horse. The fate of the
Colonies depended upon the flight of a
pellet of lead—a yard's difference in the

aim of a nameless marksman would have
made all the difference.

—Abraham Lincoln would never have
become president, had there been no seven
year old Austin Gollaher at hand to pull
the little Abe out of a creek. The fate
of the Union was at the fingertips of a
backwoods urchin; no Austin Gollaher—
no Gettysburg Address!

—By so slender a thread hangs life and
death—and Murder!

"I told you something might turn up,"
grumbles the policeman-within, "and spoil
your perfect crime!"

I say that has nothing to do with it.
Genius is not the capacity for planning
perfectly; anyone can make plans: fools,
dreamers, and failures are more full of
plans than are great men.

Genius, I say, is the capacity for
adapting the plan to the circumstance.
Stubborn, small minds "stick to it"
through "thick and thin—" come what may.
Great men know a Destiny rough-hews their

ends—and take advantage of it—make advantage of Destiny, the Fates, luck, coincidence. . . .

Something turns up—and small men shrink.

Something turns up—and Genius welcomes it.

Genius, I say, is the infinite capacity for trimming one's sails to the winds.

The policeman-within remains uninterested in philosophy. Practical fellow!

"That's all very well," says he. "But it isn't what you were letting yourself in for! You weren't going to act except on a plan approved by me. It was all to be so simple—straight-forward—no mystery about it—"

Well, yes, I was. I had such a plan— a good plan, the best plan possible—for a man going at the thing single-handed.

Other people might interfere; I knew that; obviously any drunken lunatic whirling along the highway at seventy miles an hour could interfere! Dr. Harry Rigmire

might have interfered—by returning to Altamont Saturday afternoon, say. Certainly
I had no control over other people's
lives, schemes, movements; any more than
I could control the elements—prevent a
rain, mud, if it had rained.

I said—in my critical, cautious, detec-
tive-self—that something might turn up;
I allowed for the possibility.

It did turn up, and I made use of it.

"On the spur of the moment," says the
policeman-within. He worries; he detests
brilliant improvisation—but how can you
improvise, except on the spur of the
moment?

I say this is better—better because I
didn't plan it—because nobody could have
planned it. The thing contradicts logic,
contradicts probability itself, contradicts common sense.

How is it to be unraveled by logic,
common sense, practicality?

The fact is, of course, that improbable
things continually do occur. The laws of

probability are based on the improbable,
just as much as on the probable; if nothing improbable ever occurred, it would
never occur to logical minds to construct
a law of probability. Take the extreme
case—a man falls 228 feet—falls from a
balloon—and lands unhurt, without a
broken bone, a sprain, a scratch.*

How "probable" is that? How many policemen—how many lawyers, jurors, judges
—would accept it as even a possibility?
And yet it happened.

"Believe it or not," the improbable
continually does happen—and continually
is ignored, disbelieved, forgotten; because events of this nature cannot be

---

*On June 21, 1901, George R. Lawrence "was attempting to get a
bird's-eye picture of a Chicago packing plant from a captive balloon suspended over the stockyards district. The exposure was made at 950 feet,
but as Lawrence was being drawn downward the netting ripped, allowing
the gas bag to free itself and float away. Lawrence hurtled downward 228
feet, as was determined by mathematical calculation before the debris was
cleared away. . . . The only physical effect of that terrific plunge through
space was a fierce stinging sensation on the soles of his feet."—H. H.
Slawson, in *American Photography* Nov. 1939.

An account of this incident, drawn from contemporary newspaper accounts, appears in an earlier thesis (1935) by Dr. Earl Sawyer on "Mental
Factors in 'Shock' in Accident Cases." He argued that the "mental factors" were negligible. Mr. Lawrence was so little shocked that the following day found him "photographing Chicago's old-time derby race at
Washington Park," as Mr. Slawson states.

classified, ticketed, and filed away
according to the "laws of probability."
The whole literature of psychic experience
is ignored, disbelieved, and forgotten
for just this reason. The so-called "laws
of chance" would be upset, if all the
successful predictions of soothsayers,
the curses connected with famous diamonds
and Egyptian tombs, the dreams coincident
with events transpiring at remote distances, were all to be explained as mere
"chance." Either these things are not
lucky improbabilities, or else our tables
of probability must be revised. A Pharaoh
dead three thousand years can lay a curse
on modern men—or the arm of coincidence
is longer than science supposes—the
improbable is probable.

"What's all that got to do with it?"
says the policeman-within.

I say that it has everything to do with
it. His man-made Law—its rules of evidence—its whole pattern and patter of
legality is based on logic. So-called

"Guilt" must be established beyond a
reasonable doubt.

But Destiny—Fate—Luck—Coincidence—
these concepts are neither logical nor
reasonable. The man-made Law can convict
a man only on the probabilities. Convictions are not gotten on a series of
illogical, unreasonable, improbable sup-
positions.

I say that my original Plan was a
miracle of logic; it satisfied the policeman-within; he could find no flaw in it.

But the Murderer saw a chance to base
his Crime on something better than logic.

For it was chance—the purest and
sheerest Chance—that car turning into the
lane at the exact moment that Dr. Harry
Rigmire reeled before me—struck senseless, bleeding, but still on his feet.

"You didn't know he was senseless," says
the policeman-within. "You ran away because you saw the chance of being caught
red-handed—"

Not at all. Not at all!

<u>You</u> were afraid, I say. That is to say,
there were two of us; two sides to my
nature. The artist-creator self: the
inner man of fire, imagination, audacity.
And the policeman-self: the creature of
logic, common sense, and caution.

Which of these counseled flight? Which
<u>would</u>?

Why, the policeman-within; how could it
be otherwise?

"Run!" cried Caution. "Rigmire is still
dangerous, if he gets his hands on me!"
cried Common Sense. "That car will be
here in a few seconds—you can't be caught
struggling with the Victim!" shouted
Logic.

It was a bad moment, that. Luck—the
chance that brought him to the woodpile—
played me false; but there he stood,
playing that flashlight around; he would
have found me out in the next instant. <u>I</u>
<u>had</u> <u>to</u> <u>strike</u>. I had no choice—I had
to strike blindly—the wonder is that I
did not miss him entirely! <u>It is not easy</u>

to gauge precisely with an axe a moving
target only indirectly seen behind a
flashlight. I should have gone to the
tool-shed for the hatchet in the first
place. The axe was too heavy, unwieldy,
requiring too long a stroke—and I could
not change the direction of the stroke
once well begun. The Victim cowered,
threw up his arms; and saved his life.

And, "Run!" cried the policeman-within.
"Run for your own life!"

What luck, what mischance! What could
logic, common sense, and caution do—
but run?

Nevertheless, I turned this mischance to
my own uses.

Dr. Harry Rigmire saw a woman behind
the axe. It was the rain cape—something
like a skirt, as he glimpsed it; the
rustle of a woman's dress, as he heard it.

Happy accident! Improbability of improbabilities! The Murderer cleared by the
Victim's own testimony!

"Policeman," I say, "what do you make

of that? How will you go about convicting
me <u>now</u>?"

   "You're not through with it," says he.
"Rigmire's still alive, after all."

   "That," I promise him, "won't be for
long."

IX

WHEN HE UNLOCKED THE PHOTO SHOP MONDAY morning a voice bubbled:

"Johnny-boy!"

A man got out of a car at the curb. He was a page out of *Men's Wear*. He wore blue flannels and a foulard tie and two-toned oxfords. He was hatless, and his hair was blonde, curly. He had a blonde moustache. He was very tan. His blue eyes flashed and danced, smiling.

"Johnny-boy, pal, remember me?"

"I'll be damned if I do," said Johnny Kendall.

"Friend of Macguire's," the man said. "You must've seen me and Mac around. Larry Elroy. I work out of Sherman's."

Macguire was police reporter on the *Altamont Blade*. Sherman's was a private agency.

Johnny said, "Oh, a dick."

"Sure, *you* remember," Larry Elroy said. His voice was a soft shout. He was enthusiastic. He was exuberant. He was a gorgeous blonde animal.

Johnny Kendall did not remember him at all. He knew of Sherman's. It was a well-established agency.

"Well," Johnny said, "what can I do for you?"

"Chum," Larry Elroy said, "I'd like to know. I've

been asking myself. I thought I'd ask you that, Johnny-boy."

Johnny Kendall went into the shop, and behind the door. The door was slotted: *Leave Rollfilms Here.* Sunday snapshooters had left half a dozen rollfilms, and there was an envelope besides. He tore the envelope's end, and shook out some Speed Graphic negatives.

He slid them back into the envelope swiftly.

"How do you mean?" Johnny asked.

"I thought I'd get you drunk first," Elroy said. "I thought I'd ply you with liquor, Johnny-boy. Taking drink-for-drink with you, of course. It goes on the swindle-sheet, see?" He opened his eyes wide, glowing. "You could do that much for me, couldn't you, chum?"

"At this time of the morning?"

"My God, yes," the blonde animal said. "The morning is when I need it."

"Wait'll I put this stuff in the darkroom," Johnny said. He went back through the gallery and through the light trapped doors. He switched on a bulb over the wash tank, held up one of the Graphic negatives. And then another. And a third.

These were the films that had been stolen from his drying cabinet. A thumbprint on the third was very clear.

Johnny Kendall uncapped his fountain pen. He wrote across the envelope: *Sheriff—You'll find the fingerprint of a suspected thief and murderer herewith. The moral is, Never handle film except by the edges.* He thought and added, *In fact don't handle it at all.*

"Pop!" said Johnny, from the gallery's back door.

Pop Capp appeared on the stairs. Johnny Kendall said loudly, "Will you look after things while I'm out awhile?" and winked, tapped his forefinger on the envelope before passing it up to the veteran photographer.

"The former owner. He runs the shop while I'm out," Johnny said to Larry Elroy.

"Come on," said the blonde detective. "Let's choose up sides and see what the boys in the backroom will have."

"A small beer, Mike," Johnny Kendall told Slalol.

"Make mine bourbon and ditch," Elroy said. Slalol's backroom was large enough for three tables. The tables were used by pinochle players in the evening, were built to withstand the crashing of triumphant fists. Elroy opened a door that said MEN, and looked in, and then selected a chair facing the door. His eyes twinkled merrily.

"Holy hell!" he said. "How do you stand it, Johnny-boy?"

"Stand what?"

"The goddam sunshine and fresh air and all that crap," Elroy said. "Don't it drive you nuts, though?"

"No."

"It will. You're *city.* You live too fast. You'll have this town used up in six months. Maybe three. There isn't enough of it to go around. You'll have the flesh off its bones in six months. Right now you're getting a kick of it, meeting these primitives and finding out what makes 'em tick. But the ticking gets goddam monotonous when it never changes."

Slalol brought in the small beer in one hand, the bourbon in the other.

"That'll be five dollars and thirty cents, gents," Slalol said. "Ten, twenty, and five bucks cover charge."

Elroy watched Slalol's bulk through the door. "Wait'll you hear him pull that so-called gag the ten thousandth time. Wait'll you know what every last damned one of them is going to say before he opens his face."

Johnny Kendall said, "All right, you've undermined my loyalty to Crestpeak. What follows?"

"You're a bright guy. That's why I say it can't last. It wouldn't last for me, and you're a hell of a lot brighter than I am." Elroy drank. "Who was Rigmire playing, Johnny?"

"Was he?"

Elroy drank again. He said. "Sure. I talked to the telephone operator, the girl that was on the board Saturday night. I asked her why she called Dr. Dwyer instead of some other sawbones. She said the call was *for* Dwyer. You chase that around in your brain awhile."

"Uh-huh."

"Suppose I was off some place, sixty-seventy miles from home. Would I grab the phone in an emergency and ask for a particular Dr. Smith or Dr. Jones? I wouldn't, couldn't. I'd just say, 'Operator, for God's sake get me a doctor.'"

"Yes," Johnny Kendall said.

"Local girl, then," Elroy said. "So churchy la femme, as the Frogs say. I'd even gamble she was one of Dwyer's patients, or at least he's the family doctor, since she thought of him first."

He drank.

"Strange Dwyer didn't recognize the voice, then," Johnny Kendall said.

"Maybe he ain't telling."

"Or maybe she called him because she *wasn't* his patient, and he'd not know the voice."

"Don't confuse the issue, Johnny-boy. She's not that bright, I bet," Elroy said. "A nice mountain girl. A sweet highlands lassie. A wild flower. You never heard of such?"

"I'm sorry."

Elroy pounded the table. "More bourbon and less ditch," he said to Slalol. "Make it two?"

Johnny Kendall said, "Just beer, Mike."

"You're *newspaper*," Elroy resumed. "You can dig it out, and let me tell you why. It's a story. You could buy your way back into the business with that kind of a story. Exclusive. Walk into the managing editor's desk, and say, how about it?"

Slalol brought the drinks.

"With what you can dig up, and what I can give you," Elroy said. "One hand washes the other. We could play ball. With what you can get, and what I've got."

Johnny Kendall said, "What sort of a bargain is this? I give it to you, and you give it back to me?"

"I want the dame from you," Elroy said. "That's all. And I'll give you the background. *You* don't have to tip your hand. I'll do the dirty work, and chum, it's always dirty."

He drank and said, "Don't think I can't work it out by myself. Hell, there's not more than two, three possibilities. Doc Rigmire wasn't picking also-rans. He didn't have that habit."

He drank again. "You're inside, though. I'm out. These people won't talk to me. All I'm asking you to do is listen for the gossip. Find out what probably half the town already knows."

"You're sure it wasn't an out-of-town woman," Johnny said, "who might have heard Dwyer's name mentioned, professionally or otherwise. Or perhaps just've seen his office sign, driving through town?"

Elroy's whisper shouted softly, "You mean Gene Carr."

"Do I?"

"Forget her," Elroy said. "Would you know anything about first aid, Johnny-boy?"

Johnny Kendall winced. "Just call me Johnny."

"Sure. Just call me Larry, chum," said Elroy fondly. "I took up that subject once. First aid. Did you know there was a time in my misspent youth when I hankered to be an honest-to-Gawd cop? 'S fact. Well, that's one of the qualifying exams you have to pass."

He drank.

"They *never* put a tourniquet on a wrist, Johnny. They never at all, if they can help it. But the correct pressure point is higher, between the elbow and the shoulder. So I guess we won't worry about Nursie Carr."

"Unless she deliberately—?"

"Ah, crud. You're confusing the issue again," Elroy said. "A child of nature is the ticket. A full breasted child of nature."

Johnny Kendall said, "Then, your theory is—?"

"Ah, crud, theory! That's storybook stuff. That's armchair detection. A practical dick never stoops to it. To hell with the loose ends. To hell with the if, but, and maybe crap."

Elroy drained his glass. "I'm professional," he said. "No theory for me. I get a lead, and follow the lead. Then I get another lead. Finally I get my bastard cornered. That's all there is to it. I don't give a damn about anything in the world except finding the child of nature."

He didn't, Johnny Kendall decided, give a damn about anything else—so far as Johnny Kendall was concerned. Larry Elroy's manner was tailored, like his flannels. He was an actor. He derived from the imagination of Mr. Dashiell Hammett and the pages of *Black Mask* magazine. He was a copybook private cop. There were probably scores of private detectives in the country striving to be Sam Spade and Bill Crane. Nineteen in every score were deceiving themselves; the twentieth wasn't; Larry Elroy wasn't.

"Why didn't you make the grade?" Johnny Kendall asked.

"What grade?"

"With the cops."

Elroy laughed. His teeth flashed, his eyes glittered, his shoulders shook. "I didn't have the three C's," the blonde animal said. "That was the year the alderman built a swimming pool. I understand it cost ten patrolmen and a police lieutenant promotion." He twirled the glass, empty. "Ah, well," he said.

"Yep," said Johnny Kendall, recognizing the tone of dismissal. Elroy had no intention of talking about Larry Elroy. He wanted to talk about Dr. Rigmire's paramour, if the doctor had one. Whatever else he wanted was hidden behind the man's brisk artificiality.

They stood. Slalol grinned behind the bar. "You ain't staying for the floorshow?"

"We seen it," Elroy said. "A parade of pink elephants."

He stopped on the sunlit curb. He took Johnny Kendall's arm, squeezing. "There's the pressure point," he said, beaming. He was acting harder than ever. Underneath the flashing male magnetism ran something else, a narrow dark current in the man.

He's dangerous, Johnny Kendall thought suddenly.

"I'm serious," Larry Elroy murmured. "Maybe you

don't give a damn about the exclusive newspaper angle."

He had a politician's sense.

"I tell you what," said Elroy, baiting another hook. "I'll get something out of the agency for you. We don't usually pay for information, but I think I could get you maybe a hundred fish, cash." He watched Johnny Kendall's face. "Nobody'd ever know where the tip came from. My God, I don't want to get you in bad here. After all, you're in business. You have to protect yourself, that's understood."

When they can't talk you out of your vote, Johnny thought, they try to buy it. If you're not for sale, why, two other men will be.

Johnny Kendall probed: "You want me to drop you a line, then, care of Sherman's?" He kept a careful, posed innocence.

Elroy recoiled. His expression was comic, and too large for his face. "Jesus, Johnny! They open my mail there. You want to leave me no mystery, make it look like I went out and bought an answer? You want to get me canned?"

He teetered on the curb. "Besides, you'd play hell getting a hundred bucks out of George Sherman. Squeezing a nickel out of that guy is something you do with a lasso and a tin cup. Like milking a range cow." He patted Johnny's shoulder. "No, I'm in the phone book. Call me, and reverse the charges."

Elroy got into his car. "I'm counting on you, chum."

Johnny Kendall watched the car down the street

before he turned into the Photo Shop. He said to Pop Capp behind the counter:

"What'd the sheriff think?"

"I didn't go," Pop said. He looked tired and troubled.

"Johnny," Pop said, "I guess we better talk this over. I know whose fingerprint you've got on that blamed negative. I think maybe we better go upstairs, Johnny."

X

"I'M GOING TO SHOW YOU SOMETHING," POP CAPP SAID. He took a key-ring from his pocket, selected a small key, and unlocked the desk. "Something I should've destroyed, and've been putting off." The package was large, sixteen by twenty inches, wrapped in brown paper. It had come by express, was addressed to him, and was rubber stamped *Photographs*. Pop's pyrostained fingers peeled aside the brown paper, and revealed first corrugated paperboard, and then a matboard on the back of which was pasted a green crown that said: *Exhibited, 39th Annual International Salon, G.C.*

"Vanity," Pop said. "I guess that's the text for the sermon. Pride goeth before a fall, and so forth."

Johnny Kendall stared at the small green emblem. He had heard of the Crown Society. For himself, photography was a livelihood, not an art; he did not go in for the salons. But he knew pictorialists well enough to appreciate the importance which they attached to exhibition stickers. And he knew that of all such stickers, the Crown's was the hardest come by. The Society's annual show was limited to a hundred prints, so that not more than that number of pictures ever received recognition in a single year; frequently the number was less, since no picture was ever hung without the jury's unanimous approval.

Johnny Kendall said, "Good Lord, Pop, that's tops."

"You haven't seen it yet," said Pop Capp, turning the matboard with his pyro-stained fingers.

The print itself was small, as salon prints go; it was eight inches by ten, a contact print from a view camera negative. It had the exact and literal quality, the sharp and almost steel-engraved definition that characterized Pop's best work.

"They tell you," Pop Capp said, "a nude shouldn't look like a woman without her clothes on. She should look like something you could call Arabesque or Moonlight Sonata or Adoration. Now to me, that's just plain nonsense. What else *is* a nude but a woman with her clothes off? Why in the name of heaven do you have to photograph her twisted into some crazy shape, like the radiator cap on a car?"

The photograph was of a young woman seated on a chair, drawing on a stocking. It did not look like a hosiery ad. It looked like a girl putting on a stocking.

Pop Capp said, "Darn it, Johnny. Suppose she was two years old instead of twenty. You'd say I was crazy if I took a picture of her posed like a pretzel, and called the result Odalesque or Evensong."

He paused.

"It's no use arguing, though," he said. "Either the picture tells you what I mean, or else it's just a smutty postcard to you."

It was not like any nude Johnny Kendall had ever

seen; in camera annuals, or hung on newspaper dark-room walls. It did not seek to display the model's beauty of figure at all. It had the innocence, indeed, of a two year old model.

Johnny Kendall said that wasn't his point. "I can't see why you intended to destroy it."

"You recognize her, don't you?"

"Yes. Babette Hazelle."

"Well," Pop Capp said, "that's why. I don't expect to live forever, and there aren't many people in town I'd care to find that picture after I'm gone. It tries too hard to be what it is, Babette without her clothes. I judge Crestpeak would consider it indecent. And the worst is, I expect maybe Babette would agree with them there."

"Then why did she—?"

"I guess that's why she did," said Pop Capp, sighing. "You have to remember she's the town drunkard's daughter. She's been brought up on a diet of public pity. That ain't wholesome for a high-spirited girl. If the town's standards make her an object of pity, she's bound to question those standards. I'm trying to suggest," Pop said, "having her picture taken without her clothes was, well, thumbing her nose at them."

Johnny Kendall smiled. "That's probably a pretty acute analysis. Still, let's not get into a cracker-barrel session. You didn't get me up here just to tell me about this photography angle. What I want to know about Babette Hazelle is why—"

Pop Capp said, "Now, Johnny." He gave the

younger man a deeply disillusioned look. "I wish you would forget that murder for once. For a few minutes. I phoned Babette, and she'll be here. For the time being, if you could quit treating the whole thing like a crossword puzzle."

"That," said Johnny Kendall, "isn't fair. I want to see the connection, is all."

"And I want you to see," Pop Capp said, "how it began. You've got to understand it ain't easy for Babette in this town. She can't hold a job, even. Old Hazy makes trouble; he gets drunk, goes around to people, and insists he's got the right to her wages. She worked in the drugstore awhile, and in the variety, but a business man can't have a thing like that—old Hazy coming in Saturday night and raising plumb hell. Babette has tried one thing and another; addressing envelopes at home for a mail order outfit, was one. And taking courses. Self-improvement. The girl's tied down, she's not willing to go without taking her mother; she's tried to learn things by home study, like shorthand and fashion modeling. It was the fashion modeling brought her in here—she wanted some pictures taken, to send off to a department store in Altamont."

Pop shook his head. "I don't say there's no such thing as a legitimate and honest correspondence school. But that course was a fake. She didn't know the first thing about modeling. But I told her I'd pay professional rates if she was interested in that line of work." He gestured. "I'm the one that's got to bear the responsibility. I don't know why I did it. Vanity, I guess.

I had my own ideas about salon nudes, and I wanted to prove I was right. But there wasn't any chance. No model. Oh, I could've hired a commercial model from some agency in Altamont, but she'd be no good for me. A professional'd be crammed with all the stock, phony notions I wanted to work away from. Babette looked like a Godsend."

"You don't have to explain all this to me," Johnny Kendall said. "Photography in the nude is perfectly legitimate. Anyone who can get a study accepted by the Crown jury doesn't have to apologize for his artistic standards."

"Photographically speaking," said Pop, "but we're not talking about my artistic standards now. The fact is, Babette took off her clothes in front of me. And that's a scandalous fact to be gossiped about in Crestpeak."

Johnny Kendall thought the older man overly insistent.

"I don't see," he said, "why it has to be gossiped about. I assume Babette knew about your back door key. So what? You could've left that door unlocked, after all. You don't have to tell the town all your past history."

Pop Capp was grim. "She borrowed my car Saturday night, too."

"What?" Johnny Kendall cried. He swallowed: "When?"

"When she drove out there to Rigmire's," Pop said. "You knew—?"

"She didn't say where she was going, or where she'd been. I had to put two and two together to get that answer," Pop said.

Relief. "Then you're not involved."

"In some ways, Johnny, you ain't very smart. Babette is about one-third my age. Why would she come and ask the loan of my car? Why'd I let her have it? People are bound to figure out there's something behind that."

"It's nothing to be ashamed of. You're iconoclast enough to stand up to the town with that cracker-barrel philosophy of yours," said Johnny, smiling.

"Me? I'm not worried. It's Babette. I've got to shield her from that kind of scandal if I can."

Johnny Kendall heard the shop door downstairs release its warning note. He heard the girl's heels click on the stairs. Babette Hazelle stopped in the doorway.

Pop Capp's hands hung lamely at his sides. "Some films were left here yesterday," he said. "Johnny found a thumbprint on one of them. I guess we all three know who's thumb it was."

Johnny Kendall looked at the girl, disturbed.

Babette was not a "beauty." She was "photogenic." An inexpert glance might have summed up her features, and dismissed them as plain; but she had glowing, generous eyes under a widely generous forehead. Her skin was olive, and superbly receptive to light.

She was a slim, trim brunette; her figure, too, would have fooled an inexpert eye. It was not at all a voluptuous and alluring figure. It looked athletic, and almost too economically spare.

But the merciless camera lens found the structure of her form flawless; its lines flowed smoothly, and the firm breasts were convexly Oriental.

She was angry, and frightened. She said: "Well, what are you going to do about it?"

"I guess that's more or less up to Johnny," Pop Capp observed sadly.

Johnny Kendall said uncomfortably, "Come in and sit down. Let's get to the bottom of all this." He was bothered by the direct challenge in Babette Hazelle's eyes.

He felt reproach and antagonism in her manner. Babette lived in Crestpeak hostilely, in the enemy's camp. He was an enemy. He was moreover an enemy who held in his hand the power to inflict injury.

He was conscious of acute embarrassment. It put an unhappy, bumbling edge to his voice.

"What was the trouble?" he asked.

"Trouble?"

"You and Rigmire."

Babette Hazelle sat stiffly on her chair. "There wasn't any. I went there to see him about my father."

Johnny Kendall struggled for understanding. "About—?"

"It was an advertisement," the girl said. "I clipped it out of a movie magazine. It was something to stop the drink habit. You just put it in their coffee."

"Self-improvement," Pop Capp said. "Postpaid in a plain wrapper. What'd I tell you, Johnny?"

Johnny Kendall stared at the girl. "You went there

to ask Dr. Rigmire about that advertisement?" He was incredulous.

"No," Babette Hazelle said. "No, I sent for it. I put it in his coffee. Saturday night was the first time. You know what happened Saturday night."

"He got drunk, anyway," Pop said.

"He—was worse. He was crazy drunk. I was afraid," the girl said. "Maybe the medicine contained some drug or other. Or poison, even. It didn't work the way the ad said at all. It just made him sick and crazy. I wanted a doctor for him, but not anyone here in Crestpeak. It'd be all over town. It'd make me a laughingstock on the streets. The idea of putting something in his coffee to make him stop drinking. A scream, isn't it?"

Pop Capp sighed, tired. "Now, Bab, you quit tormenting yourself."

"It's the simple truth. They'd laugh their heads off if they knew."

Johnny Kendall decided Babette had never had any genuine faith in the advertised article at all. She was ashamed of having purchased it. The act had been one of desperation, performed without hope because everything else had failed. Her emotions now were greatly magnified, those of a presumably rational scientist who has been caught walking around a ladder.

He said: "All right. You gave this 'medicine,' so-called, to your father. It made him desperately ill. You wanted to consult a physician, but not a local man. But how did you happen to hit on Dr. Rigmire?"

"I—I knew him. A—a little."

"How well?"

"Just to speak to. My father has some bees out there. That's how I happened to meet Dr. Rigmire."

"It's peculiar," Pop Capp interposed, "but bees won't sting old Hazy. He knows how to scratch them behind the ears, too."

"You mean the bees are on the Rigmire place?" Johnny asked.

"The hives are along the creek," the girl said. "It's mountain lilac honey. Dr. Rigmire was fishing when we were out there once. He talked to me a little bit then."

She hesitated.

"I thought he might help," she said, "only he probably wouldn't even remember my name. I—it wasn't exactly like calling a doctor. I was asking a favor. I couldn't very well explain all this on the phone. So I went out there."

Johnny Kendall was thoughtful. "Had it struck you, you might be held for murder—or manslaughter—if your father died?"

Her eyes became glassy. "No. It never entered my head. That wasn't my reason at all. I just didn't want the whole town laughing at me."

Pop Capp said with meaning, "You see. She's highly sensitive to being talked about."

"You didn't tell Pop where you were going when you borrowed the car?"

"I didn't want him to know, either."

"Well," Johnny said, "go on."

"That's all there's to it. I drove into the yard and there was Dr. Rigmire on the ground, senseless, bleeding. I ran and phoned Dr. Dwyer. I didn't want to stay and explain all this, why I was there, and so I left." She breathed hard. "Except one thing. I took the stuff with me. It was a white powder in a round blue package, it's called *Anti-Alcohol*. I had it in my purse. Somewhere or other, I lost it. But I didn't know that right away. I found that out after the dance."

"You went to the dance, despite your father's condition?"

"He was better. Mother had been to the jail." She faced Johnny Kendall coolly. "Yes, I went to the dance. I gave up crying into my pillow when I was fourteen years old, Mr. Kendall. Besides, I wanted to find out about Dr. Rigmire, whether Dwyer got there in time. I thought the dance was the place to hear the news."

Johnny Kendall said, "You heard it. You knew you were the mysterious woman in the case. And it didn't occur to you, you should come forward with this explanation?"

"I didn't see how anyone could connect me with it. Until I discovered the *Anti-Alcohol* vial was lost from my purse. I knew if I dropped it there, it might be traced to me."

Her lips tightened. "I remembered. Ed Bundy stopped at the dance late that night. He said you'd taken pictures of the evidence. If the vial had been found, it'd show up in your negatives. The easiest way for me to find out was by using that hidden key.

"But I didn't think of that right away. I'd just barely gotten into the building when Butch started barking. I just snatched the films and slipped out the back way as you and that Rigmire girl came in the front door."

Johnny Kendall considered. He said with careful patience, "But, Miss Hazelle. Don't you see the main point? You've told me a number of facts the sheriff ought to know. Your story clears up a number of confusing factors. For one thing, the oil drippings in the yard came from Pop's car. Then, this ends the confusion about a woman trying to kill Dr. Rigmire—and then changing her mind and trying to save his life afterward. It isn't fair to leave Frank Ellsworth fumbling in the dark about those things."

"I don't care about Ellsworth," Babette Hazelle said. Her dark eyes were moody. "He wouldn't go out on a limb for me. Why should I do it for him? And be laughed at by everyone."

Johnny Kendall sighed.

"It isn't for Ellsworth, personally. . . . Keeping still is a favor to the criminal. In effect, by withholding these facts you're helping confuse and cover up a murderer's tracks."

He searched the depths of the girl's reluctant eyes. "Babette, even if it means being laughed at you're not willing to have that on your mind the rest of your life."

"Johnny," said Pop Capp, "you've got a dangerous

gift of gab there. I hope you ain't making a mistake with it." The doubt in his voice was somber.

Babette Hazelle looked from one to the other, bewildered. "I don't know what you two want me to do."

"You've got to decide for yourself," Johnny Kendall said. "You've got to live with yourself. I think you'll decide right."

She stirred. "I'll go tell him," she said. Slowly. "If you put it that way." Her smile was small and crooked. "Nobody ever gave me that much credit before."

XI

"WELL," POP CAPP SAID, "SHE'S IN JAIL."

Johnny Kendall had taken the morning's batch of film out of the wash tank. He was about to print the negatives Babette Hazelle had returned.

"What?" he said.

Pop was a ghostly figure in the light trapped doorway.

"Babette," he said. "Ellsworth locked her up. In jail."

"My God," Johnny Kendall said. He snapped off the printer switch, flung his rubberized apron onto the hook, and hurried.

The sheriff's shape flowed and filled the wide swivel chair. "Think," the sheriff said. *"Two* women there. That's too much to ask a man to believe, ain't it? I been figuring the time element. It was five, ten minutes past nine when Rigmire went out to the woodpile. It was ten, twelve minutes past nine when Doc Dwyer got called. If he left a quarter past. Two women there inside of five, ten minutes. No, sir. That's too much to ask a man to believe."

He swayed, and the chair creaked.

"No, sir," the repetitious sheriff said. "I told you all

along. I never put any stock in that woman behind the woodpile story. One was bad enough, but, Jesus Christ, I'm not going to swallow two of them there. I'd be crazy to believe a thing like that."

Johnny Kendall's mind felt heavy, choked, sluggish. He said, "Let's get this straight," and paused. "Point one," he said. "You don't believe there was a woman hidden behind the woodpile."

"No, sir," the sheriff said. "I can tell you a dozen reasons."

"You've told them," Johnny said. "Point two. Therefore, you don't believe Dr. Rigmire when he says he went out for wood at five or ten minutes after nine."

"No. Well, the time is all right. The time checks with when Doc Dwyer tells me it happened. But the rest is wrong. That wasn't why Rigmire went outside."

"You believe he went out and quarreled with some woman who was leaving."

"Yes. I can't figure anything else."

Johnny Kendall said, "All right. Assume there was such a woman, and such a quarrel. Say she snatched up the axe, the most convenient weapon, and struck Dr. Rigmire. At nine, or nine-five, or nine-ten. Then she fled. After that," Johnny Kendall said, "Babette came, found him there, and called Dwyer. What is so improbable about it?"

"Plenty," Ellsworth said. "Plenty. There wasn't any first woman, but just suppose. If she hit him the one lick with an axe, why didn't she finish the job with a few more licks? Bless us, that's how axe murderers work."

"She wasn't a murderer. She struck in self-defense."

"Not for my money," the sheriff said. "She wouldn't've left him like that, to lay and bleed to death. If there was such a woman, supposing so."

Johnny Kendall said, "People become frightened. They lose their heads. I can see a frightened, hysterical woman fleeing from such a scene." He paused. "A few minutes before Babette Hazelle arrived."

Ellsworth shook his head. "No, sir. That's too far fetched for me. Two women there, coming and going, almost running into one another. Then, it's like Bundy says. Eleven minutes is too fast. Dwyer probably started before a quarter past nine. It was closer to ten past nine. I'd say Dwyer probably got that phone call at ten past nine, or earlier, because he talked awhile on the phone. So Babette was there by nine-five. At least that early. She was there when it happened. I can't figure anything else. No, sir."

"Why," asked Johnny Kendall, "would she have done it? Why?"

The sheriff's chair creaked. He sat forward, swept open a desk drawer. He said, "Yi, but dang it, you don't know Babette. She's a fast proposition. She's got bad blood in her. She's the most likely girl in town to get mixed up in such a mess. Yi, damn it all, she's really a proposition." He stared across the desk at Johnny Kendall. "Where does a girl get money when she ain't working?" he asked. "That's been noticed about Babette. Some man has been paying her. That's been going on for awhile, and it's been noticed around town."

Johnny Kendall supposed the sheriff meant the money Pop Capp had paid Babette for modeling.

The sheriff said, "It all points against her. Being there at all, in the first place. Running off instead of staying until Doc Dwyer came. Stealing them films she stole. It all points the same way, and look at this. Ed Bundy went down to the house after she told that story, and he found this."

The sheriff lifted Babette's dress out of the drawer. It was a trifle of rayon; it looked disheveled and almost indecent in Ellsworth's big hand.

"Spots on it," the sheriff said. "Blood, I bet. Where she tried to wash it out. Washing that dress points more against her than anything else."

Johnny Kendall said, "But she tried to help Dr. Rigmire. The blood on her dress is natural enough. And she explained why she went there."

"When you caught her redhanded," the sheriff said. "She had time to think up her explanation. She had to wiggle out of it some way."

Johnny Kendall struggled against the man's solid disbelief. He asked, "Have you forgotten it was a man who came there the second time?"

"No sir. I ain't forgot, and Babette better not, either. It'll be worse for her, if she don't remember who he was, pretty quick."

"You think she's withholding the man's name?"

The sheriff said, "She won't tell that. Not while she can figure on wiggling out of it some other way. That's the last thing she'll tell, yes, sir."

Johnny Kendall got out of his chair. He stared across the jail office at the sheriff's huge form. He said, "Do you know what ails you, Ellsworth?"

"Me?"

Johnny said, "You're lazy," bitterly. "You've got Babette Hazelle. You're not interested in looking for any other woman. It would be just too damned much trouble for you to get out and find her."

The sheriff was offended. "Dangnation. Now that's not so."

Johnny Kendall asserted, "You're mentally lazy. You don't like puzzles. Anything puzzling, you sweep aside as far-fetched, too much to believe, falsehood. Whenever you encounter a fact that would make you stop and think, you eliminate that particular fact as an impossibility."

"I try and use common, horse sense," Ellsworth said. The chair groaned away back. "Plain, common sense."

Johnny Kendall said, "You listen to me. Dr. Rigmire told you what happened at the farm that night. It was a story which the evidence failed to contradict in any particular, except one. You found fresh motor drippings in the yard. Therefore you assumed that a car had been there, that he knew it, and consequently he was lying. On that one contradiction, you founded a theory that the lodge was a love-nest, that Rigmire had

quarreled with his paramour, and that the paramour
had fled."

"Well, a married man couldn't come out and say—"

"No," Johnny Kendall said. "Forget that. For once
in your life, look the facts in the face instead of trying
to detour around them."

The sheriff sat silent, blank.

"It was a convenient theory," the photographer resumed. "It excused you from the mental labor of solv-
ing a number of factors in an otherwise puzzling
problem. As long as you could believe that, you didn't
have to assume Dr. Harry Rigmire might be telling
the truth. You weren't compelled to think through the
puzzle of why an unknown woman might have been
in the yard that night, and why she stopped short of
murdering Rigmire."

"Wait," Johnny Kendall said, "I'll finish. Now Babette Hazelle enters into the picture, *your* picture, as
that unknown woman. As simply as that. You don't
stop, think, review the whole matter, and realize that
instead of completing the picture she may change it
entirely.

"I mean this, sheriff. If it's true that Babette arrived
after the assault, then your assumption that Dr. Harry
Rigmire is withholding the truth falls to pieces. If she
came later, then there was no car in the yard when he
went to the woodpile. Consequently, he could neither
have heard it arrive nor seen it standing beside the
woodpile. You no longer have the least logical reason
for assuming that he was lying. On the contrary. The

evidence of two witnesses—Dr. Rigmire and Babette—runs exactly counter to your assumption. In order to maintain that point at all, you're forced to dismiss them both as liars."

The sheriff said, "Yi, why not? They wouldn't be apt to tell the truth about a thing like that, would they?"

Johnny Kendall said, "A thing like that." He shook his head. "You mean, an illicit relationship. But go back over that again. When did you first suspect there *was* an illicit relationship? What were your grounds for believing it?

"I'll tell you," Johnny Kendall said. "It's all based on your presumption that Dr. Rigmire is concealing this woman's identity. It's based—fundamentally—on the motor drippings. Take that away, and you've got to revise all your thinking, start at the beginning again.

"Suppose the doctor isn't lying, and you can't *prove* he is! Then Babette is telling the truth, too! And you've got to solve the enigma of some other, mysterious woman attacking the doctor for some other, mysterious reason. Unless you're going to throw away all the evidence that doesn't jibe with your easy answer."

"Bless me," the sheriff breathed. "You should've been a lawyer. You sure can twist things around."

He rested inert in his chair, and Johnny Kendall felt helpless. Johnny said, "I'm trying to help you. I was trying to help when I talked Babette into telling you her story. I'd never have done it if I'd known you were going to fix on her, and just ignore the first woman."

Sheriff Ellsworth mused. "It's funny. She ain't what I'd call pretty. It's funny what she's got that makes a man twist everything around."

A bead of moisture tracked down Johnny Kendall's cheek. It was hopeless. It was like throwing a rubber ball at a board fence. The sheriff didn't like puzzles. The sheriff was not a man who lived by logic. His mind walked cautiously and warily, where the footing was sure.

The sheriff waved his hand across the office. "Corridor door ain't locked," he said, "if you want to go back there."

"I think I owe her an apology, at that," Johnny Kendall agreed.

He went along the hardwood corridor. "I'm sorry," he said through the barred door. '

Babette Hazelle said remotely, "I bet."

There was a metal bunk in the cell, slung by chains from the wall. She sat there, rubbing out a cigarette under her toe. That was before she looked up and saw Johnny Kendall's face.

"Oh, forget it," she said jerkily. "You're not to blame for my reputation. If it was anyone else, Ellsworth might've believed it."

"Did you ever find that *Anti-Alcohol*?" Johnny Kendall asked.

"No. I don't know where I left it."

"If you remember the name of the firm," he said.

"They must keep records. We could prove that much of the case, anyway."

"It's advertised in the magazines," Babette said. "But I don't think that part's so important."

She jumped up from the bunk. "The thing is, I'm not a hypocrite. I didn't kowtow to anyone. I've always said and done approximately as I pleased, and if people didn't like it they could lump it. I don't pretend to be better than I am. I'm not one kind of a girl in Sunday school, and a different kind in a parked car. As a matter of fact, I don't know anything about Sunday school. I do know about parked cars. That's the real reason I'm here."

"Your morals don't interest me," Johnny Kendall began. "What I—"

She interrupted, "But don't believe all you hear. I've learned to look out for myself. I'm not fool enough to throw myself on any man—including Dr. Rigmire. That's Frank Ellsworth's mistake. He thinks I'm tough. He doesn't realize I'm so tough I've got my guard up all the time."

She stepped close to the barred door. Mockery burned in her eyes. "Oh, I've let lots of men make love to me. Telling me how wonderful and beautiful and sweet I am, and how crazy they are about me. *Me*. Old Hazy's kid. But that's letting them make fools of themselves. If I gave in, they'd be making the fool of me. You can believe it or not," Babette Hazelle said, "but I've never been the sucker, yet."

"I believe it," Johnny Kendall said. He added, "You poor little devil."

She stared at him.

"Getting back at the town that way," Johnny said.

She nodded. "Yes, that's why. Well, it's caught up with me. I'm in here now."

Babette Hazelle laughed.

"It's funny," she said. "I thought I knew my way around. Then you came along and appealed to my better nature. I fell for it, did the right thing, and as a result I'm in the damnedest jam of my life."

Johnny Kendall got out a handkerchief and halted a moisture bead on the other cheek. It wasn't logical any more. It wasn't a puzzle with sharply fitted edges.

"Babette," he said, "I'm going to get you out of here. I'm going to close up the shop until I do that."

XII

Dr. Harry Rigmire's wife was a large, fair woman dressed in a gown of tea-rose. She said: "I do not believe in mourning, Mr. Kendall. That is because I do not recognize the sovereignty of Death. Cousin Joe has not passed from me. He has passed into the All-Absolute, which of course includes the All-Immediate or mundane world. Our dear cousin has shed the mortal, fleshly fetters. But he is with us still. I believe that utterly."

If Mrs. Harry Rigmire realized Joe Hanlon had shed the mortal, fleshly fetters in frustrating a second attempt upon her husband's mundane existence, her manner gave no sign.

Her clear, gentle eyes stared serenely at Johnny Kendall. "Why should I put on black, the aura of sorrow?" she asked. "What men call Death is but the release of the spirit. We should not weep when our loved ones enter into the joyous freedom of the All-Absolute. For they *are* joyous there, Mr. Kendall. Believe me, I bear witness of many, many communications. There is no poverty in the realm of the spirit, no distinctions of race and class. *They* know neither illness nor the anguish of betrayal."

For an instant the fair face shadowed; then she stood, smiling. "But you came to see the doctor."

The tea-rose, Johnny Kendall decided, was less a gown than a priestess' robe. Of what cult, he couldn't be sure. The terminology of All-Absolute and All-Immediate could have belonged to any off-shoot theology. The many, many communications had clairaudient implications. The tea-rose gown, flowing majestically, led along the hallway of 12 Sussex Place to the doctor's study.

Dr. Harry Rigmire, seated at the desk, said: "Oh, yes, Kendall. You telephoned from Crestpeak, something about an arrest. . . . Thank you, my dear."

Mrs. Rigmire, dismissed, went away.

The doctor, Johnny Kendall noted, had black crêpe upon his sleeve. He wore a modest white turban of head bandage, and had his right hand in a shoulder sling.

"Something about a girl," Rigmire said. "A Hazel somebody?"

"I hope you are well enough—" Johnny Kendall ventured.

Dr. Rigmire said, "Oh, that. If it wasn't for this damned hand, I'd be back in harness." The fingers protruding from the sling were a not-quite-ripe grape color. "This Hazel—?"

The photographer told him, "Babette Hazelle." He went into details.

"Well," said Dr. Harry Rigmire, "I'll put your mind at rest on that score. There's absolutely nothing to it.

You can tell your sheriff so, or if you prefer, I'll sign an affidavit to that effect."

"Your say-so isn't enough."

"Look here, Kendall, I'm not accustomed—!" The physician's large, handsome face had become almost the color of his injured hand.

He caught himself. He said, "My boy, I'm sorry. I realize *you* are not questioning my integrity. You're on the girl's side, obviously. Let me assure you, Ellsworth can't connect me with Miss Hazelle, or any other woman. The lodge served a very different purpose. I suffer with asthma. The altitude, the air there, or it may be the escape from an allergy, those are the attractions I find at Crestpeak."

Johnny Kendall said, "I meant your say-so wouldn't be sufficient for the sheriff. It goes back to the woman at the woodpile. For with that in the record, as Ellsworth says, he's not going to swallow *two* women."

He sighed. "If we only had a little better description of her."

"I didn't see her face. Her arms were swung up behind the axe in such a manner as to bar my view of her features. She was wearing a dark dress of some material that rustled with the movement. I've gone over all this before, you know."

A thought sparked and jumped. Johnny Kendall bent forward. "Kind of a stiff rustle, maybe?"

"That would be a way of putting it."

"Blood spatters," the photographer said. "My God, doctor! I think that's it! Blood—anyone who planned such a thing—would take precautions not to be spat-tered. A raincoat—a slicker—one of those waterproof cape outfits—!"

"It is possible enough," Dr. Rigmire said, "that she wore such a garment."

"*She!* No, let's stick to the garment! It sounded like that kind of a rustle?"

"It was, as you say, a stiff rustle. A dry, somewhat papery sound."

Johnny Kendall was excited. He cried, "You say *she,* but the identification rests upon that presumed rustle of a dress! That, and in the dark, a silhouette—some-thing in skirts." He slowed his voice with an effort. "Make it a rain cape, Dr. Rigmire, and the person in-side it could as well have been a man."

Rigmire objected, "But Dr. Dwyer—" and then checked himself.

A smile ran in crinkles from the corners of his blue eyes. "Why, Kendall, that's a tremendous deduction! It's—it's simply tremendous. Dwyer of course was concerned with the woman who telephoned and disap-peared. As I search my mind now, I find a predisposi-tion to identify the assailant as a woman because I knew—through Dwyer—a woman had been present."

Johnny Kendall heard an excitement in the other's tone.

"*Now,*" the physician said forcefully, "I am asking myself in all honesty, suppose Dwyer had mentioned a man? Or no one, for that matter? Would I have so positively recalled the person at the woodpile as a woman? I wonder! Psychologically, I may have fallen into a very neat trap there. . . ."

Johnny Kendall said eagerly, "The same man—"

"No. Let's not fall into the other side of the pit. I mustn't," Dr. Rigmire urged, "let your wish be father to my second thought. Do you follow? As a matter of scientific objectivity, I can't let myself be conditioned by your inclination any more than by the good Dwyer's."

His face was solid with thought. "Suppose we keep it to the bare minimum of objective fact. The assailant was a person who wore a rustling garment, perhaps a rain cape, but not necessarily."

He drummed the fingers of his left hand on the desk. "Even so, you've won an unexpectedly large concession. Too many physicians feel they must be infallible, you know. It takes a bold doctor to say, 'I don't know,' and a bolder one to admit, 'I was mistaken.' It's a toga we put on when we take the Hippocratic oath. I have been reproached for my interest in civic betterment, Kendall. Dabbling in reform, as they call it. Getting in the way of mud balls, they mean. They don't like to see a fellow practitioner tearing the robes of his dignity in the political arena. Those robes are the common property of the profession, and the refuge of its dullards. Well—"

The big man chuckled. "Well, that's all bye-the-bye. I wonder if you're not overlooking the most important point of all, even granting that I'm not able to agree the assailant was necessarily a man?"

"I don't see—?"

"Concentrate on the objective fact, my boy. A garment rustled. You might," Dr. Rigmire said shrewdly, "put your sheriff's theory to the test there. It should be demonstrable whether Miss Hazelle's costume, whatever she wore that night, *could* have rustled. Many materials cannot, you know."

Johnny Kendall moistened his lips. "By George!" The spark jumped again, this time from man to man. He felt, for an instant, very close to Dr. Harry Rigmire. "It's your tremendous deduction this time," Johnny Kendall said. "But it's not absolutely conclusive. Except in a negative way. I mean, even if it turns out a rayon dress would rustle—!"

"It wouldn't convict her. But the contrary fact would be incontestable, I should think."

"It's worth a try." The photographer hesitated. "There's something else, doctor."

"So?"

"Madeleine. Your daughter was afraid of some scandal or other. She wanted to buy my negatives to keep the pictures from falling into the hands of some filthy true crime magazine. Now, at that time, there'd been no murder. Nothing at all in the affair that could possibly interest one of those lurid publications for a single moment. Yet," Johnny Kendall plunged, "Madeleine was willing to spend several hundred dollars to avert a scandal."

The physician said, "My daughter is young. She

hasn't your background, your newspaperman's sense of proportion. She magnified the thing—"

"No, I got the idea she was playing it down."

"Let me finish, Kendall. I say my daughter has not your experience, or mine, in such matters. As a matter of fact, I can tell you what was on her mind."

"Your personal and professional life," Johnny said. "The thing had its roots there, as she put it."

"Yes, exactly. You should know that I am—I have been for years—devoted to what it pleases me to think of as the cause of civic betterment. I won't bore you with my life story, Kendall, though at your age you should understand it. For you're a crusader, aren't you? You are carrying the banner for Miss Hazelle, and at the sacrifice of your own business interests."

He leaned back in his chair; sighed, "Well, at your age, I did likewise. I was persuaded to give a portion of my time to a free health clinic—rather an innovation here, in those days. Of course, I discovered that a very great proportion of the ailments masquerading as heart trouble and rheumatism and so on were in fact symptomatic of what we then spoke of—in whispers—as the social diseases. And I very soon recognized the futility of trying to heal individuals while the community was being continually contaminated afresh. I therefore lent my support to a campaign against prostitution—I was one of the founders of the Betterment League. A charter member."

Dr. Rigmire gestured lefthandedly. "Let me draw a parallel, maybe a parable! It is as if *you* got interested at first just in Miss Hazelle's predicament, and then found out it wasn't at all unusual. It could be charged against the county sheriff system as a whole—the man Ellsworth, and for that matter, your county attorney, too—suppose you saw *they* were merely symptomatic of the system. Because a man like Ellsworth holds office simply because he is the most popular candidate, he is bound to play up to the popular prejudice against that girl. You might conclude, Kendall, that our whole administration of justice is corrupted at *its* source; that might be why criminal trials so frequently degenerate into three ring circuses."

"I don't know what a better system would be."

The left hand waved. "It's bye-the-bye, my boy. I don't say you must reach that conclusion. The point is, if you did, and if you took up the cudgels against county political machine justice—you'd find yourself in a position analogous to mine. Quite powerful and unscrupulous men would oppose your effort at reform. Your life might be threatened. Invidious attacks might be launched against you professionally. You would discover the frame-up to be a favorite weapon of the opposition."

Johnny Kendall stared. "You think that's what's behind all this?"

"No," Dr. Rigmire said. "I don't. If it had happened twenty years ago, I should have thought so. But experience has taught me better. I've learned to disregard threats, you see. The Darrows and the Steffenses generally die in their own beds, and at a comparatively ripe age, too. I have a fancy that men forge the weapons of their own destruction, Kendall. They who take up the sword—you know. It's the chaps who try to make a racket out of reform who get riddled by shotgun slugs or are blown up by bombs planted in their cars. Your sincere reformer is generally undone by his own weapon—by words—by counter-propaganda and ridicule."

He looked tired, an ellipsis of disillusion drawing down the mouth's corners. "I expect—the League expects—to be the target of sneers. Not of axemen. I don't think *that's* behind it at all. Lord, no!" A moment slid away, and another. "But Madeleine's another matter. She's young enough to believe in that sort of thing. She was afraid, of course, that some such deadly plot was being sprung. It *would* have been clever, you know. A Machiavellian assault upon a victim who was not supposed to be killed at all—the planting of a mysterious woman in the background—and then, some trumped up badger game finale! You can see how an imaginative young girl would construe it, until Cousin Joe's death proved it *was* meant to be murder all along."

"It comes down to this," Johnny Kendall said. "You don't know what was behind it?"

"It comes down to that, yes. May God be my judge," the physician said, "I cannot conceive of any explanation of the thing. Or motive. To the best of my knowledge and belief, neither Miss Hazelle or any living soul had any sane reason to raise a hand against me.

If you ask me what was behind it, I can only say madness—homicidal madness, a demented brain, a lunatic's obsession with some crazed, fancied grievance."

He stared at Johnny Kendall. His left hand lifted and fell in a vague, uncompleted gesture.

"What's the use?" Dr. Rigmire asked hoarsely. "What's the good of our fine logic at unraveling a thing like that? Earl Sawyer says no man can evolve a cryptograph another man can't solve. But who can decipher the meaningless doodlings a madman scrawls on the asylum wall?"

XIII

Macguire of the *Blade* was a morose man. Caliper wrinkles divided his mouth from the remainder of his countenance.

"Why, Johnny," said Macguire, "I thought you quit this stinking racket."

Johnny Kendall crossed the shabby press room at Police Headquarters. "Just renewing acquaintances," he said.

"You done well to quit," said Macguire of the *Blade*. "Look at me. The Oldest Inhabitant of Police Beat Row. Thirty years in the harness. What've I got to show for it besides fifty-five bucks a week, lunchcounter dyspepsia, and bad memories? Did you know I started in this business along with Si Hector?"

"The Heck?"

"The same," said Macguire. "The guy that said General Mud would beat the Nazis in Poland, that the Mannerheim Line couldn't be cracked, and likewise mechanized war wouldn't work in the Balkans. You seen his column today?"

"No, to tell the truth I—"

"The hell with it," muttered Macguire. "I was saying we started together. On the old *Herald,* long before your time. The Heck quit, though. He went to

Paris, wrote a lousy Left Bank novel. After that he
worked awhile in a damned tourist agency. He worked
some more on a fashion magazine, and on and off,
worked for the Paris *Tribune*. You know, a four-syl-
lable bum. An expatriate."

Macguire fumbled in his pocket and got out a
package of stomach pills and ate one.

"Not me. Hell, I'm a *newspaperman*. Old dog Tray.
I didn't give the *Blade* anything but my life blood. I
say look at me, and look at *him*. Salary twelve hundred
a week, counting up the syndicate take and the radio
and the lecture fees."

He sighed, "I wouldn't give a damn, Johnny, if the
guy was a newspaperman. But he ain't, and he never
will be. I tell you, and it's God's truth, The Heck
wouldn't know a story if he saw one, much less could
he dig it out if you told him where one was buried.
Well, it's the newspaper racket. It's the way they treat
a guy. You carry the ball for them day in and day out
for thirty years—and you'd've been better off carrying
a hod all the time. On the other hand, you quit 'em
cold, write a rotten novel, and they wind up making
you a foreign correspondent."

Johnny Kendall made sympathetic sounds.

Macguire said, "You're well out of it, boy."

Johnny Kendall made sounds of agreement. "By the
way," he said, "I ran into a friend of yours the other
day. Elroy."

"Elroy," said Macguire, "is no friend to me, or to
any man."

"You know him pretty well, though?"

"It is a penalty attached to the profession," Macguire said. "A police reporter's career is infested with such vermin."

"That bad?"

"He's a louse. He stinks. I mean it, Johnny. That guy is plain poison, to be taken as externally as possible."

A reflective look did not overcome, but mingled with the police reporter's morose expression.

"In town long, Johnny?" he asked.

"Just today."

Macguire deduced, "Then it was up in Crestpeak you seen Elroy?"

"Uh-huh."

"On that Rigmire thing?"

"Well, yeah."

"What," asked Macguire, "was Elroy's in?"

"He's Sherman's man. The family retained the agency."

"Well, then," said Macguire, "the family is due to be rooked most royally, if I'm any judge of Elroy."

Johnny Kendall shrugged; asked, "How does all that look from here?"

"It's country correspondence to me," said the reporter. "Not on my beat."

Johnny Kendall said, "You don't think there's any connection with your beat? Rigmire's connection with the Betterment League, maybe?"

Macguire stared. "How so?"

"Why, the League is more or less in conflict with the underworld."

"Oh, hell!"

"You think not?"

Macguire said, "No. Those people are just a bunch of goddam fumbling idealists. You take their campaign to rid our fair city of B-girls. Look what happened there."

"I thought they enacted a municipal ordinance."

"Yeah, sure. They did. Bar girls've been out six weeks now. But if you'll saunter down the Stem, Johnny, you'll find all the joints have installed booths —curtained ones—in them six weeks. They naturally need waitresses to serve 'em. And if a guy wants to buy two drinks and give one to the girl—well, what's to stop her from sitting down behind the curtain? So that's what become of the B-girls. They're booth girls now."

Macguire was morosely cynical.

"Johnny," he said, "I've seen municipal purity legislated all my life. Its net result is generally to cover up sin somewhat—and force the sinners to pay a cover charge accordingly. And that's exactly what the underworld—so-called—wants. Make it illegal *and* expensive, see? It's the difference between a nickel schooner of suds, and two-bits a glass for needle beer in a speakeasy.

"It's my idea," Macguire said brightly, "if there wasn't any Betterment Leagues the underworld would have to invent some. They *want* wine, women, and gambling to be against the law. When such things are legal and respectable, why, hell, they can't cash in on 'em."

"It's your idea. Not Dr. Rigmire's."

"Well, no. All he can see in a pin-ball machine is a temptation to school kids to gamble their lunch nickels. It just so happens in outlawing human impulses he plays into the hands of the hoodlum element."

"If they're smart enough to regard him as· a benefactor rather than a menace."

Macguire yawned. "It wasn't any hoodlum job, Johnny. Those guys use sawed-off shotguns or Chicago typewriters. They'd got him the first time, not had to come back and kill the wrong man after all." He shrugged. "Oh, maybe some ginned up B-girl went gunning for the Doc. But I don't think so. From what I've seen of small crook psychology, and I've been watching it thirty years, they generally take it out on the special agent who testified against them. They're always innocent—framed—you see? Having that quirk in their natures, it's the vice cop or the undercover snoop they're sore at."

"The League has undercover men?" Johnny Kendall asked.

"They got a few. They turn in addresses to the Police Department. The Cadillac squad makes raids, or else the Commissioner hears from the League. A few streetwalkers land in the House of Correction that way, but it doesn't seem to bother the big houses any."

"Well," the photographer said, "Rigmire himself

doesn't feel there's any connection. I have the impression he'd like to consider himself so prominent they'd not dare attack him personally."

"I don't think it's that. What's his theory?"

"A lunatic."

"Maybe he's right. You know, there's a hell of a lot of screwballs around. They come in to report all sorts of stuff to the cops. People with persecution complexes are the worst. For awhile, for a joke, the desk sergeant used to sick some of the choice ones onto me.

"You can't tell. The Doc's prominent enough to be a target for that kind of thing. Or maybe he's got a patient that's equipped with homicidal delusions. Plenty of women fall in love with their physicians, and I imagine a crazy female could do the exact opposite."

"Are the police working on it at all?" Johnny Kendall asked.

"Why should they? It didn't happen in their backyard. They'd go out and pick up anybody, sure, if the Crestpeak authorities asked. But there hasn't been any such request, not that I know of. I don't think you Crestpeak people have done anything at all except send in some stuff to the lab. You might go up to the I.B. and ask Al Larson." Faint curiosity momentarily dispelled the gloom in Macguire's eyes. "Think something's going to break, Johnny?"

"I wish I could think so."

"Taking a personal interest?"

Johnny nodded. "The sheriff's got a suspect. He

picked up a girl—more or less my doing. I'm sure she's innocent."

"You got an angle?"

"Not yet."

"Well, I wouldn't know," Macguire said. "It's off my beat. There's nothing stirring here, so far's I see."

"I guess," Johnny Kendall said, "I'd better chase on upstairs. What's the lieutenant like, by the way?"

"Larson's a fair guy, for a cop. He knows his stuff. I'll say that much for him." The reporter dropped his voice. "I wouldn't let on I was trying to take the sheriff's case apart, though. The cops got an unwritten law, Johnny. They're loyal to the badge, no matter who wears it."

Johnny Kendall went up a flight of stairs and along a dingy hallway to the Identification Bureau. A counter divided the office from its olive drab files. A middle-aged woman indicated an inner doorway to the left.

Lieutenant Alvin Larson was a gaunt, plainclothes officer behind a shabby desk littered with Federal Bureau of Investigation report cards. The walls of his private office were hung with "wanted" posters, counterfeit money circulars, and the police target range practice schedule.

He recognized his caller. "I thought you went out with the *Herald*."

Johnny said he was in business in Crestpeak. "I've been doing a little work for Frank Ellsworth up there."

"Crestpeak," the lieutenant said. "What's the matter

with you people? Don't you believe in fingerprinting
the scenes of your murders?"

"I'm afraid Ellsworth is more interested in saving
the taxpayer's money."

"Well, it *is* expensive," Larson agreed. "You can't
hand fingerprints around a jury box, unfortunately.
You have to photograph that kind of evidence on quite
an enlarged scale. And even so, one print looks very
like another to a layman's eye. You have to make the
comparison visual, but the courts in this state won't
allow a marked photograph in the evidence. The photograph mustn't show anything which alters the evidence at all. I've got around that by devising a method
of presenting comparisons on translucencies. I enlarge
each print on Diafilm Opalin and bind them in a
frame backed with a third sheet on which the comparison chart is photographed. The three have to be
in perfect register, naturally. It's an exacting job, and
it does cost money. And I can't draw on the Department's budget to stand the bills for some upstate sheriff's office.

"But all the same, Ellsworth should have had the
job done. It wouldn't have cost much to have had the
place searched for prints, and we could simply have
held onto the negatives in case he wanted to use them."

"He did send in the axe and hatchet," Johnny Kendall said.

"Yes. But the findings didn't amount to much."

"No prints?"

"I found a few blurred specimens. They were Rigmire's own, probably."

"Probably?"

"At least a dozen points of identity must be established to prove anything legally," the lieutenant responded. "These were so blurred I couldn't find more than three or four such points. To that extent, so far as I could tell, they were Dr. Rigmire's prints. You would expect it, considering the axe and hatchet were in everyday use about the place."

"That means," Johnny Kendall said, "the assailant came equipped with gloves."

"It suggests so." The lieutenant stood. "Come along, will you?"

He opened another door, this one into the Identification Bureau laboratory.

"Look at these boxes," Larson said. "Keep them in mind, if you're going to do any more work with Ellsworth. You fellows shouldn't go throwing exhibits of this nature into the rumble compartments of your cars."

The axe and the hatchet were separately crated. A noose of wire netted about the head of each was guyed to the box-ends. Other strands of wire were wound about the handles and carried out to the box-sides. The articles were suspended in space.

"Broom handle wire is a good thing to use," Larson advised. "It's soft enough not to scratch a surface unnecessarily."

He turned to the smaller box.

"Now, this is your best specimen. There's even a

hair or two from the victim's head on that hatchet blade. If you had to, you could determine by microscopic examination those hair ends were severed by crushing blows. Then, you can see the directional blood sprinkles. It fairly squirted out along the blade and against the handle. They look a lot like exclamation marks, don't they? There's nothing like that on the axe, because the axe got a regular blood bath. It must have been lying in a puddle of the stuff."

Johnny Kendall stared at the hatchet. "It squirted, all right. The murderer must have been dripping." He hesitated. "You could tell, couldn't you, whether blood sprayed like that onto a garment, or was merely daubed on?"

"You just find the garment," said the lieutenant confidently.

"But if it had been washed?" The photographer was thinking of Babette Hazelle's rayon frock. "Could you tell then?"

Larson's lips puckered. "As a rule, no. Anyone who goes to the trouble of washing out bloodstains doesn't generally leave any physical evidence. What you find are chemical traces, and it takes extremely delicate tests to find those. Any actual physical blood is generally to be found only by opening the seams of the suspected garment."

He shrugged. "The main thing is, the garment *was* washed. That's pretty strong evidence by itself."

"That would be more true," said Johnny Kendall,

"if innocent persons never tried to escape being connected with crimes."

The I.B. officer's interest was languid. "Well, it's out of my field. It isn't my job to say why people do the things they do. I'm only concerned with establishing the fact of a fingerprint or a bloodstain. How those things came to be there is the Homicide Detail's worry, not mine."

He pointed a long index finger at the smaller box.

"Now, you take that hatchet," he said. "I can tell you it's a fairly new one, one of the best on the market. I know who manufactures it, who the wholesaler is, and I could find out which store handles that line of merchandise in the Crestpeak area. I can tell you that the blued finish has been scratched away from the nail claw on the inner blade surface. The helve has been strengthened in a slipshod manner by nails driven into the head.

"But," said Lieutenant Larson, "that's all the expert testimony I could give in a court of law. It's up to someone else to deduce that this hatchet was purchased by a man who didn't mind paying for the best, but who wasn't well-acquainted with the use and care of woodworking tools. He used it in rough carpentry, pulling spikes which he should have drawn with a pinchbar, and as a result loosened the head. Of course, driving in the nails was a makeshift for replacing the handle.

"Now, the axe is an older and inferior tool. It has been whetted, but failed to take a good edge. Those are the physical facts. You can infer that a former owner probably left this axe lying in the shed. The same man who bought the expensive hatchet wouldn't have turned around to buy a dozen year old axe at second hand. Nor would the man who repaired the hatchet in such a slipshod fashion have gone to the trouble of trying to sharpen a dull axe. If you check up on it, you'll probably find Dr. Rigmire happened on the axe and gave it to a carpenter to be whetted. But I don't guarantee it.

"And," said Larson, "the same holds for the garment you mention. If the fabric contains enough blood to react to leuco-malachite or a Teichmann test, I'll establish that fact. How the blood got there and why an effort was made to remove it is none of my concern."

XIV

Johnny Kendall stood on the sidewalk in front of Police Headquarters, and tried to cast up accounts. He had been in rather a bright mood when he left 12 Sussex Place. On the favorable side of the ledger, he had gained a good deal by extracting from Dr. Harry Rigmire the admission that the mysterious personage at the woodpile *might* have been a man.

Johnny Kendall told himself it *was* a man. He argued that the man had been frightened away when Babette turned Pop's car into the lane. Perhaps he had thought Rigmire dead, anyway. Later he had learned his mistake, returned to finish the job, and again been intercepted—the second time, by Cousin Joe Hanlon.

It was disheartening to discover absolutely nothing in Lieutenant Larson's physical evidence to support this theory. At the best, there was nothing in the evidence to disprove it, either.

He trudged toward the Medical Arts building. Dr. Earl Sawyer's name, he observed, was not on the directory board. It was not on the frosted glass door, either, when the elevator had whisked him to the ninth floor.

The waiting room was chastely Early American, with samplers on the walls, with the kind of chairs that are commonly found with velvet ropes drawn across their arms, in museums.

Miss Geneva Carr appeared at the sliding window which was the room's one utilitarian note.

"You!" Miss Carr said, almost shrilly. Her eyes, by daylight, were a glinting malachite green.

"Sawyer in?"

"This way," the nurse said. She opened a door, led Johnny Kendall along an inner corridor. The room was small. The helmet shape of an X-ray machine gargoyled over a rubber-sheeted table. There were no chairs, only white enamel stools.

"Dr. Sawyer is with a patient," Geneva Carr said. "Cigarette? They're Turkish." She slid onto a stool, pleasingly. Her rump was a nicely rounded one. The stool also made the most of her legs.

Johnny Kendall refused the cigarette, then lighted one of his own defensively, as the Turkish fumes assaulted his nose.

"Go ahead," Geneva Carr said. "Apologize."

He stared at her.

She said, "Oh, I know. It was on the radio. I hope now you're heartily ashamed of yourself."

"What," Johnny Kendall asked, "was on the radio?"

"Why. They've got one of the pair. The girl," Geneva Carr said. She added with arch mockery, "Don't deny it, *you* suspected me all the time. Now didn't you?"

"Suspected you of what?"

"Of being the Woman in the Case, at least." The

green eyes became roguish. They tantalized. "Maybe we could call it square," the red-haired nurse teased. "I had my ideas about you, too."

Johnny Kendall watched intently. She turned a little on the stool. The profile of her figure was emphatic. She contrived to wear her professional white garb like a drum majorette's attire.

He protested. "I don't know what you're talking about."

"Oh, well," said Geneva Carr lightly. "It doesn't matter now, does it? It's just that we both showed our claws in the beginning."

"I don't get it at all."

A breath lifted the profiled breasts. "Think back," she said. "It was the watch, of course. You were looking at it."

He frowned, "What?"

"When you drove into the yard. You looked at your watch before switching off your headlights. You said so, but I'm afraid I didn't believe it."

Johnny Kendall felt his throat swell against his collar. "Go on."

Miss Carr smiled. "You see, I didn't go *straight* from the shed to the house. You were driving up the lane. I stopped to watch. I even stood there awhile right in the headlight beam to see who'd get out of the car. You must have noticed me, I thought. And then, when you told that other story about first seeing me backing out of the doorway—well! I imagined you were willing to distort the truth just to involve me!"

She jumped down from the stool.

"You see how silly we've both been," Geneva Carr declared. "Heavens, I should have known. . . . But coming on top of that little idiot Madeleine ringing up the wrong number—involving me that way—!"

"You didn't tell any of this at the time," Johnny Kendall asked.

"Well, no one asked. It was all about what happened after the scream. If I didn't think of it then, that was because I was wondering what *you* were up to. That's the trouble with being innocent. You know you are, so your interest is in what other people have to say."

The photographer considered. Geneva Carr had changed, enlarged, her account to include this detail. It was a very convenient addition, since it put her safely clear of that doorway.

She was smiling. "But what's the difference now? It's all over and done with. We needn't argue about whether you noticed me or not."

It would be even more convenient, Johnny Kendall said to himself, if she could induce him to accept this revised explanation without argument.

He shook his head. "It's no good. It won't wash, Miss Carr."

"Why won't—?" Her voice broke away.

The voice from the other room was emphatic. It declared, "That can't be true! We've got to put a stop to it! It's too absolutely scandalous to even think about!"

Johnny Kendall sprang past Geneva Carr and whipped open the door of the X-ray room.

"What isn't true, Miss Rigmire?" he asked.

Madeleine Rigmire jerked her blonde head around and stared at him. She said, "Those things you people in Crestpeak are saying about that girl with the Frenchy name and my father."

Dr. Earl Sawyer made a reproving sound. "I don't think Mr. Kendall is interested in our personal feelings, Madeleine."

Sawyer was a little stockier than Johnny Kendall remembered him. The cut of his brown herringbone attire was single-breasted and ultra-conservative. The photographer wondered for a fleeting instant whether the moustache and the temples weren't artificially greyed.

Johnny Kendall said, "I'm interested in Madeleine's sensitivity to scandal. This is the second time I've heard her express her personal feelings on that subject."

"You're a suspicious beast, Mr. Kendall," said Geneva Carr. "Earl, he's just as good as called me a liar."

Madeleine Rigmire's color rose. "How was that?" she asked.

Earl Sawyer gestured. "Step in here, Kendall—all of you."

The elaborate office was evidently Dr. Harry Rigmire's private, consulting chamber. It struck a neat balance between being a doctor's office and a gentleman's den.

Sawyer looked around, a bar of light flashing on his

eyeglasses. He said composedly, "Now, one at a time. Mr. Kendall—?"

"One thing at a time is good," Johnny Kendall asserted. "Just what I was going to say. Because just so many things can happen in a minute and a half."

"I beg your pardon?" said Earl Sawyer.

"I base that on Miss Rigmire's statement. She was close behind my car, something less than a mile behind. She was driving forty miles an hour. At that rate, you drive a mile in a minute and a half."

"Oh, yes. Sunday morning, you mean."

Johnny Kendall said, "Now, Miss Carr, you were in the car—in the shed—with Sawyer when you saw me turn into the lane. You stick to that, do you?"

"She has said so," said Dr. Sawyer. "I think your tone is just a bit unnecessary."

Johnny Kendall drew a deep breath. "And there was time for one of you to make a remark about its probably being Madeleine's car?"

Earl Sawyer said, "Yes. I remarked on it."

"All right. And there was time for Miss Carr to get out of the machine. There was time for you to say you'd get her suitcase out of the trunk, and for her to tell you not to wait. There was more time for you to look for a flashlight, which you couldn't find, and for her to reply she didn't need one.

"And then," said the photographer, "she had time to walk about forty yards away from the car shed. Not only that, but to stop on the way and wait 'awhile' to see who'd get out of my coupé.

"All that before the scream.

"And there was the 'minute' she told Ellsworth it took her to run up onto the porch and fumble at the door and finally get it open.

"While that was going on, after Joe Hanlon screamed, there was time for him to be killed, and for the killer to run out the back door and around the house.

"There was time for him to knock me off my feet, and for me to jump up and find the gun and snap a shot over his head.

"There was time after that for Miss Carr to tackle me.

"And for you, Sawyer, to run to the house after you saw the guy escape.

"All in the minute and a half, maybe less, it took Madeleine to drive a mile, or under a mile.

"It's incredible," Johnny Kendall said. "It's impossible." He peered at the red-haired nurse. "And you know it's incredible and impossible," he said. "You can't have all of that. Some part of it has got to be dropped to make room for the rest."

Geneva Carr was silent.

Dr. Earl Sawyer took off his eyeglasses, tapped them in his palm, said, "I'd like to comment on that, Kendall."

"I'm asking *her*."

"I can't tell you anything, except that's the way I remember it," the nurse said.

Earl Sawyer said, "I'd like to say this. It's unfortunate, perhaps, we're not equipped with any special sense organ for the measurement of time—as our eyes evaluate physical distances, or our ears determine the volume and direction of sound. To a youngster, the longest days of the year are the days before Christmas. The shortest are the days of the summer vacation. The five minutes a tardy friend keeps us waiting on a streetcorner are literally five eternities. But five minutes, when you're hurrying to catch a train, is no leeway at all. We pick up a book, and a whole evening passes —as we say—without our knowing it. In general, time passes rapidly when we are employed and drags when we're merely waiting."

"Now," said Dr. Earl Sawyer, "to apply that practically. As it seemed to you, Kendall—grabbing that gun and racing to the house—the passage of time was instantaneous. But to Geneva—on the porch, fumbling to find the doorknob, thinking (as she says) her patient had fallen out of bed—the same period seemed an eternity. It might very easily appear to her she'd spent a 'minute' trying to get the door opened, whereas the actual, measurable interval amounted to only a few—a dozen or fifteen—seconds."

Madeleine Rigmire said, "Why, of course. It certainly sounds reasonable to me."

Johnny Kendall said, "Uh-huh. You've thought it over, and decided you don't want your minute *after* the scream. You can't have both, so you'll have it before."

Geneva Carr said, "You do love to be disagreeable, don't you?"

"It's the truth that disagrees with you," the photographer retorted. "You're trying to juggle this thing, trying to keep it within the time limit Madeleine established, and at the same time give Sawyer the minute *he* says elapsed before the shot was fired. You tried to use up that moment after Joe Hanlon screamed, and when you found that wouldn't stick, you tried to push it in before. You want it anywhere except where it belongs."

"I don't understand this," Madeleine Rigmire protested. "Why do you say—?"

"I say it because I was driving fast. I drove that quarter-mile lane in fifteen or twenty seconds. I was racing against Doc Dwyer's time, trying to see if it was possible at all. Miss Carr would still have been inside the shed, if she'd stopped there and gone through all that talk about who was coming, and getting a flashlight and all that. That part is no good.

"And," said Johnny Kendall grimly, "the part about loitering in the yard is no better. Actually, I fired that shot within twenty to thirty seconds. I had time to look at my watch, time to grab the gun, and time to run a hundred feet. I was knocked down, and I jumped up and fired after the fellow before he'd had time to run more than a hundred feet the other way."

He paused. "The fact that you're trying to disguise," he said, "is that it took Earl Sawyer a full minute to do anything about the scream and the shot."

Madeleine Rigmire's eyes widened. "Oh! But that's—!"

"That's the fact. He ran up just as you drove into the yard, Miss Rigmire, and not an instant before. That's the part they can't explain, and to cover it up, Miss Carr has to invent a delay somewhere earlier along the line."

The green eyes flashed. "You make me out quite the clever moll, don't you?"

"You're not clever, Miss Carr—just in love with the guy."

Madeleine Rigmire said faintly, "No, that'd be too much—" and stopped, staring at Geneva Carr.

Earl Sawyer had been listening quietly. He said, "I see what's in your mind, Kendall," and appeared to give the matter respectful attention, such as he would bestow upon a patient's symptoms. But it was impersonal attention.

"That's quite ingenious," the young physician said. "I was the chap who knocked you down. You give me just time enough to dispose of a bloodied outer garment—a waterproof, a surgical gown, something of the sort. I could have done so, you know. Chucked it into your coupé, Kendall, if you'll let me dress up your idea a bit. While Geneva, as my accomplice, pinned you to the ground."

He smiled around at the two silent young women.

"But at the same time, it's highly ingenuous, too," said Dr. Earl Sawyer. "For you've practically got to assume that I was responsible for the first attack, haven't you? And leaving aside the question of an alibi for that, Kendall, you run into real difficulty there. There's the first difficulty of establishing any motive for such an attack. And if you could establish it, there'd be a still greater difficulty ahead.

"Because, you know, Madeleine's father wasn't killed after all. Joe Hanlon was killed. And Cousin Joe's presence on the scene wasn't premeditated by anyone. He came on his own invitation. You can count on the fingers of one hand the persons who knew he *was* there. The Rigmires, Dr. Dwyer, myself—since I'd talked to him on the phone—and Geneva Carr.

"So," said Earl Sawyer, "if you operate on the theory that one or more of us is responsible, then you've got to abandon your whole theory that Cousin Joe died resisting an intruder. For he wouldn't have resisted. He expected me—and Geneva—and Madeleine. Had he wakened and found one of us in the room, he'd merely have turned over and gone to sleep again.

"You see where it puts you, Kendall. It's not possible to argue that Hanlon was killed to cover up an assault on Dr. Rigmire, either, for as a matter of fact the assailant never reached Rigmire's bedside at all. Didn't, because Cousin Joe prevented it. As he'd not have tried to prevent me or Geneva Carr.

"In fact," Dr. Earl Sawyer concluded, "if any of us is guilty, why, it must have been our intention to murder Joe Hanlon all along. And Dr. Rigmire as well. So that you've got to deduce a vendetta against all the male members of the household."

"Of course," said Madeleine Rigmire. "It's unthinkable. It's just ridiculous."

Johnny Kendall said, "I didn't say you killed anyone, Sawyer. I asked what you did with that minute after the shot, and you still haven't answered."

"Well," said Dr. Earl Sawyer, "I have answered. As I told the sheriff, I thought the minute elapsed between the time you drove into the yard and I heard the shot. There's a gap in your time schedule that you've not taken into account."

"I'd like to know where."

"I can tell you where. That chap knocked you dizzy, Kendall. You were dazed. It took you longer than you suppose to snatch up the gun again. I should say you lost a half minute of your time right there."

Johnny Kendall was incredulous. "You think it took *him* half a minute to run as far as the shed—running for his life?"

Dr. Earl Sawyer nudged his moustache. "To be frank, no. To be perfectly frank, it wasn't the chap at all. You fired at me, Kendall."

"Running away?"

"It would have seemed so to you. At the time, my movements didn't seem to me to be any concern of your sheriff's. I suppose I shall sooner or later have to make a full statement. The fact is, I did hear that scream."

"You denied that once!"

"Yes," said Earl Sawyer. "But I heard it. Only I thought it came from your car. Madeleine's car, as I supposed. So that's where I went. And then the man went dashing away across the yard. It took me a moment to decide—just what to do—and then I saw this other car coming into the lane—finally, I ran after the fellow. And you fired after me. So I dropped down. Then Geneva called for help, and I jumped up again and ran back to her."

DEATHDEALER'S DIARY

Tuesday, Oct. 21, '41

Dr. Harry Rigmire can wait.

For once, I and the policeman-within are agreed.

That damned snooper—why did he have to take his hand in the game? Why must <u>he</u> play the interloper?

He compels me to take heroic measures. He's the sort—even more conclusively than the estimable medico—that requires handling in the one, firm, final way.

He will learn that it is Death who deals the cards in this little pastime.

Openers, has he?

Well, it is my turn to draw now. . . .

XV

"You see," Johnny Kendall urged, "that dress doesn't rustle. She can't make it rustle."

The sheriff looked at Babette Hazelle and said nothing. The dress had shrunk in the washing. Jim Wallach, the county attorney, replied earnestly: "That's a good point, Kendall. I'm obliged to you."

He uncapped a fountain pen and wrote in a pocket memo book.

Across the sheriff's office, Babette Hazelle asked: "Shall I go and take it off now?"

Wallach said, "No, wait, there's a few other things." He re-read what he'd written, then tore out the memo page and handed it to Ed Bundy. "Right away, Ed."

Johnny Kendall watched the deputy walk out of the office. Then he peered at Jim Wallach. Wallach was a youngish, roundish lawyer who, in private practice, had specialized in grazing lands and water rights litigation. He owed his election to the popular feeling that the county attorneyship ought to be "passed around" among the Crestpeak attorneys.

The photographer said, "I don't see what else. She's put on the dress. She's gone through the movement of swinging an axe. The rustling sound is the main feature of Rigmire's testimony—the one thing he'll swear to. Without it, you've got no identification at all."

Wallach said, "She's still under arrest. She was out there that night. You admit that, don't you, Babette?"

"I told you why," the girl said.

"Well, yes, you did. People who get into trouble generally put one interpretation upon their acts. The State may put another. The whole question hangs on which the jury is going to believe, on which interpretation stands most convincingly in the light of the evidence. Now the evidence here," observed Jim Wallach, "is that at about nine o'clock last Saturday night, Dr. Harry Rigmire received serious and incapacitating wounds on the hand and head from a lethal weapon: to wit, an axe. And that, at about three o'clock of the following Sunday morning, a relative charged with attending the patient received similar, in fact fatal wounds, from a similar weapon: to wit, a hand hatchet.

"Those are the facts, Babette. You can't deny them, and Mr. Kendall here can't deny them for you. They're basic, and as county prosecutor I've got to view your story in the light of 'em. Now, step by step, what is your story?"

The question was rhetorical. Without pausing, Wallach continued:

"Firstly, by your own confession you were on the scene of that axe assault. And secondly, likewise by your own confession, you fled from the scene in order to keep secret your identity. You have confessed to those facts, haven't you, Babette?"

This time he paused.

Babette Hazelle said, "I've told you why, over and over again. It was because I didn't want to be a public laughingstock."

"I know, I know. But I'm talking now about the facts, the various movements you made. The next, thirdly, is that you attended a public dance in order to get the earliest news of this Dr. Rigmire's condition. That's what you told Ellsworth, isn't it?"

Babette nodded.

"Fourthly, then, you did obtain—because Ed Bundy went to the dance later on—the information you were after. You learned that Rigmire's condition was possibly grave. It was sufficiently so for Dr. Dwyer to remain at his side until after midnight. You understood that a specialist was being called in by the family. Didn't you?"

Johnny Kendall said, "But it wasn't that bad."

"It was bad enough," Wallach asserted. "After all, in cases of that kind, it's as much a question of shock as anything else. A lot depends on whether or not the patient can throw off the effects of the shock. It often happens, in hospitals, they don't make any effort to treat the actual injuries until a person has come out of shock.

"But that's not my point. I'm saying that, firstly, Babette was there and she saw him in that condition— bleeding to death, as she told Dwyer on the phone. And fourthly, later on, what she heard at the dance must have confirmed her impression that it *was* serious, and might turn out to be fatal.

"And fifthly, she found out that a woman was known to be involved in the thing."

Jim Wallach turned to the girl.

"Sixthly, then. After the dance, you found out you'd lost—misplaced—some article of yours. At the Rigmire place, you thought."

"The *Anti-Alcohol*," Babette Hazelle said. "That just goes to show I'm telling the truth. About my interpretation, I mean."

"Yes and no," the attorney said. "Whether it was really that, we don't know. Nobody has seen the *Anti-Alcohol* from that day to this. But it was certainly something you lost—or left—somewhere. So—seventhly—you confess you illegally entered Kendall's photo shop and purloined his negatives. But in the eighth place, it turned out the missing article wasn't photographed among the evidence. Which brings us to the ninth step."

"I washed my dress," said Babette Hazelle wearily.

"Not that, yet, either. Let's keep things in their order. You washed the dress Sunday forenoon. Nine o'clock—Rigmire was assaulted with an axe. Ten o'clock, you went to the dance. Around midnight, you got Ed Bundy's story. Around one, the dance broke up. It wasn't until after one, then, you learned you'd lost this article—whatever it was. It wasn't until after two that you stole the negatives. That's five hours, Babette, in which this thing was building up in your mind, and continually getting worse, too. And your acts show it *was* on your mind, driving you to commit this act of burglary."

Babette Hazelle said, "But I didn't intend to steal anything. I didn't intend to take the negatives. It was just that Kendall and that Rigmire girl came in, and I was forced to."

"That's true," Wallach acknowledged. "You didn't *intend* any of this, in my opinion. You were forced, as you say. Caught, and driven into an unpremeditated act. It's an old, old story. It reminds me of the farmer who wouldn't let the young couples park in his lane. He was afraid they'd get to hugging and kissing, and from that they'd go to drinking out of pocket flasks, until finally somebody'd dare to smoke a cigarette— and set fire to his fields."

Frank Ellsworth gurgled with merriment. "Babette has heard the story told different than that, I bet."

The county attorney said, "I bet, too. But it shows how one thing leads to another. In this case, ninthly— the missing article wasn't in Kendall's negatives. It wasn't in your room at home, or in the car you used— Capp's car. That would lead to just one conclusion. Your *Anti-Alcohol,* if that's what it was, must be still at the Rigmire place. Now, Babette, don't you admit you thought of that?"

The brunette girl nodded. "Of course I thought of it."

"You went over and over it in your mind. The places you could have dropped such a thing. The woodpile. Or in the house when you used the phone. One or the other," murmured Wallach.

Babette Hazelle said, "There wasn't anything I could do. I certainly couldn't walk fourteen miles out there, and fourteen miles back."

"There was no way of getting a car?"

"Not at two o'clock in the morning. How could I?"

"But you thought of it—how nice it would be?"

"I wished," Babette Hazelle said, "I had a car. I hadn't, and that was that."

Jim Wallach began smiling. "You know lots of young fellows around town. One of your admirers—"

She interrupted. "As if I'd be fool enough to trust anyone that far!"

"I think you've got one admirer you could trust," said the county attorney. He glanced at Johnny Kendall. "Maybe more. Take the fellow who wrote this."

His brief case lay on the sheriff's desk. Wallach pulled it onto his pudgy knees. He fumbled, tugged out an envelope.

Johnny Kendall stood, walked over. The envelope was a three-cent stamped one, having a Crestpeak return printed in its upper left corner. The postmark was Crestpeak, too. Wallach's name was blocked in sprawling capitals across the face: JIM WALLACH, COURTHOUSE.

"Came in the morning mail," the county attorney said.

The enclosure was a single sheet of coarse, blue ruled

paper—torn from a school tablet, Johnny Kendall guessed. In the same blocked, sprawling capitals it said:

JIM, YOU ARE DEAD WRONG. THAT GIRL WAS HOME DURING THE MURDER. YOU BETTER BELIEVE THIS FOR I WILL TAKE THE STAND AND MAKE A MONKEY OUT OF YOU. IF YOU GO AHEAD YOU AND YOUR DUMB SHERIFF WILL BE THE TWO SICKEST BABOONS THAT EVER TOOK TO THE TALL TIMBER AND YOU WILL NEVER HOLD OF-FICE AGAIN SO LONG AS YOU LIVE. I DON'T WANT ANY TROUBLE BUT I SWEAR TO GOD I WILL BLOW YOU SKY HIGH TO STOP THIS INJUSTICE YOU ARE DOING AN INNO-CENT GIRL.

The last lines were crowded. There was no signature, nor room for any.

Frank Ellsworth said, "Yi dang it, now, you didn't write that, Kendall?"

Wallach said, "No, he didn't. Kendall's open and above board. This chap is anonymous, and he has to stay that way."

"Meaning," the sheriff said, "he's in it up to his neck?"

"I imagine it's the same man, yes," said the county attorney. "Whoever it was. The man who drove her out to the Rigmire place between two and three o'clock Sunday morning. She admits she thought of such a plan, and it's my contention that's what happened. They slipped into the house, hunting for whatever it was she lost. Joe Hanlon woke up at the wrong time, was all."

The girl swallowed. "You're making that all up, Mr. Wallach."

The county attorney said in grey, neutral tones: "I don't claim you intended to. Your hand was forced again. You were caught and driven into this thing. Because the one thing under God's heaven you could never explain was being in that room at such an hour. If Rigmire died, and for all you knew he likely might."

Babette Hazelle's dark eyes veered to Johnny Kendall. Tired and bitter, she commented: "I told you how it would be. Everything I say, they turn and twist into something else. What they can't make me say is just as true in their minds as if they saw it happen."

Jim Wallach sighed. "Don't take on that way, Babette. I don't want to persecute anybody. I don't like the job, and you won't believe it, I'm trying to be your friend so far as the law and my duty allow."

"My friend."

"It's no pleasure to me," he insisted. "But what I've said is consistent with everything else you already admitted. It's consistent with the main facts. It explains that six hour delay between those attacks, makes that part all neat and logical. And there's something else."

The county attorney swung to Johnny Kendall.

"Your story."

"Mine?"

"You were there. You heard Joe Hanlon's dying

scream. You grabbed a gun and ran about a hundred feet to the house."

"Ten seconds," the sheriff said. "You claimed it was."

"Well," said Jim Wallach, "that's not long enough. A man can't be two places at once. He can't be chopping Joe Hanlon's head with a hatchet, and running away at the same time. I've thought on that, and I can't see any way out but one. The man was never inside the house at all. He stayed outside while she sneaked in, and then he ran away when the trouble started. And I figure Babette got away afterward, during all the ruckus."

Johnny Kendall's brain spun.

"That's only circumstantial evidence," he managed.

Wallach said, "I know the answer to that one, too. I got it put away in a book somewheres. It was circumstantial evidence when Robinson Crusoe saw that footprint in the sand."

He shrugged.

"Still, I don't want to go in front of a jury and ask for a death penalty here. It wasn't premeditated, and on that basis—on a guilty plea—I'd settle for as light a sentence as a judge would give. Twenty years. And people do get paroled, Babette." He broke off as Ed Bundy tramped into the office.

"Well?"

"I had to get a bigger size, 18, all they had," Bundy explained.

Wallach opened the package.

"It's the same dress, from the same store." He crushed the rayon in his hand. "You hear that? It rustled when it was new, before she washed it."

Johnny Kendall said nothing, helplessly.

XVI

"WHAT DO YOU MAKE OF IT?"

"That note to Wallach?" Pop Capp said. "Well. Whoever wrote it, doesn't know Jim. He isn't going to be scared that way. It'll put his back up, if it does anything."

Pop leaned on the Photo Shop counter and considered the grey Wednesday forenoon.

"It won't do her any good," he said.

"Maybe," Johnny Kendall said, "that was the idea. To put his back up."

"Sounds a little overdeveloped to me," Pop said.

Johnny Kendall muttered: "I'll tell you what I make of it. The note said Wallach was wrong. Next it said Babette was home during the murder. The man who wrote it, if it was a man, pretty obviously knew Wallach's theory. His notion Babette went back to the Rigmire place that night."

"They throw that theory in with a haircut, around town," said Pop Capp. "With a permanent wave, too, I guess."

Johnny Kendall argued, "My point is this. If the note's author knew Wallach as well as he knew his theory, the thing could have been a deliberate effort to force his hand. Couldn't it?"

Pop Capp said, "It sounds overdeveloped to me."

He sighed.

"It's human nature," Pop said. "You get a negative that isn't fully exposed and you try to force it, try to bring out something that's not in the film at all. Your result is a hard, contrasty picture without any proper middle tones.

"Photographically," Pop said, "I don't have to tell you that. Only maybe you never stopped to think, it's as true of ideas as of snapshots. You take what this town has done with Babette Hazelle—convicted her even before the inquest today, and practically without any evidence. The evidence isn't in the picture—and they've strained so hard to see it there, the whole picture has gone hard. Folks've overdeveloped their notion of Babette Hazelle until the human, middle tones aren't in their portrait of her. She's all black shadow and glaring highlights, as they see her now. The roundness and natural modeling are missing. She's a black-and-white caricature instead of a human being.

"And," said Pop, "I don't know but you're making the same mistake, in a contrary way. You've dwelt on this thing until it's gone black-and-white in your mind, too. This note isn't white, can't be because it hasn't helped Babette any; so you've got to have it solid black, a deliberate effort to drive Jim Wallach into indicting the girl."

Johnny Kendall said nothing; and after a moment, Pop continued musingly:

"Whereas, it's probably just grey. It was intended

to be white, intended to help her; but it didn't turn
out that way—it fogged and veiled-over, photographically speaking."

Johnny Kendall said: "This is another cracker-barrel
sermon. Well, what's the text?"

Pop Capp rubbed at his chin with pyro-stained
fingers. "I don't know if it has such a thing. As I look
at it, Johnny, we've taken it on ourselves to act as
Babette's sponsors in this thing. We're going to see
her through it, as I understand."

"See her out of it," the young man amended.

"Well, then, that. I don't think we can swing it if
we can't hold onto some sense of proportion. We don't
want to see an excess of highlight and shadow every-
where we look. We've got to see the picture pretty
much as it is, seems to me. With the half tones left in."

"Well," said Johnny Kendall, "a good detective suspects everyone. Until it's proved otherwise."

"I don't believe in that," Pop asserted. "You're only
looking for one murderer, aren't you? There's a dozen
people more or less mixed up in this, and I don't think
you'll get a very accurate picture by assuming they're
all guilty. I don't see how you're going to get the picture at all, when you start out by admitting you're determined to be wrong about eleven out of your twelve.

"Why," said Pop Capp, "I'd call it a better policy to
assume everybody concerned is innocent. You'd at least
start eleven-twelfths right, instead of eleven-twelfths
wrong!"

"That's ridiculous," Johnny Kendall said. He considered. "It's the germ of an idea, though. I wouldn't overdevelop it, Pop."

The phone was ringing.

Johnny Kendall went to it.

He said to Pop Capp, "It's Ellsworth. He's apologizing all over the place."

Then he said:

"My God! Sherman's man—Elroy—he's turned up something—a confession or diary of some sort—!"

XVII

JOHNNY KENDALL, COUNTY ATTORNEY JIM WALLACH, and Sheriff Ellsworth entered the Detective Division office in the City of Altamont Police Headquarters building.

Already seated about the room were Dr. Rigmire, Lieutenant Alvin Larson, Inspector Clay, and Mr. George Sherman, of the Sherman Agency.

Johnny Kendall looked around and observed: "No Elroy?"

George Sherman was a small, spare, secretive man who wore horn-rimmed eyeglasses and a tight expression.

"No," Sherman said. "I haven't seen him in two days. This thing came in the mail."

The envelope lay on Clay's desk. It was a manilla clasp envelope of nine by twelve inches; it was addressed to Geo. Sherman, personally.

Clay handed the diary to Jim Wallach.

"See what you fellas make of it," the inspector said.

The diary was in the form of plain white bond paper sheets, pierced with three holes along the left margin for insertion in a looseleaf binder. The pages were typewritten, double spaced.

"It's not signed," Wallach said. "Who wrote it?"

"Find Larry Elroy and ask him that one," replied Inspector Clay. He ran his pipestem along his lower teeth, noisily. Clay was the officer in charge of the Bureau of Internal Security, which included the Bureaus of Identification, Missing Persons, and Homicide; he incidentally exerted supervision over the licensed private detective agencies. He was an old man, with close-cropped, bristling white hair and the complexion of a boiled lobster.

"Damn it, man," said Clay to Sherman. "What kind of a business do you run, anyway?"

"Now," murmured Sherman. "Now, now." He had the air of a man who was determined to be reasonable in the face of any opposition.

Clay raged. "So far as I can see—hell—you don't know *what* your louse was doing. You haven't known from the start. The case came into your office, and you turned it over to the guy. He could kick it around any damn way he pleased. For all you knew or cared. So far as I can see."

Sherman said quietly and appeasingly, "It was unusual, Inspector. It wasn't a routine case at all. It wasn't a case where I *could* give an operative a definite assignment, such as to shadow so-and-so a certain number of hours and turn in a report at the end of that period." He spread out his hands. "How could I sit at my desk and direct an investigation of this nature in detail? I did the best with it I could. I had a competent man on the job and let him dig up as much as he could find, where he could find it.

"And," concluded Sherman, "he did. He at least got this diary, and that's a great deal more than anyone else among you has to show."

Clay's pipestem rattled. "But you don't know where he got it. You haven't got even a general idea of what course his investigation was taking. Have you?"

Sherman said, "He'd been up to Crestpeak. He talked to some people there locally. He'd gone over the case with Dr. Rigmire here, and Miss Rigmire, and with Dr. Sawyer and Miss Carr. But as a matter of fact, he'd made no progress with it, up to the last two days."

"That's," said the inspector, "as far as he told you."

George Sherman said patiently, "I'll tell you what I believe. Larry was stumbling around, more or less blindly, and then—*bam!*—he jumped a hot clue. He found this diary. He dropped it into the mails, I presume, because it was a good deal too important to risk carrying around on his person. And he was right—he ran into trouble—the man was gunning for him. The diary says so, and I believe it to be so."

Clay said, "Yeah. Only I'm not sure you're in just as much trouble. That agency of yours has been lone-wolfing this proposition. It looks to me like you've got your rear end in a sling, and you want the Police Department to get you out."

George Sherman gestured.

Dr. Harry Rigmire was frowning under his turban. "I don't follow."

"Well," said Clay, "it wouldn't surprise me. It wouldn't surprise me if a deal was cooking here. If

Sherman and his louse knew damn well who wrote this thing, and turning it over to us was just a part of the squeeze."

"Blackmail?" Dr. Rigmire exclaimed.

"They got a more polite word for it. They call it retainer fee. They get the goods on a guy, and then hire out to protect his interests."

"Those remarks," said George Sherman, "classify under the head of criminal libel." He became grim. "In front of witnesses."

"Yeah," said Clay. "Well, don't forget this. I've had my eye on your stinking agency a long time, Sherman. I've had my eye on Mister Elroy, too."

Sherman said hastily, "It's possible I've reposed a mistaken trust in Elroy." He was reasonable again. "But if there's anything like that in the wind, Inspector, I assure you it's entirely without my connivance."

Jim Wallach had been reading the diary. As he finished, he passed the pages separately on to Ellsworth. When the sheriff had read, he in turn handed the sheets to Johnny Kendall.

Johnny found that he read a good deal faster than the sheriff. It gave him an opportunity to watch Clay and Sherman rather closely.

"Well, hell," the inspector now said, with finality, "if Elroy had the time to mail this thing, he had the time to pick up a phone and call a cop. He knew who wrote it, all right, but he was holding out—he was trying to pull a fast one."

Dr. Rigmire asked, "There's no doubt it passed through his hands?"

"It's his handwriting—the address is," Sherman said. "The postmark reads Altamont, 11 P.M. That got it onto my desk the first thing this morning." He was speaking to Clay. "I read it carefully, attempted to get in touch with Larry, and found he'd not returned to his apartment at all last night. After that, I came directly to Rigmire. I advised him to put the matter into the hands of the authorities. I don't see, on that basis, how you can accuse me of holding out in the matter."

Lieutenant Alvin Larson made a throat-clearing sound.

"I don't think there's any question Elroy mailed it," he said. "I've slit open the envelope in order to examine the inner surface of the flap. If you've ever watched anyone seal an envelope, you've noticed how the envelope is generally held for the purpose. As a rule a person grips the envelope by the ends, with the fingers, using the thumbs to hold the flap up to the tongue. In this case the mucilage was hastily wetted and not moistened to the extreme corners. I developed quite satisfactory latents upon the mucilage itself. We've Elroy's prints on file—every licensed operative's in the city, in fact—and I'd say without any hesitation, Elroy not only addressed this envelope but sealed it as well."

From Ellsworth came a murmured, "Dangnation, now that's smart."

Wallach agreed it was. "We've got another envelope might be worth looking into. But what about fingerprints on the diary itself?"

Lieutenant Larson responded negatively. "The identifiable impressions appear to have been left by Sherman and the doctor here, both of whom, of course, handled the pages this morning. There were other smudges, but nothing identifiable."

"But doesn't a typist generally leave prints on paper?" Wallach asked. "I know my office girl does."

"Your girl uses carbon sheets," said Larson. "You'd not notice genuine latent prints. As a general thing, smudges of that sort aren't particularly valuable from a scientific point of view. Bloody fingerprints, for example, are a great standby for Hollywood purposes. But in technical fact, prints daubed in blood aren't of any great value. That's by the way, for your information."

He mused.

"Actually, I'd be surprised to find the chap who wrote this thing leaving any prints about. I don't see" —frowning—"why he let the diary itself go undestroyed."

Dr. Rigmire said, smiling, "Why, the man's insane. I've said so all along, Kendall knows. I should say so far as this diary is a record of anything, it's the record of a schizophrenic mind at work."

"You mean split personality," said Lieutenant Larson. "The Big Me and my Policeman-Within act?"

The physician said:

"Well, yes, that's a very fair layman's analysis. We might go a step farther, from a psychiatric point of view, and say that the subject's simulation of qualities which he does not possess is the essential element. We are all split personalities, more or less, Lieutenant; but, on this side of sanity, we don't inflate our personalities into fire, imagination, audacity and—how does he put it?—patient artistry."

"He's got delusions of grandeur," said Larson, trying to follow. "To write that crud."

"Yes," said Dr. Rigmire, "from the layman's point of view, a man must be mad to write of himself in that vein. Your psychiatrist, I suppose, would put the compulsion on the other foot. The man is mad and *must* write 'crud' about himself. The compulsion to interpret himself in those terms is every whit as important to him as the murderous impulse itself. *You* would say the man wrote the diary to justify the crime of murder. Whereas the psychiatrist might argue, the man committed the crime to justify the diary."

"That's too deep for me," grumbled Jim Wallach.

Lieutenant Larson turned to the county attorney. "I can see where the psychiatrist would have an argument," he asserted. "This bird isn't just a murderer. He's one with a capital M. He's pretty special, isn't he? When he hits a man over the head with an axe, that's no ordinary, run-of-the-mill killing. It's a Fine Art, no less. And when he kills the wrong man by mistake— why, that's Genius!"

And Larson laughed.

Clay said glumly: "Hell, they're all crazy to hear the brain bug doctors tell it. Every killer that ever came down the road."

"The definition of legal insanity in this State," said Jim Wallach, "hangs on whether or not the accused could distinguish right from wrong. If he knew the nature and quality of the deed, or knowing it, knew he was doing wrong."

Dr. Rigmire's lifted left hand demanded their attention.

"I don't mean to quarrel with your definitions," he said. "What I've been speaking of here is the medical fact. I'm speaking, strictly, of psychosis rather than insanity. I mean that the individual we're talking about here suffers from mental illness of a definitely schizophrenic nature. He is no longer oriented to realities. His behavior is motivated by delusion rather than by external circumstances. He lives, and his diary demonstrates this, in a world of his own.

"Now," continued the physician, "it's basically a definition of delusion! It's a question of whether his beliefs are sane or insane, as you would use the term in everyday speech.

"In general, psychiatry recognizes three tests for the identification of psychotic delusions. In the first place, are the patient's beliefs obviously untrue, improbable in the extreme, or even utterly impossible? And secondly, are they susceptible to an appeal of reason? And thirdly, are they beliefs one would normally associate with the individual's education and environment?

"Unfortunately—in the absence of the individual, we can apply neither the second nor the third of these tests. But what we do have, in this diary, is a record of deluded belief that is obviously untrue, improbable, and impossible. Take, for example, the accusations he levels upon my head."

Dr. Rigmire smiled broadly. "My professional standing. What does he allege? Why, I am an impostor—if I get a difficult case, I refer it to a specialist—and split the fee. My sole qualification to practice medicine appears to be—that I have a competent assistant! I needn't go into detail, since you've all just finished reading the thing.

"It's enough to ask whether these beliefs are *facts*—such as could be ascertained by making inquiry of the State Medical Society. Of course, they are nothing of the kind. I am *not* a family doctor, to begin with. I am, and I have been for years, a diagnostician. It's my business to refer my patients to the appropriate specialists; that's what they come to me for.

"But these *facts* don't exist for the author of this diary—he must distort reality—he must cling to his fantastic falsifications. His thinking is obsessive, rather than logical."

"He takes a crack at my racket, too," said Lieutenant Larson reflectively. "Where is that? Hand it here, Kendall. 'The detective-mind has a fondness for maps, plans, diagrams, sketches, and enlarged photographs. One wonders why?' "

Larson tossed down the diary.

"I'll tell him why! It's because maps and plans help win convictions in court. They have the practical purpose of informing a jury. We're not just a bunch of kids amusing ourselves with playthings, as he seems to think."

Dr. Harry Rigmire said that was the point. "Your practical purposes, Lieutenant, haven't any reality to a schizophrenic brain. That diseased condition renders the individual impervious to reasonable consideration. You've got the same motif reappearing in the imputation that I owe my professional success to a fortunate marriage, and so on. Reality must fly out the window when it conflicts with the deluded imagery, feeling, and psychotic urges of our subject.

"Your maps *are* playthings, in his distorted view of the matter. Your behavior—hurtling around in siren-screaming cars!—is malicious behavior, malicious caprice, when it threatens his safety. It's a personal affront, in short."

"Persecution complex," muttered Lieutenant Larson.

"There's a systematized delusion of persecution, yes. Since the grievance doesn't exist in actuality, he's under the compulsion of inventing it. That's what makes his conduct so inexplicable and so utterly unmotivated, by a rational standard of judgment."

"Well, Doc—" Inspector Clay's pipestem rattled briskly—"well, how many screwballs like that do you know?"

Dr. Rigmire said, "The schizophrenic psychosis is frequently masked by the retention of quite normal, superficial personality traits. Schizophrenia is a disorder you expect to encounter in adolescence. When it occurs in later life, it's rather characteristically paranoiac. Paranoia, you know, is hard to detect. The insane suspicion and conceit may be concealed under an appearance of complete normality in thinking, willing, and acting."

Clay stared. "You mean you can't tell?"

"*I* could tell. The condition might escape the notice of an untrained observer. There are more or less definitely indicative clues. I should expect this subject has hallucinations of hearing. I should expect, too, a marked emotional deterioration. He would be apathetic, rather than warm, in his personal relationships. I should expect to find him indifferent to society, insensitive to the social atmosphere, careless of other people's opinion. The man is extremely introverted, beyond doubt."

"Yeah," said the inspector, "but who would you say answers that description—that you know of?"

"I can't name anyone who does."

"But the guy knows you!" exclaimed Clay. "He's been out to that mountain place you own. He knows the whole layout there."

Frank Ellsworth said, "But, damn it all, he doesn't. I can put my finger on one place where he slipped. There's no twelve or fifteen cabins out that way. I can count up seven. By Jupiter, he slipped there."

"Still—" this from Johnny Kendall—"he's got the quarter-mile lane correctly. He knows how that road

came to be oiled. He's right about the Ghost Canyon
bridge and the Stokesville road. He knew about the
woodpile and the axe—and the hatchet in the shed.
You'd say he'd been there at some time or other,
wouldn't you?"

Dr. Rigmire said, "I don't see any difficulty there.
The trout stream's not closed. Anyone can fish it, and
a great many people do. I should think almost anyone
might have been over that road, and paid the shed a
visit, too. There's no one about the place, except week-
ends."

Ellsworth stirred his bulk restlessly. "Yi—but just
anyone—it don't make sense to me."

The physician peered at the sheriff. In dry tones he
replied, "Yes, yes, I know *your* theory." He looked
around at the other. "Why did Booth shoot Lincoln?"
Dr. Rigmire asked. "Why did Czolgosz kill McKinley?
As it seems to me, assassination has its own abnormal
psychology! Some profound, psychotic urge impels the
assassin to destroy another personality in order to exalt
his own! I suppose this man, whoever he is, is obsessed
with an insane hatred of medical men. He picked me
rather than Sawyer—or your Dr. Dwyer, sheriff—
because I happen to be a bit more in the limelight. I
am the scapegoat for the entire profession, I presume.
Just as an assassin with another obsession might consider a Morgan or a Ford a scapegoat for the sins of all
the capitalists."

"Well, hell," said Inspector Clay, "it's your life. If
you don't know who's gunning for it."

The inspector's thought hung in silence.

"I've arranged with Sherman to have the house watched," Dr. Rigmire said. "There's probably not much more that can be done. Unless this diary can be traced?" to Lieutenant Larson.

The I.B. officer was pessimistic. "I can't see how, unless some one's able to recognize its source from the internal evidence. That reference to the gardener's rubber gloves, for instance?"

No one answered.

"Well," said Larson, "the paper is ordinary sixteen pound sub bond. It's a dime store brand. You know, no girl is going to remember a purchase like that among the hundreds of transactions at a ten cent store stationery counter every day."

"An envelope of that size can't be quite so ordinary," suggested County Attorney Wallach.

Larson said, "Well, if the envelope was purchased specially for this job, of course Elroy did the buying. If it wasn't, if he just picked it up along with the diary, we've got no reason to suppose it hadn't been lying in a desk drawer for weeks or months."

"That leaves the typewriter," said Wallach.

"Yes. I can tell you it was done on a Corona machine, one with pica type," Lieutenant Larson said. "It's an old machine, since it's quite out of alignment. The type were cleaned recently, as the impressions show. It has a fresh ribbon."

"I understood," the county attorney said, "typewriting can be traced as readily as handwriting."

"I wouldn't say traced. I'd say identified. In cases of this kind, the typewriting becomes tremendously valuable—once you've nailed your man. It'll link him positively with the diary then.

"But—" said Larson—"to *trace* such a thing is something else, and not so very feasible. It's like having a bullet from a corpse. It's worthless until you've got a suspect's gun with which to fire a comparison bullet. I'd say you've got to find a suspect who owns a Corona machine."

Jim Wallach pushed back his chair and stood.

"Well," said he, "that's not what I expected. I've been sitting here, turning this thing over in my head, and I've got to say I'm not satisfied at all."

Lieutenant Alvin Larson said, "I'm sorry, but that's the way it is."

Jim Wallach replied that wasn't what he meant. "I postponed the inquest on this account," he asserted, "considering new evidence had come to hand. But now, in my opinion, this thing isn't evidence at all. It might be introduced at the inquest, maybe. At the trial, no."

Johnny Kendall's heart sank.

"How do you mean that, sir?" asked Dr. Rigmire.

"I mean," said Wallach, "Babette Hazelle's trial."

The physician exclaimed, "Good God! Do you intend to indict the girl in the face of this?"

Wallach was grim.

"As county prosecutor, it's my duty to do so. The law requires it, as I understand the law. I can't be swayed from that duty by anonymous threats I get through the mail—and it seems to me, this 'confession' here doesn't amount to anything more than that!"

He shook his head.

"Come right down to it," he said, "what *does* it explain? About the murder? Why, the perfectly tremendous fact that he killed the wrong man doesn't make any impression on the fellow at all!

"That Sunday morning part of it—why, he doesn't seem to know there *was* that mistake!

"And," said Wallach, "the only 'improbable accident' which pressed on *his* mind was the 'accident' of Babette Hazelle arriving there at the lodge when she says she did.

"No mention at all of the immensely greater improbability of Earl Sawyer and Geneva Carr, Johnny Kendall, and Miss Rigmire arriving there at exactly the time of the second attempt! There was the thing that really contradicts logic, probability, and common sense!"

Johnny Kendall said:

"Well. Could *Sunday* A.M. mean between Saturday midnight and three o'clock of that morning?"

"I don't see how," responded the county attorney. "He mentions Dr. Rigmire's mistake—the rustle of a woman's dress—he dwells on that.

"But who knew it, between midnight and three A.M.? Madeleine—and she phoned her mother. Sawyer and Miss Carr—they'd phoned Joe Hanlon.

"And who else? You did, Kendall. Ellsworth here,

and Doc Dwyer, and Ed Bundy—and Babette, she found out through Bundy.

"That's a pretty tight little circuit! It doesn't include any insane schizophrenic cases, either."

Johnny Kendall said, "Everyone who was at the dance might have known. Your circuit's wide open there."

"If you please, gentlemen," said Dr. Rigmire. "You've got to realize these pages aren't the record of a crime. They're not even a record of reality.

"I said before—and it's essential to remember—this man utterly disregards *facts* when fact conflicts with his fantasy.

"It's even possible the madman doesn't know me personally—that he killed Cousin Joe under the impression he was killing me."

Jim Wallach smiled.

"Well, yes. And it's possible some nut wrote this stuff based merely on what he read in the newspapers. It seems to me I've heard of some special kind of craziness that specializes in just that kind of stunt!"

"I don't think," objected Sherman, "Elroy would be taken in quite that easily."

"Elroy!" exclaimed the county attorney. "That's another thing! How does it happen the one man who could identify the source of this document disappears so abruptly—I might add, conveniently?"

Johnny Kendall was fingering the diary.

He noticed—there were a good many typographical mistakes in its early pages. Quite frequently a lower case *q* was dropped in the left margin, fronting the paragraph indentations.

Later on, that didn't happen at all.

"No—" said Wallach—"it'll take more than that to convince me! I'd like to see Babette produce that *Anti-Alcohol,* for instance!"

He picked up his briefcase.

"All right, Frank."

The sheriff stared at Johnny Kendall.

"I'm sorry," said the photographer. "You two will have to catch the bus."

"Yi. You were glad enough to drive us down here, though."

Johnny Kendall said, "I've got things to attend to, now."

XVIII

M<small>R</small>. T<small>HEODORE</small> G<small>ARRANT</small>, <small>OF</small> G<small>ARRANT'S</small> (T<small>YPE-</small> writers Sold—Rented—Repaired) barely glanced at the press card. Which was as well, since Johnny Kendall's press card was a souvenir of the defunct *Herald*.

"No, sir," said Mr. Theodore Garrant. "Not last week. But do you know, young fella, speaking of used Coronas, there was a funny one yesterday?"

"It would have to be last week," Johnny Kendall said.

"Well, I can't help you there. The only portable I sold last week was a Remington. A rebuilt one. Come right down to it," said Mr. Garrant, "as a rule we don't handle used machines, except rebuilt ones. We take them in for rebuilding. It isn't very often a party trades in a machine that's in good enough shape to resell, as is. As I was saying, a deal as funny as that one doesn't happen often in this line of business."

Mr. Garrant was a man who liked to tell a story. He held Johnny Kendall with a confiding eye.

"You ever bought a typewriter?" he asked. "A rebuilt one?"

Johnny Kendall said he'd always made use of a newsroom machine.

"Well," said Mr. Garrant, "when you do, I can tell

you how you'll go about it. You'll walk into a shop
(my shop, I hope) and try out the machines on the
counter. Actually, as between factory rebuilts of the
same model, the difference is all in your hat—you
could take any of the lot—actually. But you'd try them
out, anyway. You wouldn't walk in here, point out
that one, and lay the price on the counter—without so
much as tapping a key."

"Is that what happened yesterday?"

"No—it was funnier than that. The fella yesterday
phoned in, he wanted to rent a portable. At once, in a
rush. As it happened, our pick-up man was out of the
shop; and as it happened, too, we had that one Corona
in here. I went around with it myself to oblige the
fella—it was only around on Riverbank Street.

"And," said Mr. Garrant, "do you know what? I
walked up—it was one of those apartment buildings
there—and rang, and he called me in. He'd changed
his mind and decided to buy the machine outright.
The money, sixty dollars, lay right there on the table.
He told me to take the price out of that. You won't
believe this—but the fella was in the shower at the
time. Taking a bath, mind you. He didn't so much as
put his head around the door. He didn't (and I'm telling you the truth) even look to see what *make* of machine he was getting for his money."

Johnny Kendall stared.

"You didn't see him at all?"

"No," said Mr. Garrant, "and it struck me so odd, I

stopped by the bank afterward. The money was all right, though. Nothing queer about *it*."

"He mention any name?"

"Sherwin, 111 Riverbank," said the typewriter agency man, "and that address was another thing. Those apartments rent by the week. The fella might have moved in under an alias. I wouldn't have left a rental machine without a good reference, or else a good big deposit."

He smiled, a smile tinged with apology.

"Maybe I'm too hard on him," said Mr. Theodore Garrant, "but you know, at one of our Kiwanis luncheons we had a talk by an ex-con man. A fella who's reformed and is going around the country exposing the methods of swindlers and short change artists. He said something I've never forgotten—and it'll pay you to remember, young man."

A pause.

"It's this," Mr. Garrant confided. "We all have our own routine ways of running our places of business. But those rascals don't do business *our* way. It has to be done *their* way, or their little stunts won't work. So beware of the stranger who walks in and upsets your normal routine of business!"

Johnny Kendall nodded.

It couldn't be the same Corona, could it?

He ventured, "I suppose you clean up your rental machines and put in fresh ribbons—as a matter of routine?"

"What? Oh, yes. But I didn't mean that. It was buying the machine sight unseen, you know."

It certainly sounded like the same Corona.

Johnny Kendall thought of the *q* dropped in front of the paragraph indentations. The diary's author had stabbed that letter when he reached for the neighboring tabular key.

As if the machine was an unfamiliar one—and he'd only gained familiarity with it as the diary progressed!

"I'll take one of those brushes," said Johnny Kendall.

Mr. Garrant expressed surprise. "I thought you didn't own a typewriter."

"It's to clean a camera," said the photographer.

He went outside, thoughtfully.

Yesterday! But if this *was* the Corona, then *Sunday morning* meant nothing; the diarist's knowledge of Dr. Rigmire's mistaken identification meant nothing, either; long before yesterday, Tuesday, the facts had been published for all Altamont to read.

Assume this—and the diary ceased to be a diary or the outpouring of a psychotic urge; it was neither a plan for a murder, nor the projection of a schizophrenic personality.

If written yesterday, the thing was a masquerade. It was a fabrication. It was a hoax.

Johnny Kendall could imagine, he could hear Jim Wallach saying, that the hoax was nothing more nor less than a companion piece to that anonymous letter.

So Babette Hazelle was by no means out of the

woods yet! She was not going to be satisfactorily
cleared by another anonymous and patently false communication, if that's what it came to.

Johnny Kendall could hear Pop Capp reminding
him he'd undertaken to act as the girl's sponsor.

"Sherwin," he thought. "111 Riverbank."

He walked, hurrying. Ahead of him, Capitol Hill
ascended from the river's loop. Railroad tracks followed the river; a semi-slum of warehouses, transient
hotels, poolrooms, pawnshops, toggeries, eateries, and
flats smoked and brawled and decayed in the Capitol's
shadow.

Riverbank—a sidestreet. It had the architectural ele-
gance of an old shoe. It smelled as city alleys smell. It
was the kind of street that art students paint. One of
them was at work now, as Johnny Kendall entered
Riverbank. Your portrait 50¢, incidentally.

111. This was the Capitol Arms. (There was a Capitol theater and a Capitol Bowling Alley—a Senate hotel and barbershop—in the adjacent blocks. The
district clung to this nomenclature, as a poor relative to
a distinguished family name.)

It was a dingy brick building. It had a small, tight,
shoebox size of foyer with mailboxes and a row of push
buttons opposite a list of tenants' names.

E. Sherwin opposed 2-B.

Johnny Kendall thought awhile. And then he didn't
ring the bell, after all.

He walked back along the street and inspected the
art student's easel. On the canvas, by a peculiar twist

of perspective, the Capitol's dome was made to loom goldenly at the extreme end of a painfully literal Riverbank Street.

"You want to make some money?" Johnny Kendall asked.

The art student gave the photographer a long look.

"Woof?" he asked. "Woof? Go to hell."

Johnny Kendall said, "Uh-uh." A pedestrian came toward them. "Take one look at that guy," Johnny said. "Now, do his portrait. I want to see if you can."

"You want to see fifty cents' worth?"

"Five dollars' worth," said Johnny Kendall.

The student's crayon flew. What he handed over was a recognizable representation of the pedestrian.

Johnny said, "Okay. Now get out of that smock. Take this box. There's a brush in it. You're a delivery guy from Garrant's Business Supply. A Mr. Sherwin at 111 bought a machine from them yesterday. You think he didn't get a brush with it. You give him the brush. You got that?"

"No," the student said. "I don't get it."

Johnny Kendall said, "Then you come back and draw me a picture of Mr. Sherwin. That's where the three dollars come in."

"You said five."

"I'm giving you two in advance."

The art student shrugged, sighed, and accepted the typewriter brush box.

"But I don't get it," he said.

"It's just a gag," Johnny Kendall said. "I need a picture of the guy to pull it."

The youth went down the street. He was gone perhaps two minutes. When he returned, the box was still in his hand.

"Nobody in?" Johnny Kendall asked.

"He was in. He didn't know anything about any typewriter, though."

The crayon made dashing movements across the paper. A face formed. It consisted of shaggy eyebrows, full-blown cheeks, a small and womanly chin. The artist roughed in a few wrinkles, and the features aged. It was a face Johnny Kendall had never before seen.

"There's your five dollars' worth," said the student. "What kind of a gag is this, anyway?"

"That would be telling," said Johnny Kendall.

He walked to the Senate news store on the corner, entered a phone booth, and told Lieutenant Alvin Larson.

XIX

THE POLICE SERGEANT INTONED: "EDWARD SHERWIN. Alias Elesander Shaw. Alias Professor Elesander Stanley."

Edward Sherwin's height was five feet and three inches, as indicated by the white ruled lines at the rear of the police line-up stage. A series of brilliant lights in front of him, at knee level, made it impossible for him to see anyone except the uniformed sergeant at his side.

He was a roly-poly little man of perhaps one hundred fifty pounds; in the glare of these lights, his clothing looked threadbare. His expression was sad and resigned; he seemed to expect the worst of life, while deserving the best. His expression was, in a shabby, shoddy, second-hand way, a saintly one.

Miss Geneva Carr said to Dr. Earl Sawyer: "Poor thing."

Lieutenant Larson bent forward to say, "That's the typical con man mug, lady. How many people do you suppose they'd fleece by *looking* like crooks?"

The sergeant was reading from a card in his hand. "Arrested May, '32. Charge, larceny. *Modus operandi*: Faith healer, laying on hands, laid hands on victim's wallet."

"The charge was dismissed, officer," said Edward

Sherwin in a resigned voice that was nevertheless resonantly musical.

"Dismissed," the sergeant agreed jocularly. "How come, Ed, you give the guy back his money?" His tone reverted to the official. "Arrested, March '36. Charge, practicing medicine without a license. *Modus operandi:* Posing as professor of psycho-analysis. Disposition: Six months in House of Correction."

"Suspended," murmured Edward Sherwin.

The sergeant continued reading. "Arrested September, '39. Charge, ditto. *Modus operandi,* ditto. Disposition: One year in State Penitentiary—you didn't beat that rap, Ed. You served eight months, released May, '40."

Edward Sherwin said, "The voice of organized intolerance was raised against me."

Johnny Kendall heard Dr. Earl Sawyer whisper, "He means the State Medical Society."

Sherwin heard, too.

"Read Matthew 10:6," he said. "Jesus commanded them, saying, *Heal the sick.* He didn't say anything about being a member in good standing of the State Medical Society to do it."

"Listen," said the sergeant, "to the divil quote Scripture."

Inspector Clay said out of the darkness, "Skip it. Just answer what you're asked to, Sherwin. What've you been doing since you got out of stir?"

"Living," said the suspect, "according to my Light."

"Yeah? On what?"

"Luke 9:3-4. It is written, *Behold, I send you forth as lambs among wolves. Carry neither purse, nor scrip.* Likewise Matthew 6:25-26. *Take no thought for your life, what ye shall eat, or what ye shall drink. Behold the fowls of the air; for they sow not, neither do they reap . . . yet your Heavenly Father feedeth them.* If you ask how I live," said the little man, "it is by Faith."

Inspector Clay grunted.

"Where were you," he asked, "last Saturday night, about nine o'clock?"

"I entertained a friend."

"All night?"

"No."

"Can you produce the friend?"

"I might," said Edward Sherwin, "if anyone was to tell me what all this is about."

"How about yesterday, 2 P.M.?"

"I was at home."

"Yeah. Having a typewriter delivered, wasn't you?"

"No."

"Give him the paper there," said the inspector.

The sergeant handed the suspect a piece of paper.

"Read it," directed Clay, "and then say what's on it."

Edward Sherwin turned a little in order to study the page. Having done so, he declaimed resonantly:

"I've changed my mind. I'll buy it. The money's on the table for you."

"All right, sergeant," said the inspector, "take him away."

Edward Sherwin was led from the stage; he said

over his shoulder, as he was thrust through the side-door: "II Corinthians 11:26—*in perils among false brethren!*"

The strong lights died away; other, overhead lights swam into being.

Inspector Clay looked around. "Well? Any of you place him?"

Neither Johnny Kendall nor Miss Carr, nor Doctors Rigmire and Sawyer responded.

Inspector Clay asked, "Well, then, you recognize the voice?"

And Mr. Theodore Garrant said, "No, no. It was a different voice than that, entirely different."

"That might be due to the acoustic properties of the shower," Lieutenant Alvin Larson remarked. "Maybe if we tried him out under the same conditions—?"

"Well—maybe—we can give it a try," said the inspector.

Miss Geneva Carr brushed against Johnny Kendall at the door. "I'd like to see you later," the red-haired nurse said under her breath, "about all this."

Mr. Theodore Garrant said to Johnny Kendall, "I want to cooperate with you fellas. It's just, damn it, it was a different voice altogether."

"Come along," said Lieutenant Larson, behind them.

Presently a police car pulled up at 111 Riverbank. Inspector Clay got out first; then Edward Sherwin and a detective named Hanty; the trio went up the steps.

A second police car followed the first; Lieutenant

Alvin Larson got out of it, followed by Mr. Garrant and by Johnny Kendall.

Hanty held the foyer door open, fell in step behind them. They went up a flight of green carpeted stairs. Inspector Clay, using Sherwin's keys, unlocked 2-B.

Mr. Theodore Garrant said in a thin, startled voice: "But it wasn't here—it was upstairs."

"What the hell?" cried Clay.

"I tell you it was upstairs—above here—not this apartment at all."

Clay decided, "Hant, you stay here with Ed."

They went upstairs to 2-C. No one answering his knuckles, the inspector said to Garrant, "I hope to hell you ain't daydreaming this," and went in search of the building manager.

A stout woman in an unclean apron unlocked 2-C for them.

Clay, going in first, came to an abrupt stop.

"Jeezus Cor-risttt!" said the inspector.

There was a typewriter on the table. There was a vial of something or other beside the typewriter. Also on the table was a headset of earphones.

Clay's exclamation had been occasioned by none of these things.

He was staring under the table. Larry Elroy lay there. His blonde hair was bloodsoaked. The blood was a tarry brown in the hair, and where it had pooled upon the carpet, was purplish with dye absorbed from the fabric.

The body had begun to decompose. Veins like

greenish-blue worms wriggled beneath the skin of an outflung hand. There was an odor of death in the room.

"Outside, outside," said Lieutenant Larson. The heel of his hand pressed against Johnny Kendall's chest. "Nobody touches anything in here."

There was just time for Johnny Kendall to jerk his eyes up from Elroy's body to the vial on the table. *Anti-Alcohol,* the label said in pink-printed letters.

XX

Dr. Earl Sawyer said, "I'm not a psychiatrist. But in my opinion that diary was never the work of a diseased brain. Never."

Johnny Kendall had gone around to the Medical Arts building, found Geneva Carr already gone for the day, and had remained to interrupt a blood smear examination. Dr. Sawyer wore a knee-length laboratory smock; his arms were bared to their elbows: he toyed with an inch square glass slide, and the muscles played visibly in the forearm.

"With all respect to Harry Rigmire," said the younger medico, "I'm astonished he could be taken in so easily. Of course, he graduated from medical school a quarter of a century ago. At that time psychiatry was a more or less foundling science that had been left on the doorstep of the profession. Its antecedents were looked upon with a very grave suspicion."

Johnny Kendall said he should have thought Dr. Rigmire had kept well abreast of the times.

Earl Sawyer looked non-committal.

"Hasn't he?" pressed the photographer.

Earl Sawyer said, "Now, understand me. That infernal diary is utterly unfair to Rigmire. There's not a word of truth in it, as you and I understand truth.

237

And yet there *is* something—an obverse of the truth—the other side of the coin, so to speak. If I make myself clear."

"You don't," said Johnny Kendall.

"Why," said Earl Sawyer, "you speak of keeping abreast of the times. But—this isn't original with me—the day has passed when even an Aristotle or a Newton could keep abreast of the times, really. You've got to think of medical science as being a mine sunk into an enormous mountain of conceivable knowledge. A hundred years ago that mine was a comparatively simple, single shaft. Shafts began to branch from it, however. And other shafts branched from those shafts, and so on.

"A man could spend a lifetime exploring any one of a thousand tunnels in the mine. Men do.

"Why," said Earl Sawyer, "you could devote your lifetime to the study of shock, for example. Not only that, you could devote a lifetime to the study of traumatic shock. And then you could give another lifetime to the study of toxic shock, and another to hæmorrhagic shock. And yet another to *my* interest, which is protein shock."

He shook his head. "That's if I'm lucky enough to land a fellowship with the Greeley Foundation. But that's by the way.

"The point is, of course Rigmire hasn't kept abreast. How could he? Look at the time he's given to municipal affairs. To say nothing of having been a sick man, actually flat on his back, needing a nurse in attendance

—for months at a time. Besides the Medical Society itself, and all the executive and organizational detail that's got to pass through his hand.

"No," said Earl Sawyer, "Dr. Rigmire belongs to your man Dwyer's generation. They were classmates in medical school, did you know?"

He paused.

"The difference, Kendall, is this. Dwyer doesn't pretend to be anything more than a country practitioner. Harry Rigmire does pretend—*must* pretend. He's got to sit here in his office and, because his extremely wealthy patients demand the 'best that money can buy,' he *must* pose as the very fountainhead of medical progress. He's obliged to go through the motions, write his book reviews, preside at the Society's dinners, and so on.

"There," said Earl Sawyer, "is the other side of the coin. The chap who got up that diary wouldn't understand it, but in a sense Harry Rigmire is an impostor. Only he's an honest impostor. Or he'd never have been so sublime an ass as to toss off a verdict and pronounce that diary a psychotic document.

"Psychotic, my eye! Why, the thing's no more genuine than Beryl Rigmire's blathering about the All-Absolute and All-Immediate is genuine!"

And Earl Sawyer tossed aside the bit of glass.

Johnny Kendall asked, "You didn't tell him what you thought of it?"

"I tried in a diplomatic way," said Earl Sawyer. "He's a hard man to unhorse when he takes a fancy to tilt with windmills, though. And to be perfectly frank with you, I've got no chance on earth of landing that fellowship without his recommendation. I have to be diplomatic, you see."

Johnny Kendall considered implications awhile.

"Getting back to the diary itself," he suggested.

"It's a hoax. It's a barefaced, unmitigated series of lies from start to finish. The truth simply isn't in it."

"Or the obverse of the truth?" asked Johnny.

Dr. Earl Sawyer's face became grim.

"I've thought of that," said he. "To begin with, it's pure rot that anybody tried to kill Harry Rigmire because he 'consulted.' In effect, that's saying the assassin had no motive. Obversely, there was a damned good motive."

"Point one."

"Point two," said Earl Sawyer, "there's no mention of Joe Hanlon. Obversely, Joe Hanlon was just as much in the assassin's mind as Rigmire himself."

"And three?"

Dr. Earl Sawyer said, "It wouldn't surprise me a damned bit if that diary turned out to be a ruse to disguise the assassin's sex."

XXI

"YOU LOOK LIKE A MAN WHO COULD USE A DRINK," Miss Geneva Carr diagnosed. "Scotch, rye, bourbon?"

Johnny Kendall said it didn't matter.

"Scotch, then." She went away into the kitchenette of 1234 Buxton Street, apartment 3. Sounds came, of clinking ice cubes, the swish of siphoned water.

Johnny Kendall looked around the melodramatic room. Stiff, cherry-colored drapes fell from ceiling to floor. An ugly, Haitian mask stared from the wall. Leather clad hassocks were strewn about the bare, black-painted floor.

The room had a headachy, stale scent of Turkish cigarettes.

He lighted a cigarette of his own, defensively. Miss Carr returned and pressed a square tumbler into his hand. "I did it myself," she confided, glancing around. "You like?"

"It's interesting."

Geneva Carr chose a hassock for herself. "It's dirty and germy and I love it," she said. "My God, I've spent my life in sterile, white-painted, antiseptically scrubbed surroundings. Do you know why I smoke those dreadful gaspers? It's because I found out years ago how nicely they overcome the smell of drugs."

Miss Carr's red hair flooded onto the shoulders of a yellow housecoat. Improbable dragons pursued each other around the garment. The dragons were as green as Miss Carr's eyes. She tugged the hem about her curled ankles. The housecoat had a V-front. It was possible to observe the suggestion of a shadow separating the suggestion of her breasts.

"You didn't want to talk to me about interior decoration," said Johnny Kendall.

"No," Geneva Carr admitted. She sighed. "You don't like me *or* my apartment."

He did not deny this. He tasted the Scotch and waited.

The nurse said, "I wish you'd relax and be a human being for ten minutes."

He tasted and waited.

"Or better yet, think of me as a human being for ten minutes," the red-haired girl said. "I know—we got off on the wrong foot. But if you'd just get it out of your head I'm a villainess with a guilty secret to conceal."

"I'm listening, if you want to convince me."

Miss Carr attacked her own Scotch. "Look," she said. "I'm not the Florence Nightingale type. I didn't become an R.N. to play the ministering angel, nothing of the sort. As a matter of fact, my folks had money enough. They lost it in 1929. I was eighteen years old. I had to earn my own living. It was pound a typewriter—or something. I could have gone to business school. It didn't make sense, when experienced girls were being let out on every side, every day. On the other hand, depression or no depression, it seemed a reasonably sure thing people would go on falling sick."

"Well?"

Geneva Carr said, "It was foul. It was perfectly filthy. It was like joining the army and getting K.P. and nothing but K.P., and worse than that. Being a student nurse, I mean."

"Uh-huh."

"I tell you, I hated it. I hated the hospital. I lived for the day when I could break away from it, and take private cases. That was the first step. Only it turned out to be pretty loathsome, too."

She brooded.

"Never mind, Kendall, I don't expect you to be interested in my life story," she said. "The point is—I've gone through all that. I've been through the mill once. I don't want to go through it again. I've got a pretty good thing as it is, and I'm not fool enough to throw it away."

"You're talking about your job now?" Johnny Kendall asked.

"Yes, my job. Office hours. This apartment. My salary. I like it, and I don't intend to lose it all. I'm not going to talk out of turn, Kendall."

He stared at her.

"That means you could, if you wanted to!" The ice rattled in the square tumbler. "Well, why spring that on me now?"

Miss Carr shrugged, a thoroughly feline movement on her part.

"You're pretty friendly with the police, Kendall?"

He waited.

"I think you could tell them something," Geneva Carr said. "But it mustn't come from me. You'll have to promise. Will you promise?"

"I'll do my best."

"That's not the kind of a promise I mean."

Johnny Kendall said, "I'll do my best to keep your name out of it."

She considered.

Finally she said, "All right. It isn't all I wanted, but it's something—coming from you."

She jumped up from the hassock. She went to a desk in the corner of the room. She turned the pages of the telephone directory and found a letter.

"Here."

He peered at the envelope. It was addressed to Jos. E. Hanlon, Esq., 12 Sussex Place, Altamont. The return address in the upper left corner read: Office of the Attorney-General, The Capitol, Altamont.

"It hasn't been opened," Johnny Kendall said.

Geneva Carr said, "There's a Federal law about opening other people's mail."

"Where'd you get it?"

"It was in the Monday morning mail."

"At Rigmire's home?"

She nodded. "I stopped by with Dr. Sawyer that

morning. Before going to the office. It was on the hall table with the other letters."

"And you picked it up?"

Geneva Carr said, "It followed me down the street, barking."

"Why did you take it?"

"Why do you suppose Cousin Joe wrote to the Attorney-General?" she retorted.

"I don't know. Do you?"

Miss Carr lowered her lashes. "I could think of several excellent reasons."

Johnny Kendall walked over to the desk lamp. He held the envelope over the top of the shade. The tightly woven envelope was opaque.

"Well?" he asked.

Geneva Carr said, "This is in strict confidence now. You promised."

"Go ahead," he said impatiently.

"I happen to know the family pretty well. I lived with them awhile. That was when I took private cases. The doctor's asthma was very bad then. Afterward he went on a new diet, and his health improved, but then I'd often have to get up in the night and give him morphia, when he had the attacks. He used to talk to me about things. Madeleine was away at school, and there was no one else for him to talk to, I suppose. I—well, that's one reason. It wouldn't be very ethical for me to bring up those things now."

"Yes," said Johnny Kendall. "And what things did he tell you?"

Miss Carr said, "Don't get the wrong impression. He—we didn't gossip. When you get to know Harry Rigmire better, you'll realize he's quite a philosopher. He likes to dig down into things and get at their hidden meanings. But when a man does that, he's apt to let little things slip."

"For instance?"

"Well, for instance, he once asked me how I came to be an R.N. I told him just what I've told you. About my family losing the money. That got him to philosophising about money, and what losing it did to different people, how it affected them."

Miss Carr's auburn brows frowned.

"Cousin Joe," she said. "Now, Cousin Joe was an independently wealthy man at one time. Unfortunately, the Hanlon family included a black sheep. I don't suppose you've ever heard of the uncle, 'W.F.' That's one of the family scandals, one thing Madeleine is so anxious to keep out of sight. Of course, you can't blame her. If I had an uncle who'd died in the State Penitentiary, I wouldn't be anxious to advertise the fact myself."

Johnny Kendall said, "But what's this letter got to do with all that?"

Miss Carr smoothed the shining flanks of her housecoat. "I'm trying to give you the family background," she said. "Old W. F. Hanlon was a perfect brigand, by all accounts. He swindled Cousin Joe out of his every cent. It was some sort of stock promotion. Dr. Rigmire's wife was in it, too, or rather her parents were.

Swindled, I mean. As a matter of fact, her parents died immediately afterward. It was hushed up, but I think her father killed her mother and then himself. As Dr. Rigmire said, it showed what a thing like that would do to a family. Cousin Joe turned out to be an absolute bum. And of course, that's when Beryl, Mrs. Rigmire, went crazy."

"Mrs. Rigmire—!"

Miss Carr said, "Oh, she is. On that one subject. You talk to her sometime."

"I *have* talked to her," said Johnny Kendall.

"I mean really have a heart-to-heart chat with her," said the red-haired girl. "Get her to tell you about her 'communications.' She has them, you know. Of course that all started when her father died. You can imagine how it embarrasses the doctor. His wife running around in those other-worldly robes of hers, and 'testifying' in season and out.

"But that's all past history, isn't it? The important thing is that old W.F. finally *did* die. That's where the letter comes in."

She paused.

"He left the money to Beryl, and his business to Cousin Joe. Only he didn't really leave it. What he did was write identical letters to each of them. There was no regular will at all. I suppose," Geneva Carr said, "he did it on purpose. Because Mrs. Rigmire's share amounted to around a hundred thousand dollars. But Cousin Joe's wasn't worth a red cent. The old scoundrel ran a song publishing racket, you see.

The Federal Government cracked down on that with a cease-and-desist order. So all Joe Hanlon could possibly get out of it would be the office furniture and the sucker list."

"*Would* be?"

"The estate hasn't been probated yet," Miss Carr said, "and that's one thing this letter might be about. Cousin Joe might have been taking steps to get half of the money."

Johnny Kendall said, "My God!" He rubbed his jaw in bewilderment. "How could they keep all that quiet this long?"

She said, "By not talking about it. They're ashamed of W.F., and you can't blame them. He was in prison on a morals charge—a man his age, past seventy. Dr. Rigmire, of course, wouldn't have anything to do with it, if it was ten times the money. The trouble was—is —his wife. It's her inheritance, not his. And she means to have it. As I understand it, she's had 'communications' on the subject."

"You're kidding! That's laying it on too thick!"

Miss Carr's green eyes were cool. "It's the solemn truth. She's been in 'communication' with W.F. The old goat has seen the light, in the All-Absolute, or whatever she calls it. He's not only assured her that the money is hers, but told her how to spend it. He wants to make amends for his sins."

"Well—how—" Johnny Kendall struggled—"how in the name of God, do you know all this?"

"She explained it all to Madeleine. Madeleine went

to Earl Sawyer with it. Earl talked it over with me.
The thing is—you can't go to Dr. Rigmire—what can
you do about it?"

Johnny Kendall was incredulous. "Rigmire doesn't
know?"

"He doesn't know the important thing," said Geneva
Carr. "Not unless Elroy told him. And from my—
from what I've seen of Elroy, I don't suppose he did."

"Elroy!"

Miss Carr said grimly, "When you turn a detective
loose on a thing like that, the first thing he does is
check the alibis of everyone concerned. Now, what do
you suppose is Beryl Rigmire's alibi for last Saturday
night?"

"She was with a Betterment League committee, at
the Capitol."

"She was nothing of the kind."

Johnny Kendall moistened his lips.

"I *know*," Geneva Carr said intensely. "Harry Rigmire is president of the League. The committee reports are made to him. I've seen that committee's
report. *She* didn't attend. I called the secretary to
make sure. And I found Elroy had been around asking the same question."

Johnny Kendall asked, "Did he tell the secretary he
was a private dick?"

"I don't suppose he—" she stopped abruptly.

"You knew he was?"

Miss Carr stared steadily at him. She said, "Listen,
Kendall. The doctor and I were friends—once. He

was sick and lonely. Under those circumstances, it isn't unusual for a man to be attracted to a nurse. But that was all over—long ago. The craziest thing his wife ever did was sick a private detective onto me at this stage of the game."

XXII

JOHNNY KENDALL WENT AROUND TO THE *Blade* AND besought the use of a darkroom. He put the envelope into a printing frame, backed it with bromide paper, and placed the frame under a white light. He could only guess at the exposure; he guessed a minute.

It wasn't enough.

With a second sheet of sensitized paper, he doubled the exposure. Now, as he rocked the developing tray, white letters appeared against a blackly burnt-out background.

That the letter had been folded didn't particularly matter: the letter was a brief one, and so folded that the typewritten body of it stood superimposed against the Office of the Attorney-General's letterhead.

He studied the wet bromide.

My dear Mr. Hanlon (Edward Thatcher had written):
Replying to yours of the 9th, instant, may I state that Standard time dates from the International Meridian Congress of 1884, if this is the meaning of your query.

Standard time was, however, adopted by the railways of the U.S. and Canada in the previous year, 1883, if that is what you mean to ask.

If by officially you mean legally, no single date may

be cited, inasmuch as it devolved upon the several
states to enact the appropriate legislation.

In this State, Pacific Standard time became effective
as of midnight, March 31, 1885.

Trusting that the above satisfies your requirements,
I remain,

> *Your ob'd't servant,*
> EDWARD A. THATCHER
> LIBRARIAN
> *For the Office of the Atty.-Gen.*

Johnny Kendall reflected that the contents of this
letter could have been ascertained as easily by means of
X-ray photography.

Miss Carr, then, might have known very well its
contents. Indeed, Johnny Kendall felt sure she knew.
"Why do you suppose Cousin Joe wrote to the Attorney-General?" she had asked, and the slip of her
tongue argued she was quite well aware this letter
came by way of reply to *yours of the 9th, instant.*

He went upstairs to the *Blade's* clipping morgue and
reference room. When he emerged from an hour-long
bout with the encyclopaedias there, his mind was dizzy
with time—Standard, mean local, astronomical (mean
solar time reckoned from noon), nautical (which was
the same except that the date of the day agreed with
the civil or ordinary time for the morning hours, while
astronomically reckoned the date agreed in the afternoon hours), and sidereal (which he did not understand at all.)

XXIII

D<small>R</small>. R<small>IGMIRE</small>'s wife murmured, "The will? Oh, dear. But that's preposterous. I don't see whatever put such a tiresome notion into your head."

Her clear, gentle eyes stared serenely at Johnny Kendall.

"It's natural to be interested in wills when people die," said Johnny. "Especially when they die violently. You've got a copy of this one around?"

Mrs. Rigmire said, "Dear me. Is there, Madeleine?"

Madeleine Rigmire said, "Yes, in father's study." Her trim figure moved away.

"It's a pity," Mrs. Rigmire said, "Harry isn't here. He could explain it all so much better. I'm afraid I'm terribly dull about mundane matters."

Dr. Rigmire, she went on to say, was at Police Headquarters.

Madeleine, returning, handed over a typewritten page. "It's only a copy," the girl said. "The original is in the hands of mother's attorney."

Johnny Kendall studied the copy. It was dated at the State Prison, as of January 2nd, 1940. The superscription ran, "To my Niece, (Mrs.) Beryl Hanlon Rigmire & my Nephew, Joseph Elliot Hanlon."

I am leaving this (2 copies) with the Warden to be forwarded to you after my death. I am dividing my property between you two as my nearest kin; for that reason only. I know what sentiments you both entertain respecting your Jailbird Uncle. & and on my part, I despise milksop piety the same a spendthrift profligacy. Therefore I am apportioning my estate on the basis of age—First Come, First Served—and on no other basis whatsoever.

I declare this to be my last will and testament.' I give and bequeath to the older of you all of my property of whatever kind and wherever situated; except that I give and bequeath to the younger everything I own under the name of W. F. Hanlon Publishing Co., its stocks, inventories, accounts receivable, and assets of whatever nature.

             (signed)   Walter Frank Hanlon

Johnny Kendall, having read, asked: "And you regard this as a legal will?"

"Yes," said Beryl Rigmire. "The lawyers say so. Don't they, dear?"

"It's a holographic will," declared the girl. "The original was entirely written, dated, and signed by Uncle Walter in his own handwriting."

"But it's not even witnessed."

"Holographic wills do not require witnessing," said Madeleine. "It's really very simple. The attorneys explained all that. If it's in your handwriting, it doesn't matter about the form. It's a legal will if it appears that the writer intended to make a testamentary disposition of his property."

Johnny Kendall peered at the girl. "Oh," said he.

"Uncle Walter could be trusted to know the law, and of course he did," said Madeleine, a bit grimly. "It seems that holographic wills are hardly ever contested with any success."

"Yes," said her mother. "It's the other kind, where you hire a lawyer and have the witnesses and everything, that leads to all the lawsuits."

Johnny Kendall was willing to admit that Uncle Walter had, in all probability, been acquainted with the law.

"That may be," said he, "but in this case what he bequeathed to the younger heir was nothing at all—or next to nothing. Don't you think that might make a difference?"

The girl shook her head. "It wouldn't," she said, "because it's what's called a specific legacy."

"Meaning what?"

Madeleine Rigmire smoothed her skirt upon her knees. "Why," said she, "it's a legacy of a particular thing, specified and distinguished from all others of the same kind belonging to the testator. The will specifies the nature of the bequest clearly. Uncle Walter wanted Cousin Joe to have the W. F. Hanlon Publishing Company, as distinguished from the remainder of his property. It wasn't a demonstrative legacy at all, you see."

Mrs. Rigmire observed, "Gracious. I'm afraid I'm not very good at all those queer legal terms, are you, Mr. Kendall?"

Johnny Kendall said, that may have been Uncle Walter's wish at the time. "But the publishing company folded up. The Federal Trade Commission put it out of business."

"Well," said the doctor's daughter, "that doesn't affect the legality of the will. Ademption of the specific legacy would be accomplished by extinction of the thing or fund bequeathed. That was all settled by a famous lawsuit years ago. *Dobbs vs. Dobbs,* if you care to look it up."

"I don't see how in the world—" murmured Beryl Rigmire "—lawyers remember all those old cases. I know I couldn't, possibly."

"The long and short of it is, anyway," said Johnny Kendall, "this will can't be broken?"

"It might be, I suppose," Madeleine told him, "if Uncle Walter had been of unsound mind. Only he wasn't. The court held he was sane in sending him to prison."

Her mother said, "He was examined by those foreign-sounding creatures, what do you call them?"

"Alienists," the girl said. "And the only other thing would be, impossibility of execution. If it couldn't be determined which of the heirs was the older, then the testator's intention could not be fulfilled."

Mrs. Rigmire said: "Well, I'm the older. That's always been understood in the family."

"Understood?"

"Well," said Madeleine, "it's in black-and-white, too. Father had photostats taken."

"Could I see those?"

"There's nothing secret about it," said the girl, "and I thought you'd ask that. Here is mother's birth. It's from the family Bible, you see. March 10, 1885, at 1:53 P.M. Grandfather Hanlon wrote *that* down because he was interested in astrology."

"You mean, wrote down the exact time?"

Beryl Rigmire said, "Do you know, he insisted on casting Harry's horoscope before he'd give his consent to my marriage? But it wasn't very accurate, after all. The doctor didn't know the hour of *his* birth, only the date. And of course, a few hours makes all the difference."

"Well," said Johnny Kendall, "did Cousin Joe's father cast horoscopes, too?"

"He didn't," said Madeleine, "and if he even owned a family Bible, I've never heard of it. But he kept a diary that ran into, oh, volumes."

Johnny Kendall stared at the second photostat.

"March 10, 1885," he said.

Mrs. Rigmire asked, wasn't that a coincidence. "Our birthdays falling together. But, as I say, a few hours makes all the difference."

Johnny Kendall peered at the crabbed, angular handwriting. *Born this day,* the photostat said, *a Son, 7 lbs. 2 oz. At Sunset (6:03) & hope this not a Bad Omen. Wind Bearing NWW. Fair and Colder.*

He moistened his lips. "Where—?"

"Their birthplaces? Mother was born here, in Altamont," said Madeleine. "Cousin Joe in Maine, on Willard's Island, in Penobscot Bay."

"Then," said Johnny Kendall, "you have to allow for the difference in time to determine which was born first?"

Mrs. Rigmire asked, "Do we have to go into all that again? It's too deep for me. I can't even figure out daylight saving time—when it changes, you know. Whatever becomes of the hour."

Her daughter said, "It doesn't matter. From 1:53 to 6:03 is 4 hours and 10 minutes, and since there's 3 hours difference between Pacific and Eastern time, mother is still 1 hour and 10 minutes the older."

Johnny Kendall said: "Only that was before Standard time was legalized in this State, wasn't it?"

"Was it?" said Mrs. Rigmire. "Well, after all, what is time? It doesn't exist in the All-Absolute. I mean, it's just something that people make up. What does the Good Book say about a minute being a million years in the hereafter?"

It wasn't—Johnny pointed out—a question of hereafter. "It's a question of what time was meant by those records. It was local mean time." He turned to Madeleine Rigmire and told her, with satisfaction: "That was based on the relation of the meridian of a particular place to the sun, noon being defined as the moment when the sun passes over the meridian of any location on the earth's surface."

"Yes," said Beryl Rigmire. "You mean sun time. I can remember that. We used to go to the country in the summers when I was a child. The farmers set their watches by the sun in those days."

"That would be mean local time, roughly gotten at," agreed Johnny Kendall, "although civil time was never based on the apparent sun. They assumed a mean sun, as I understand it. Anyway—this is the point—you've got to allow for the deviation of local mean civil time from Standard time."

"Well," said Madeleine, "go ahead."

Johnny said: "The deviation is four minutes for every degree of longitude west. In Altamont, we lie roughly 5 degrees east of the Pacific time meridian; that is, we're 20 minutes off; local mean time would fall 20 minutes earlier than conventional Standard time here."

Madeleine said, "That's still not enough. 20 minutes from 1 hour and 10 minutes leaves 50 minutes. Mother is still that much the older."

"Granted—" said Johnny Kendall "—but you've got to make the same allowance for a difference between Eastern Standard and mean local time at Willard's Island."

The girl said, "You can, but why do all that computation? The difference, as you say, amounts to four minutes to a degree of longitude west. All you've got to do, really, is subtract the one meridian from the other. Assuming both were using mean local time, the difference would be that much, multiplied by four."

"You have a globe?"

"If you'll come into the study," said the girl. "Willard's Island lies at 67 degrees West. The difference is 67 from 115, or 48. However much that comes to."

"48," said Johnny Kendall, "times four is 192 minutes. 3 hours and 12 minutes."

"Yes," said Madeleine Rigmire. "That's the difference in mean local time, and it doesn't amount to the 4 hours and 10 minutes in the birth records, does it? You can work it out that way, and on that basis, mother is the older by nearly an hour, still."

Johnny Kendall rubbed a hand across his chin.

"There's another possibility, you know."

"Dear me. I can see," said Beryl Rigmire, "you two do love figures."

"Standard time," said Johnny Kendall, "was actually in use by the railroads after November 18, 1883, by act of the General Railway Time Convention. So that Standard time might very well have been adopted in Altamont, and been in popular use before it was actually legalized. Grandfather Hanlon's watch may have been set by Pacific Standard time; his 1:53 could have meant that."

"A difference of 20 minutes," said Madeleine, nodding. "If you reckon Standard time here as against mean local time at Willard's Island. Even if you deducted that much more, you'd not overcome your hour's handicap. But should you deduct it? It seems to me, since Pacific time is earlier than local mean time in Altamont, the difference is in mother's favor."

Mrs. Rigmire declared, "You see, it's just as I said! Time's only something that people make up to suit themselves. I'm sure I don't care whether I was born 20 minutes before Cousin Joe, or an hour and 20 minutes, or whatever it is."

"Or—" said Johnny Kendall "—it may have been the other way around. It might have been mean local time here, and Eastern Standard at Willard's Island."

"A difference of 8 degrees that Willard's Island lies east of the 75th meridian," Madeleine Rigmire observed. "That's 32 minutes, and it falls in Cousin Joe's favor, but it doesn't overcome the handicap, either. 4 hours and 10 minutes is the apparent difference in the recorded times; by mean local times, the computation is 3 hours and 12 minutes; that makes mother the older by 58 minutes. Let it be mean local time in her case, and Eastern Standard in the other—32 from 58 is 26—she's at least 26 minutes Cousin Joe's senior."

Mrs. Rigmire stood.

"Really!" said she. "I simply can't fetter myself with that sort of detail. The only thing which matters to me is that *Uncle Walter means for me to have his money.* He's told me so, over and over again."

She caught Johnny Kendall's bewildered expression.

"Oh, I know what you're thinking. The tone of that will—but he's changed his mind about so many things since. He has, indeed. He's found a great joy—a great peace—and it simply *shines* through his every word now."

"But—!" Madeleine Rigmire said helplessly. "But, Mother—!"

Beryl Rigmire wasn't to be stemmed.

"I had such a *wonderful* communication last Saturday night—"

She saw his jaw slacken, and she put out her hand impulsively, and cried tremulously:

"Mr. Kendall! I know, I know! It *is* hard to believe! So terribly hard to cast off the coils of one's mortal error. But if you'd only be open-minded about it—if you'd only come and share the experience. Why won't you? Why *don't* you? If you'd only let *dear* Poonghee Sherwin show you the Way!"

XXIV

On Thursday morning, the middle-aged woman in the Identification Bureau was uncertain. "He's terribly busy. I don't know if he'll want to see anyone."

Lieutenant Alvin Larson, however, received Johnny Kendall cordially. He listened to an account of Beryl Rigmire's invitation with a smile.

"I'd go; why not?" said the I.B. officer. "That is, if her dear Poonghee manages to stay out of jail. He's in this thing deep, for it seems Larry Elroy rented that upstairs apartment ten days ago. He had a headset there, and an 'ear' that he could drop down outside Sherwin's window. It was a stake-out, you see."

"Did the agency know all that?"

"The apparatus was theirs. But Sherman claims Elroy took the equipment without his knowledge or consent."

"The typewriter—?"

"It's the same Corona. But Elroy didn't use it. He was killed about the time it was delivered, or possibly before."

" 'With a blunt instrument,' " said Johnny Kendall, from having read the *Blade*.

"With a pistol barrel, I shouldn't be surprised."

"Well," said Johnny Kendall, "is it your theory that the Poonghee killed him?"

Lieutenant Larson shrugged. "It seems Mrs. Rigmire went to Sherman several weeks ago! Elroy was put on the job and he did exactly what so many private ops do—devoted most of his time to investigating his client! He found out about the Poonghee, and apparently his motive was to chisel in on Sherwin's take. But I don't set up the theories. Any statement of the kind you want would have to come from Inspector Clay.

"And—" abruptly "—he wants to see you. He was on the phone badgering me a quarter of an hour ago."

"I'll drop around."

Johnny Kendall went along the hallway toward the Bureau of Internal Security. The door opened before he quite reached it, and Madeleine Rigmire emerged. The girl hesitated, and then came up to him, smiling.

"Hello," she said. "I've just been in and confessed my sins."

"All of them?"

She laughed. "Well, at any rate, I owned up to the *Anti-Alcohol!*"

He stared.

She said, "I found it on the telephone shelf when I went into the kitchen that night. I suppose the Hazelle girl was carrying it in her hand. She must have put it down when she rang up Dr. Dwyer."

She could stand here and admit . . .

Johnny Kendall asked, "Didn't you know you could

get yourself—and other people—into serious trouble, taking evidence away from the scene of a murder?"

"Nobody'd been murdered then."

"Yes. But you didn't mention it after the killing, either."

Madeleine Rigmire said in a small, stony voice: "I told you, I wasn't satisfied with Ellsworth. I thought a private investigator would do better."

"You mean," corrected Johnny Kendall, "you thought a private dick would keep his mouth shut about certain things. You knew, didn't you, your mother had already put a private investigator to watching Geneva Carr?"

Madeleine Rigmire's somewhat extreme make-up did not conceal a blush.

"That's perfect nonsense!" she said. "There's nothing to that at all. Mother *means* well. But she's credulous. She can be led around by the nose by certain people."

"Poonghee Sherwin?"

"Well, yes. I think she got that idea through him."

Johnny Kendall said, "The point is, she got the idea. And when a woman hires a private dick, the thought in the back of her head is to accumulate evidence leading toward a divorce."

"But the evidence didn't exist."

"You're sure?"

"I'm as positive as I am that I'm standing here."

Johnny Kendall mused. "Because your feminine intuition warned you Miss Carr was really *your* rival, and not your mother's?"

"What—what makes you say that?"

"Well," said Johnny Kendall, "when an attractive girl goes in for exotic cigarettes, makes herself up to look older than her age, it's a fair guess she's trying to outdo a more sophisticated rival."

Madeleine Rigmire gasped.

"It seems to me," said Johnny Kendall evenly, "you've done your best to become Geneva Carr's type. And I can't see why, except that her type obviously has an attraction for Earl Sawyer."

Madeleine Rigmire said something under her breath, and suddenly flung past the photographer. Grinning wryly, he went on into the B.I.S.

Inspector Clay, behind a desk piled with divisional reports, was puffing a matutinal cigar. By his expression, one or the other was not very much to the white-haired veteran's taste.

He growled. "Siddown, Kendall." He leaned back, laced his fingers behind his head, and stared at the younger man. "Rigmire's kid was in here."

"Yes. I understand she admitted finding the *Anti-Alcohol* vial."

"That ain't all she admitted."

Johnny Kendall was puzzled by the gleam in the inspector's eye.

"What else?" he asked.

"She told me all about that talk she had with you in the Commercial Hotel," declared Clay hostilely. "I gather you just took those pictures on spec, as a free-lance photographer."

"Well?"

The inspector exclaimed, "But you walked in here and told Larson you were working for Ellsworth, acting as his representative."

"Just the first part. I told him I'd been working with Ellsworth."

"You led him to believe you were a duly deputized representative from the sheriff's office. That's the impression *he* got. Or for God's sake, would he take you into his confidence respecting his work on the case?"

Johnny Kendall thought rapidly. He didn't want to make trouble for Alvin Larson.

"I may have given that impression—indirectly," he yielded.

"You may—Judas X. Priest! You may have impersonated an officer!" Clay came out of his chair. He crashed his fist onto the desk. His eyes burned with morose wrath. "Don't you realize, boy, you've committed a *penitentiary offense?*"

Johnny Kendall did not like the sound of it. Still, he had been a newspaperman long enough to appreciate the subtleties of the police approach.

He became wary.

"Do you mean I'm under arrest," he asked, "and anything I say may be used against me?"

Inspector Clay swallowed. "Look here! There's one thing I won't put up with, and that's amateur meddling in a case of mine! I'm continually cracking down

on the private agencies for pulling that kind of stuff!
I won't have it—"

He paused.

"—but at the same time, I realize you have been of
some help to us. I don't want to be tough about this.
I don't want to arrest you."

"Then," said Johnny Kendall, "what do you want?"

Clay said, "I want you to get out while you can. Lay
your cards on the table. Quit trying to pull this lone-
wolf stuff."

"Such as?"

"Such as," said the inspector, "going to see Geneva
Carr last night? What was all that about?"

Johnny Kendall said, "Uh-uh."

"What the hell do you mean, uh-uh?"

"Well," said Johnny Kendall, "in the first place, I
didn't impersonate an officer. I didn't employ false
credentials. I wasn't asked for any credentials, in fact."

"That," grated Clay, "was a piece of goddam negligence on Larson's part."

"It was just as much your negligence," said Johnny
Kendall. "You were in command when we went to
111 Riverbank, and you didn't object to my going
along."

"I figured, hell, you represented your county sheriff's
office."

Johnny Kendall said, "I don't, in the sense of being
a deputized officer. But Ellsworth has retained my
professional services. He has instructed me to accom-

pany him to certain places, and he has directed me to take certain photographs at those places."

"But you weren't representing him at all! You were representing that Hazelle girl—as near as I can figure out!"

"Well," said Johnny, "I was representing Justice, to the best of my ability. That's what Frank Ellsworth and you and your Police Department are supposed to be doing, isn't it? We're allies, as I understand it."

He stood up.

"But I'll be damned," he said, "if I'll let you pull that stool-pigeon technique on me. You can go ahead and make the arrest, if you think you can make it stick. But you won't get one word about Geneva Carr—or anybody else—out of me by doing it."

He started toward the door. He had the sensation of walking on extremely thin ice.

XXV

"You mustn't—" said Beryl Rigmire warningly "—expect too much. The afternoon liturgics aren't ever as successful. It's because the neighbors haven't the proper respect. Their children knock on the door and yell, 'Spook!' in the Poonghee's face when he answers. Of course when we have our fane, all that will be changed."

"I beg your pardon?" said Johnny Kendall as he opened the street door at 111 Riverbank. "Fane?"

"The sanctuary," explained Mrs. Rigmire. "Our temple-to-be."

She gave the bell button three light jabs and then a longer one. The mechanism of the inner door began to clack threateningly. Beryl Rigmire, as her robed figure swam past Johnny Kendall, provided further explanation. "It will be underground. So in case of a war, there'll always be a shelter for our Band.

"Mr. Wilbur's idea," said she, proceeding up the stairs. "*He* was killed—oh, dear, I mean transmigrated —during the bombing of London. So of course he knows. The walls will be reinforced concrete two yards thick. Then the interior is to be paneled in bleached birch."

That, it appeared, was only the beginning. There

would also be parquetry floors, modern plumbing, a private electric plant, and forced ventilation. They had reached the door of 2-B before the description was finished.

Johnny Kendall ventured to remark he should have thought such mundane luxury a matter of indifference to the transmigrated Londoner.

"But *they* are the ones who want it. They're even drawing the plans, the darlings."

"And are they putting up the cash?"

Beryl Rigmire's glance was momentarily suspicious, and then again tranquil.

"In a sense they are," she replied. "Since it's Uncle Walter's money, after all."

The door opened—was opened by a plump man who was (Johnny Kendall imagined) Poonghee Sherwin's assistant.

Mrs. Rigmire stopped on the threshold.

"Meditation," she murmured.

Meditation was in progress; the Band of the faithful squatted in a circle around Eddie Sherwin, alias Elesander Shaw, alias Professor Elesander Stanley, and (now) alias the Poonghee. That little man's five feet and three inches were disposed on the floor in a pose that had obviously been borrowed—with modifications —from Indian occultism.

"It's his Third Position," Beryl Rigmire whispered. "Now—if you want a communication—you've got to concentrate on that person."

Johnny Kendall thought he could use a communication from Cousin Joe very nicely.

The plump assistant closed the door; they advanced into a yellow, jaundiced gloom. Johnny Kendall sat down awkwardly on the floor, Turk-fashion.

... There were Seven Positions.

Johnny Kendall had grown very tired of examining his surroundings by the Fifth.

Thick yellow drapes were tacked over the windows; these stirred from time to time; the drapes let in not very much light; about as much light as one would find in a movie theater.

As in a movie theater, the eyes presently got adjusted to the gloom.

The Poonghee wore a loose-sleeved ceremonial robe (which robe rather resembled Miss Geneva Carr's housecoat, except that it was adorned with the signs of the zodiac.)

Johnny Kendall transferred his attention to the Band.

Other than himself, he fancied, there was not a soul under forty present.

He was a little surprised to discover that, by actual count, males outnumbered females.

He listened for the creak of a footfall overhead that would betray one of Inspector Clay's plainclothes officers.

His legs drowsed.

He drowsed. ...

His head came up with a jerk at the sound of the Poonghee's resonant, chanting voice.

"Communications!" whispered Mrs. Rigmire, under cover of the recited abracadabra.

This was it.

Now the plump assistant stepped to a corner of the room, unlocked a cabinet, and took therefrom a stack of slates, a bit of cloth, a black scarf, and a short, fat candle.

Johnny Kendall made inventory of these articles as the assistant placed them in the middle of the floor. That gentleman lighted the candle, and then withdrew to a corner of the room.

The slates were about eight inches by ten in size; the slate was of a grey color; the edges were rather thickly padded with yellow binding.

They weren't very clean slates. They had been chalked up at a previous séance (presumably) and very imperfectly erased.

Poonghee Sherwin attended to that detail by taking the bit of cloth (which was damp) and proceeding to scrub both surfaces of the uppermost slate.

Then—without actually submitting himself to the indignity of repelling a suspicion of unfair play—he held up that slate for inspection, turned it this way and that in the candlelight, as if to satisfy himself (and incidentally, the Band) that it was in fact a clean slate.

After which he laid it on the floor.

And so with the next. Until eighteen or twenty slates were stacked in the middle of the room, one atop the other.

Next, he placed a slate pencil on the uppermost slate.

And finally, spread the black scarf over the whole.

Johnny Kendall had detected no trickery thus far. As a matter of fact, what he anticipated was a fortuitous (apparently fortuitous) interruption in the guise of an urchin knocking at the door.

Nothing of the kind happened.

What did happen was that the Poonghee assumed an Eighth Position, squatting at two yards' distance from the cloth-concealed slates: with his head bowed, and his arms so folded upon his chest that his hands were disposed upon the opposing shoulders.

He recited sonorously.

The Band waited.

. . . "Dear me," whispered Beryl Rigmire, "I was *afraid* of this!"

As if the All-Absolute had been sufficiently rebuked, the awaited event now occurred.

There came a sound as of pencil upon slate. Johnny Kendall fancied this sound emanated from within the folds of Eddie Sherwin's robe; he could not be sure.

It presently ceased.

Now, to the accompaniment of a general, stirring sigh, the Poonghee advanced upon the slates—laid aside the scarf—picked up and examined the first slate—and handed that to his assistant.

The writing was on the underside of the third slate.

Johnny Kendall craned forward to stare at the crabbed, angular handwriting. It was a signature of some sort. It was—

"Capt. George Hanlon," read Poonghee Sherwin.

"Gracious!" murmured Mrs. Rigmire. "Whoever asked *him* to come?" And then, to Johnny Kendall: "Why, *you* must have!"

"I—?"

"It's Cousin Joe's father. He was a sea captain, you know. I suppose," muttered Beryl Rigmire, "you wanted to ask him whatever time he used."

Johnny Kendall shook his head.

"Who," asked Poonghee Sherwin, "summoned Captain Hanlon into our midst?"

No one replying, he then said:

"Well, it must be the captain has a message for some one present."

He tendered that slate into the hands of the assistant —who thereupon withdrew—and replaced the pencil on top of the remaining slates, and covered the stack with the black scarf.

The Poonghee again assumed the Eighth Position. Hardly had he done so when the sandpapery, scratching sound became emphatically audible.

Sherwin—as before, laid aside the scarf. Again, as before, there was no writing upon the uppermost slate. He therefore handed that slate to his assistant.

It was necessary to examine a second, a third, and finally a fourth slate before discovering the message. Which (as before) had been inscribed on the under surface.

"My son is here," read out the Poonghee.

"Why—" exclaimed Mrs. Harry Rigmire "—he means Joe!"

Johnny Kendall moistened his lips. It was a betrayal that did not escape Poonghee Sherwin's notice.

The little man looked straight at Johnny Kendall. "Who," he asked, "summoned the captain's son?"

"Well," said Johnny, "I thought of him. I don't know that I exactly summoned him."

"You wish a message from him?"

"Well," said Johnny Kendall, "yes, I do."

"Your psychic powers are evidently very great," said Poonghee Sherwin. "First Meditations are almost always fruitless. . . . Is it a question you care to speak aloud? Or would you prefer to put it in writing?"

"I can't just *think* of it?"

"Why," said the Poonghee, "you can try, if you like. It's extremely difficult and confusing for your etheric guest, though. Now Captain Hanlon has gone to all this trouble, and it *is* a trouble and hardship to return to the All-Immediate, and he has even guided his son here, too, especially for your benefit. And what is the result?

"Why," said the Poonghee sadly, "instead of being grateful, you only want to pile hardships in their way. Instead of helping and cooperating and assisting in every way possible. No, you want to make light of it all. You want to make a *test* of the matter. Of course, it is easy for you to *think* your questions, but what an agony for them to try and receive your mundane, worldly thought on their plane of astral existence. It's all the difference between long and short waves in radio.

"No," said Poonghee Sherwin. "It's as the Good Book tells us, *Ask,* and it shall be given you; *seek,* and ye shall find; *knock,* and it shall be opened to you. Matthew 7:7. It's not taught that you don't have to *ask.*"

A murmur of agreement ran around the Band. Of agreement and indignation, as it seemed to Johnny Kendall.

"Well," said he, "I'll write it, if that's easier."

The assistant handed over a slate and pencil. Johnny Kendall wrote, *Who killed you?* and returned the slate to the assistant, who in turn handed it to the Poonghee.

Sherwin put this slate (if there had not been any sleight of hand trickery) on the top of the stack, and replaced the black scarf.

But this time he remained in the Eighth Position a full five minutes without the faintest sound being heard.

Finally, shaking his head, he uncovered the stack of slates, this time handing the scarf to his assistant. He picked up the topmost slate, looked on both sides, and remarked:

"At least, the question has been received. It is gone, you see."

He took the scarf from his assistant, meanwhile handing over the blank slate, and having recovered the stack, resumed the Eighth Position.

A minute or so elapsed, and then the familiar sounds began—although slowly, and punctuated by pauses.

The message was on the underside of the top slate.

A single word had been printed in shaky, childish letters.

" 'Indian,' " said Poonghee Sherwin, handing this slate to Johnny Kendall. "Well, sir, is that a satisfactory answer?"

"No," said Johnny, "it isn't."

"I advise you to think the matter over carefully. You must understand that *their* minds work different from yours. There is very often a hidden meaning. The fact is that *they* think in a more or less subconscious way, using symbols instead of words. That is necessary because there is no such thing as an English language or a French language or a German language in the Beyond. Now if you think hard, perhaps you will see what the symbol is meant to stand for."

Johnny Kendall shook his head.

"I asked who killed him. I don't believe an Indian did that."

Poonghee Sherwin considered the matter.

"It may be symbolic of something else. Indian—tomahawk—scalping—something along those lines. Would that fit?"

"He was killed with a *hatchet!*" breathed Beryl Rigmire triumphantly.

"But I didn't ask what. I asked who." Johnny Kendall broke off, listening.

The sandpaperish, scratching sound had resumed. He stared at the stack of slates. They were uncovered now; the black scarf was draped over the plump assistant's arm.

By the startled intake of breath around the Band, he knew this was extremely unusual.

Poonghee Sherwin lifted the top slate, turned it over, and said:

" 'Rug.' Does that help you?"

" 'Indian rug,' " murmured Beryl Rigmire. "Whatever could—why, I know. It's the doctor's Navajo blanket, of course!"

Johnny Kendall gulped, "Oh, Lord!" and got up, and stumbled out of that room.

"Mr. Kendall—wait!" cried Beryl Rigmire.

Johnny Kendall heard a door flung open upstairs.

He ran.

It wasn't ice under his feet any more. It was mush.

He fled to the Senate news store on the corner and its phone. "Operator! Long-distance! I want to speak to Pop Capp in Kendall's Photo Shop in Crestpeak—yes, person-to-person—and reverse the charges—"

Waiting, he cursed fervently the moment of weakness in which he'd yielded and given Geneva Carr his pledge. He wasn't her lawyer, privileged to keep her communications in silence! He was practically an accessory after the fact right now . . . if it was a fact.

He thought of Inspector Clay's wrath, and shuddered.

XXVI

Johnny Kendall stared across the chaste, Early American waiting room. He breathed hard.

"Can't you see it's the last chance—" he said urgently — "*now?* For both of you?"

Geneva Carr's wail was a sound of feline frustration. "But you *promised!*"

Johnny Kendall said grimly, "I can't help that. Great God! Don't you realize Clay's Homicide cops were in that stake-out upstairs?"

Dr. Earl Sawyer said, "You've got the wind up, old man. The police aren't going to be taken in by all that clap-trap. I'm amazed at you, Kendall."

He smiled cheerfully.

"Slates," he said. "Candlelight. Robes. An accomplice in the background. You don't imagine it needed Cousin Joe Hanlon to write those messages, surely?"

"No," said Johnny Kendall. "I don't."

"Of course not. There was some sort of chemical writing on the slates in the first place. Then the cleansing rag was impregnated with a developing agent. Or," said Earl Sawyer, "Sherwin and his assistant practiced sleight of hand. You imagined you saw the Poonghee remove a slate from the stack and hand it over to his accomplice; of course he examined it closely, and you did, too; you weren't watching his other hand at all. You saw what he wanted you to see, not what he actually did. Or possibly the prepared slates were handed back and forth under cover of the black cloth. It was one or another or all of those methods."

He shrugged.

"I know, Kendall. Beryl Rigmire's dragged me to a séance, too. You sit there until you're torpid, physically; your legs fall asleep, and your whole system's half suffocated with bad air; that's the main purpose the Meditation serves. And then the Poonghee's a practical psychologist—his sort always are. He's quite shrewd enough to see what *you*'re up to; and he plays on the fact, crowds you onto the defensive, arouses feeling against you. And naturally, you're embarrassed— that's what he wants, to rattle you.

"While," said Earl Sawyer, "it's the most natural thing in the world there should be a message from Joe Hanlon. Considering the man's not been dead a week. And with Beryl Rigmire in the room. I should say a ten-year-old child, in Sherwin's position, would be prepared to produce *that* spirit. And naturally—under the circumstances—the first question anyone *would* ask is exactly the one you *did* ask."

Johnny Kendall shifted his weight restively as the young physician's voice ran on and on.

"Yes—" the photographer burst out impatiently "—I thought of all that! And a hell of a lot more!"

He moistened his lips.

"Sherwin wasn't merely *prepared* to produce that message. He was *determined* to do it.

"Great heaven, Sawyer! Can't you see it's not a question of fooling *me?* I didn't have to 'summon' Cousin Joe's 'etheric self.' I didn't have to ask any question, either! 'Cousin Joe' would have volunteered the information, just as 'Captain Hanlon' had already volunteered his.

"By hook or crook," said Johnny Kendall, "willynilly, the Poonghee was going to have that Indian rug revelation!

"Of course no 'spirit' wrote it! It was Sherwin's own deduction—the smartest deduction anyone has made yet in this whole damned affair!"

Dr. Earl Sawyer asked, "Well, why do you think he—?"

"Why? Because it wouldn't get him anything to just tell the cops. Because he saw a chance to boost his professional reputation—with Mrs. Rigmire, especially—by staging that séance today."

"I still don't see," protested Sawyer, "why that's any concern of mine. Or of Miss Carr's."

Johnny Kendall exploded.

"You can't be that dumb! This thing's going to mean your arrest—and a 100-to-1, your conviction!"

Geneva Carr swayed uncertainly, looked at Earl Sawyer, then regained her self-possession.

The physician had never lost his.

"That," said Earl Sawyer, "is ridiculous."

Johnny Kendall drew in his breath.

"Do we have to go over all that again?" he asked despairingly. "You were both on the scene. You were there ahead of anyone else. Miss Carr was in the doorway of the lodge itself.

"You could have been the man who dashed out the back way and threw a football block into me. Whereupon, *she* jumped in to stop me from giving chase.

"And you've done nothing since but tell conflicting stories about what you were doing!"

Sawyer was unmoved.

"The authorities have rejected that theory," he replied.

"Yes, but why? Because there was no blood on either of you after that hatchet killing.

"Take that away—use the blanket as a shield—and the rest fits like a glove!" cried the photographer. "Like a rope around your necks!"

Earl Sawyer stroked his moustache.

He was still unmoved.

He said, "The blanket is merely Sherwin's deduction. Any blood on it may have been there since nine o'clock. That slate-writing doesn't constitute any sort of legal proof."

Johnny Kendall's smile was more nearly a grimace.

"It can be proved, all right," he snapped.

"How do you mean?"

The photographer said, "Do you remember those negatives Babette Hazelle took? Because I'd lost them, I went back to take the shots of the woodpile scene again. Because I made prints from the second negatives, I never got around to making prints from the first batch. I was going to, and then Ellsworth arrested Babette, and I didn't."

Geneva Carr cried out involuntarily. She flung a desperate glance at Earl Sawyer.

She found no moral support there. Sawyer's own eyes were glassy. His attempt at speech resulted only in the sound of a dry swallow.

Johnny Kendall said, "So if there were stains on the blanket after Joe Hanlon's death which *weren't* there after the attack on Dr. Rigmire, the photographs will prove it."

The pair stood stunned.

Johnny Kendall said, "Make up your minds. I phoned Pop Capp as soon as I left that séance. I told him to make those prints and to call me back here.

"If you want to say anything, now is the time. I don't think Clay or Ellsworth or a jury will give one damned bit of credence to anything you say later. I won't, myself."

Geneva Carr's mouth was a slash of agonized color.

"Earl—hadn't we—maybe—?"

She stood trembling.

Earl Sawyer was just as shaky.

He said, "I'll handle it. Listen, Kendall. We're— we're innocent.

"We weren't even in this State when that attempt was made to kill Harry Rigmire. We were across the line, in Twin Falls."

Johnny Kendall stared. Twin Falls was an approximate hundred and twenty miles from Crestpeak.

He said, "Why in the hell didn't you say so?"

Earl Sawyer replied, "Because we were married there by a justice of the peace."

"Married—!"

Johnny Kendall heard a small, muffled sound.

He whirled around.

He jerked open the waiting room door.

He stared in the wide, unseeing eyes of Madeleine Rigmire. She had been standing outside that door—for how long, he didn't know. She didn't remain to explain.

"Oh!" said Madeleine Rigmire. She turned and ran down the corridor.

Johnny Kendall drew the back of his hand across his mouth. He swung around and faced Sawyer and the red-haired nurse.

"Married!" he said. "Why couldn't you say so?"

Sawyer opened his hands.

"I told you—in another connection. I'll never get that Greeley fellowship without Harry Rigmire's help and influence. I also told you he's a hard man to unhorse when he gets an idea.

"The trouble," said Dr. Earl Sawyer, staring at the corridor door, "was Madeleine. Harry Rigmire's idea was that I should marry *her*."

The bride's green eyes were grim. "You mean it was her idea. She deliberately threw herself at your head."

Earl Sawyer said judicially: "Don't be too hard on

Madeleine, Gene. She's too damned devoted to her father, and her father's interests. Considering the mother she has, that is perhaps natural. But the fact remains, she's entirely under paternal domination.

"To her, Harry Rigmire is a regular tin god. Everything that he is and has, is to her the most wonderful thing in the world. I don't believe she was ever in love with me. She was in love with his conception of me as his junior partner.

"As he has said over and over again, *his* objection to the fellowship is that he can't afford to lose me from this office. Madeleine hears things like that, and it makes me a kind of minor tin god in her sight."

He paused.

"Of course, if I disappointed her Harry Rigmire would regard that as absolute moral infamy on my part. She'll go straight to him now, and of course I'll never get the fellowship."

Johnny Kendall said to the red-haired young woman:

"Then when you told me you didn't want to throw away a good thing, you meant you didn't want to throw away your husband's chances?"

She nodded.

"Well," said Johnny Kendall, "that apparently covers the *first* attack satisfactorily. But it's no alibi for the second."

Earl Sawyer sighed.

His voice came resignedly.

"It's not an alibi, but it's the explanation. The fact

is, we reached the lodge ten or fifteen minutes before three o'clock. We parked in the lane and talked this whole thing over.

"You know, Kendall, I'd talked to Hanlon on the phone. He told me the sheriff had an investigation on foot, and that Harry Rigmire wasn't satisfied with it, and that Madeleine had gone to Crestpeak to push things along.

"We both knew that—as a formality—we might be asked to supply an alibi. We talked it over and decided not to mention the marriage. Because of the fellowship, you understand?"

Johnny Kendall asked, "And *after* you talked it over?"

Sawyer's face flushed.

"Well—" he began.

"No, Earl," said Geneva Carr Sawyer. She stared steadily at Johnny Kendall. "We saw your headlights down the road. I thought it was Madeleine's car coming, and I didn't want to turn on our lights and let her know we'd been parked there. So I told Earl to drive into the yard without turning on his lights at all."

She paused—and went on determinedly.

"He stopped in the yard, and I got out there, and then he drove on into the shed. That's what he's been trying to hide from you. That I didn't have to walk from the shed at all."

"Go on."

"I stood there and waited for him. He had trouble getting the car into the shed beside Dr. Rigmire's car, in the darkness. He got in too close, and couldn't get his door open on that side.

"That," she said, "was what kept him from coming when he heard the scream.

"I was waiting for him until you drove into the yard. Then I went on up to the porch. And that's when I heard the scream."

She released a deep breath. "Now," said Geneva Carr Sawyer, "I've told the truth. Now it's off my mind."

Johnny Kendall nodded slowly.

"You'd better get it on Inspector Clay's mind as rapidly as possible," he said. "It's not in his precinct, but you can make a statement there—before this thing breaks wide open."

"Earl will go to the police. I," said the bride, "am going straight to Dr. Rigmire. Perhaps there's still a fighting chance for that fellowship, if I can talk to him before Madeleine poisons his mind."

Her green eyes had become calculating.

"You can wait for your phone call, if you like," she told Johnny Kendall. "Just press the button on the knob when you leave. That locks the door."

"If a patient comes in—?"

"There aren't any appointments after three o'clock. It's 3:30 now."

It lacked five minutes of four o'clock when the phone rang.

Pop Capp, at the Crestpeak end of the wire, said: "That was a halfway good guess, Johnny."

"There *was* more blood on the blanket?"

"There was," said Pop, "but let me tell you the other half. It's a funny thing. That wood ain't piled the same."

A pause lengthened itself.

"Johnny?" said Pop.

"I'm here. I'm thinking."

"The trouble with you," said Pop severely, "you've got city ideas. Thinking to yourself at 65¢ for three minutes. Think out loud, Johnny."

Johnny Kendall said: "I'm starting for the Rigmire lodge. You meet me there with those pictures. Pick up Doc Dwyer. I want to go over that story of his again, on the ground there."

XXVII

HE DROVE THE GHOST CANYON SHORTCUT.

At the bridge, he turned into the lane beside the trout stream. Two sandy ruts wound into the thicket. Blackened circlets of stone betokened forgotten fires over which freshly taken fish had been broiled. Beer cans rusted among the mountain lilac.

The lane stopped after a hundred-odd feet.

Johnny Kendall got out of his coupé. He glanced at his strap-watch. The time was 5:17. He had driven from Altamont in an hour and a quarter.

He lifted his Speed Graphic case from the coupé's rear window shelf.

A few of Old Hazy's bees turned above his head as he trudged along the creek toward the Rigmire lodge.

He looked at his strap-watch again as he entered the yard. The time was now 5:24. It would have taken longer in darkness, of course.

Pop Capp and Doc Dwyer had not yet arrived.

Johnny Kendall walked to the woodpile, looked that over. The wood was partly lumber that had been torn out of the remodeled farmhouse, partly odds and ends of new lumber left over from the remodeling, and (for the larger part) consisted of saw lengths of native timber. The pile stood as high as Johnny's shoulder. The wood was neatly stacked, in tiers. The front, outer tier was perhaps a bit less neatly stacked.

He stood on tiptoe, and peered into the pile.

An ungentle muttered sound lingered awhile on his lips.

"Great hell-l-l!"

There were brown traces on the sawed surfaces of the timber lengths. Then there was a large, brown, crusty blob on a peeled projection of log.

In short and in fine, there were bloodstains in the woodpile.

Johnny Kendall backed away. He lifted a hand and drew the back of it across his lips. His lips were tight, puckered.

His nostrils tightened, too. They wrinkled. He sniffed.

The breeze was westerly. He was down-wind from the shed.

Johnny Kendall stared at the shed doors. They were closed. But he went around to the other side of the woodpile to kneel down, take the camera from its case, thrust a holder into the back.

He avoided the bare, gritty yard. He made his way across a carpet of brown, dry, autumnal grass.

A smaller door was open in the shed's side. A biting odor of gasoline came from it.

Inside, on a platform of 2 x 8 planking, stood the gasoline-motored unit which manufactured the lodge's electricity.

The camera clicked.

The man with the pliers didn't hear, didn't look around.

Johnny Kendall said, "Doctor, I wouldn't disconnect that wire."

Dr. Harry Rigmire turned. There was no expression on his large, broad, well-fleshed face. There was a streak of grease that began at the left cheekbone and quartered up across the turban of his head bandage.

"Do you know how to repair these damned things?" he asked.

Johnny Kendall said, "I know better than to disconnect that wire. If you did that, you'd have a fire in here. You'd burn down the shed. That would set fire to the grass. You'd burn down the woodpile, too."

Dr. Harry Rigmire looked at him. There was no expression whatsoever on his face. Well, he tried to assume one. He tried to smile.

Johnny Kendall said, "Come on, doctor. We'll go inside."

"Oh," said Dr. Harry Rigmire. "Yes, I had better phone for a repairman. I should have done that in the first place."

They crossed the yard. Dr. Rigmire's manner was indifferent; Johnny Kendall's abstracted, as they entered the lodge.

"Never mind about phoning," said the photographer.

"I beg your pardon?"

"Your hand's a lot better, isn't it?"

"I've taken it out of the sling," said the physician, "as you see."

"Uh-huh. And you were using the pliers with it out there."

Dr. Rigmire's blue eyes examined the younger man. "Incised wounds have been known to heal in the course of time," said he dryly. "The hand is better. I don't quite see what point you're trying to make, Kendall."

Johnny Kendall put one foot on the seat of a rustic chair, his elbow on that knee, and his chin on his knuckled fingers.

"I've been thinking about that attempt on your life Saturday night," he said. "The first one. I think I know now what happened there."

Dr. Harry Rigmire leaned against the rustic fireplace.

"Well?" said he.

"I presume it gets chilly in here, evenings. You decided to build a fire. I suppose you went out for some wood. Of course, building a fire involved splitting kindling."

"Of course—" said Dr. Rigmire "—and as I told you, I was looking around for the axe."

"That's what you said. But it seems to me, if you wanted kindling you'd split some of that scrap lumber lying there. And for that kind of a job, your hatchet would be as handy as an axe. Handier, at night, working by a flashlight. And then the hatchet was sharp, and the axe wasn't.

"So I think now—you took the flashlight *and* the hatchet when you walked out of the house."

Dr. Rigmire said calmly:

"I didn't, but go ahead, what's in your mind?"

"This," said the photographer, staring at the other. "Your hatchet had been weakened by misuse. Its head was loose. I suppose you started to split kindling— drove it into a board—and jerked to get it out. You got it out, all right. But not attached to the handle any more.

"It flew into the air. Where, you couldn't see in the darkness. You flinched. You turned away. You threw up your hands. Well, it hit your hand—it glanced off —struck your head besides. That's all."

Dr. Harry Rigmire said, "I don't see how you can think that, Kendall." He changed his position; one shoe made a scuffing sound on the pegged plank floor. "Not seriously."

Johnny Kendall was serious enough.

He insisted, "I figure it that way, now. The diary contained what Earl Sawyer called an obverse of the truth. There *is* such a thing as improbability; there has to be; or nothing could be probable, could it?

"I don't mean—" said Johnny Kendall "—an accident like that would be improbable. What I mean is, there was Babette Hazelle driving up the lane at approximately that time. It's the one coincidence in the whole affair, so far as I can see. Although it wasn't coincidence, strictly speaking. I believe it was a circumstance, not anything you could plan for. You could plan *from* it, though.

"Because," said Johnny Kendall, "the instant that

happened, you thought: 'It *might* have killed me!' And
right after that, you thought of something else:

"'It could be made to look like an attempt on my
life!'"

Johnny Kendall paused.

"Everything starts from that," he said. "The head of
a hatchet flew off, and from there on, it's all clear
enough. It was too serious to be a deliberately self-
inflicted wound—all the rest develops out of it."

Dr. Rigmire said, "That's exactly where you're out
of your depth, Kendall." He smiled. "You don't pro-
fess to be an expert on medical matters, I hope? Of
course my *wounds*—and that's plural—were too serious
to be self-inflicted.

"Or," said Dr. Rigmire, "for me to have 'instantly'
thought this, that, and the other. I was knocked unconscious, that's the medical fact of the matter."

Johnny Kendall shook his head.

"Babette Hazelle isn't expert, either. She was excited, besides. I don't think she could tell whether you
were unconscious, or just feigning unconsciousness."

"I won't argue it," asserted Harry Rigmire. "Dr.
Dwyer attended me. It appears that he would know,
and that he regarded the matter as serious enough."

"I'll argue it," said Johnny Kendall, "because you
didn't feign unconsciousness when Dwyer got here. He
can't say whether you were or not. You said you were;
that's all Dwyer knows."

He stared into the physician's blue eyes.

"Take that hand wound, in the first place," he said.

"How serious was it? As I understand it, you weren't bleeding to death. Babette didn't apply a proper tourniquet—didn't find the pressure point at all—so in fact what she did for you was nothing at all. Still you lay there on the ground—senseless, as you say—without any very serious ill effect—for the course of a quarter-hour. I'd guess your hand got a nasty flesh wound; it couldn't have amounted to much more than that, surely. Your ear's cut, but I have an idea whatever else's under that head bandage isn't too ghastly, either."

"Pressure point! Bah!" interrupted Dr. Rigmire. "Boy Scout stuff! Dwyer didn't tell you that, did he?"

The photographer shook his head:

"No, I think it boils down to about this. Dwyer examined you—your wounds weren't so serious—so far as he could see. But your symptoms were, as you let on. He had no reason to suspect a fellow practitioner, an old classmate, too, of malingering. So he assumed some hidden, out of sight, internal injury *must* exist.

"Dwyer was puzzled, as I see him—*now*. He was up against something he didn't understand. He made all the allowances he could—bleeding, shock, and the rest of it—and it still left something over, inexplicable to him, something it would take a very high-powered specialist to explain away."

Johnny Kendall shrugged.

"Or a high-powered cop," he said. "A man like Alvin Larson. For of course if Larson had heard that story, and found only an axe with blood *smeared* on it, he'd have looked around for some other weapon that had the proper, *directional* bloodstains. And he would have found the broken hatchet, where you'd chucked it away into the woodpile—to conceal the fact that your injuries were sheerly accidental."

Dr. Harry Rigmire was not so much moved by all this as Johnny Kendall thought he should be.

He stepped away from the fireplace, lowered himself into a chair behind the small table, leaned back in the chair and wriggled his feet under the table.

"As for the rest," said Johnny Kendall, "of course you dropped the head injury theory as soon as X-rays could be taken. It was just your hand, then. I suppose there were ways it could be made to look worse than it was. You could discolor it. You could tighten the bandage temporarily and get an unpleasant-looking effect that way, I should think."

Dr. Rigmire said, "Why don't you drop the medical aspects of the thing? You're only guessing, anyway. What I'd like to know," said he, "is *why*. My motives, as you imagine them."

"Well," said Johnny Kendall, "when you add it up, it's your whole life."

Harry Rigmire smiled.

"Inclusive," said he, "but evasive."

Johnny drew a long breath.

"Go ahead," said the physician. "I'd like to see myself as other people see me. This is more to my taste. Really."

Johnny Kendall shook his head.

"No," he said. "I wondered how to begin, and I

guess you knew it. You tried to put me off just now, didn't you?"

Dr. Rigmire compressed his lips. It was, Johnny Kendall thought, the first involuntary move the man had made.

That blow had told.

"It isn't how others see you," said the photographer. "It's how you see yourself, what your life has been from your point of view. So Dwyer was right. The trouble was inside, hidden away, after all."

He reached for a chair, swung it around, sat facing the physician.

"Well," said Johnny Kendall, "what has your life been? You started from scratch with Dwyer, as I understand. Only you were smart enough to see that one hour spent at a committee meeting of the right sort would do you more good than a day devoted to your professional practice.

"What it comes down to is that you pushed yourself in, you gave yourself to this and the other 'movement' —always of course a movement that had its wealthy backers. Nowadays, charity doesn't begin at home. Organized charity doesn't, at any rate. It begins with the well-meaning rich. So that when you got interested in a free clinic, it was mainly an interest in whatever dowager was backing the thing.

"But," said Johnny Kendall, "dowagers don't work. Committees don't, either. There always are the invaluable individuals who pitch in and get things done. You were such an individual; but you were a politician, too.

You got to be president of one and another of those extremely respectable and well-meaning organizations. You got your pronouncements into the newspapers. You got yourself up a name. So that, when the dowagers ailed, they thought of calling you in. I imagine that's the story of your professional life, as you yourself see it. By the way," said Johnny Kendall, "how old are you?"

"Fifty-one," said Dr. Rigmire, surprised.

"Well," said Johnny Kendall, "then you married a woman five or six years older than yourself. I gather that your interests lay poles apart. You're not wrapped up in occultism, surely?"

Rigmire said quickly, "Beryl wasn't, when I married her."

"No. That came after her parents' deaths. It also came after her parents' money was gone. You married into a wealthy family, and then that turned to ashes before you realized anything on the investment," said Johnny Kendall grimly.

Dr. Rigmire's eyes narrowed. "You make me out a charlatan and a fortune-hunter. What more?"

Johnny Kendall said that was not his intention and meaning.

"Not at all," he said. "This is as you see yourself. You're an extremely brilliant and able man who has forced his way up the ladder of success by unremitting effort, even though you've cracked a shin on an occasional broken rung along the way. Mrs. Rigmire is simply the most painful and embarrassing of the broken rungs."

Dr. Harry Rigmire moistened his lips.

"You've had some bad breaks, doctor. Your failing health—although that wasn't such a bad break, you may have thought. It put you flat on your back. It gave you a chance to review your life, look for a meaning in it, and begin to formulate a philosophy of your own. It gave you a chance to do a little reading; I suppose historical reading; I assume that's when you brushed up on the details of who pulled Abe Lincoln out of a creek and who killed McKinley. And, finally, it threw Geneva Carr into your way."

Johnny Kendall gestured.

"I don't know exactly what you *did* philosophize about life—I've got a general idea, though. It was a philosophy which justified your taking Geneva Carr as your mistress.

"Only that blew up when Earl Sawyer came into your office.

"Because he fell in love with her, and she with him.

"I don't suppose," said Johnny Kendall, "it was love at first sight. I see it coming on slowly, and I see you fighting against it. Your philosophy becomes clearer as I see you making Madeleine a pawn in that game. Your philosophy and your methods. Keeping Sawyer on, when any less astute man might have given him walking papers. And not only that, but dangling the prospect of a Greeley fellowship over his head; so he couldn't reach for it and Geneva Carr, too, at the same time."

Dr. Harry Rigmire remarked, "I wondered. So I owe this flattering portrait to Sawyer, do I?"

"I picked it up from him, and from others. Pieces of it. I'm fitting them together here," said Johnny Kendall, "into a photomontage. The picture of a wise guy who got to feeling sorry for himself. A wise guy trying to scheme life into something it couldn't be.

"Because you'd never have got Geneva Carr away from him, anyway."

Dr. Rigmire said, "Well, I'm apparently very stupid. From the sound of all this, I should have killed Sawyer. Or my wife—not my wife's cousin." He added hastily, "If that's what you're getting around to."

"You had to kill Joe Hanlon, too."

"Why?"

Johnny Kendall said, "Because he was older than your wife, and therefore entitled to all that money."

Dr. Rigmire opened his eyes widely.

"Nonsense!" he said. "Even allowing for the difference in local times—it's absolutely impossible. I've gone into all that thoroughly. I assure you, the difference is at least twenty-six minutes in Mrs. Rigmire's favor."

"Well," said Johnny Kendall, "if you've gone into it thoroughly enough to consult the *Nautical Almanac* you've got on your bookshelf here, you damned well know the difference is twenty-two *hours*—in Cousin Joe's favor."

He stood up.

"I got the essential fact out of an encyclopaedia, although it was just so much irrelevant information until I learned Captain Hanlon was a seafaring man."

Dr. Harry Rigmire was on his feet, too. The eyes hunting out of his blanched features indicated he knew too well. . . .

Johnny Kendall said, "That diary—which you've kept out of sight except for the one photostated entry —was an old seadog's log. Captain Hanlon reckoned time after his lifelong custom, according to the practice of his profession. His day was an astronomical day of twenty-four hours reckoned from noon to noon.

"Captain Hanlon," said Johnny Kendall tensely, "reckoned March 10th as beginning noon the previous day. The sunset *he* recorded fell, by mean solar time, at 6:03 on the evening of March 9th, 1885!"

XXVIII

"WELL," SAID DR. HARRY RIGMIRE, "I'M THROUGH insulting your intelligence! Suppose we switch up the lights, and have a drink, and go over this together from *that* point."

"You may need a drink. I don't."

"A light at any rate." The physician touched a wall switch. "I suppose," said he, chafing his left fingers upon their thumb, "it would come under the heading of the gruesome to suggest a fire?"

"You may be feeling chilly," said Johnny Kendall. "I'm not."

Dr. Rigmire resumed his chair.

"Come, come, my boy," he said. "After all, you've only demonstrated a conceivable motive—shall we say?"

Johnny Kendall said he thought he'd demonstrated much more than that.

"When you concealed your broken hatchet in the woodpile," he asserted.

"If I did, you mean. After all, again, it's drawing a long bow to suppose I knew in advance Joe would come here that night."

"I don't think you did. All you hoped for, originally, was to set the stage. An attempt had been made

303

on your life. The next attempt—resulting fatally for Cousin Joe—could have happened any time.

"Only," said Johnny Kendall, "he did come here. So that you didn't have to wait."

"Really? Well; go ahead."

"You got rid of Madeleine. That idea of buying my negatives—all of that—you produced simply to invent an errand and get her out of the way."

Dr. Rigmire said, "I see. And I suppose I also prevailed upon Dwyer to put me under the influence of a hypodermic? That was clever of me, extraordinarily so."

Johnny Kendall said, "Oh, hell. Geneva Carr was giving you morphine for your asthma five years ago. You've developed a tolerance for the stuff. You'd get just a pleasant reaction out of enough of it to put an ordinary man down."

Dr. Rigmire no longer looked amused. "Now, I am a drug addict," said he.

But there was little flavor in the irony.

"I don't say you are. But even taking it medicinally, you'd acquire the tolerance."

Dr. Rigmire offered neither rejoinder nor rebuttal.

Johnny Kendall said: "So far, then. You were here alone with your victim. Your problem was how to kill him without drawing suspicion upon yourself. Or your motive, either.

"You thought of another attempt upon your life, terminated by the arrival of somebody at the opportune moment.

"It worked before; why shouldn't it again?

"Well," said Johnny Kendall, "somebody was going to arrive, certainly. There was Madeleine, for one. And Sawyer, for another.

"You'd heard Cousin Joe talk to Earl Sawyer on the phone. You knew how long it takes to drive from Altamont. You could predict within, oh, a quarter-hour, when Sawyer would arrive.

"That was all you needed to know."

He watched Dr. Harry Rigmire steadily.

The physician said, "This is ridiculous, Kendall. I don't see how you can imagine anything of the sort in your wildest dreams." He wetted his lips. "To suppose I whacked Cousin Joe with the hatchet—dashed outside and knocked you down—got rid of the blanket and—jumped into bed again?"

"That wasn't what happened."

Johnny Kendall shook his head.

"Not at all," he said. "What happened is that Joe Hanlon fell asleep on the divan here.

"You slipped out your bedroom window. You circled the house, to the woodpile, and unstacked the wood to get the hatchet again. You took the hatchet into the shed and drove nails into it, fixed the head on firmly.

"Then, with the hatchet and the Navajo blanket you returned to the bedroom.

"You propped yourself up in bed and waited."

Dr. Harry Rigmire gave a little start.

He looked disturbed.

That detail was not to his liking.

"Why?" he asked, and there was a hint of trepidation in his voice.

Johnny Kendall said, "You were watching for headlights. The road past here is scarcely traveled at all, and certainly not at that hour.

"When you saw lights—and you could see them several miles away, on the hilltops—it'd be almost certainly either Madeleine's car or Sawyer's."

He paused.

"You didn't expect Sawyer to come the other way, from Ghost Canyon. You didn't know when he pulled into your lane and parked.

"Your attention was two miles away.

"And when you saw *two* headlights, two cars, it must be both Madeleine and Sawyer—you thought.

"That was your signal."

They stared at each other. Dr. Harry Rigmire's eyes did not flinch. They were stony.

"Then—" said Johnny Kendall "—you had three or four minutes in which to act.

"You stepped into this room where Cousin Joe was soundly asleep.

"Then you ran out to the woodpile, put down the blanket there where you'd found it. And got snugly back into bed before you heard the first of two cars drive into the yard.

"You waited for a footstep on the porch—Geneva Carr's.

"And then—

"You screamed!"

Johnny Kendall relaxed from his strained, tiptoe position. He was pale. Sweat had come on his forehead as he talked, and on the backs of his hands.

Anyone would have thought he was the guilty party; would have thought Rigmire the cool, implacable accuser.

The physician's face was expressionless.

"Then," said he, "how do you account for the man who ran into you?"

Johnny Kendall said, "That was Larry Elroy, of course."

"Elroy?"

Johnny Kendall gestured. "You know your wife had him shadowing Geneva Carr. He followed her and Sawyer that night. He was, I suppose, a half mile or more behind them.

"He saw their car turn into the lane, if you didn't.

"He parked his machine, probably at the bridge, and came the rest of the way on foot. I gave him ten minutes to get into the yard here.

"He was here in time to see you run out with that blanket."

Dr. Harry Rigmire assumed a thoughtful look. He shook his head. He said, "And by an incredible coincidence, I went to that very agency and was assigned that very detective."

Johnny Kendall shook his head in return.

"I don't believe you intended to go to *any* agency, doctor. I think Elroy forced your hand. He compelled you to engage Sherman on the case. That he'd get the case from Sherman was a cinch, since he'd already been making an investigation in the family.

"That gave him a hold over you, since he could then legitimately expose you as a result of his investigation.

"He couldn't admit, of course, he'd practically witnessed the murder.

"But he knew who did it.

"He was in Crestpeak on Monday, trying to dig up the dirt on your private life. He wanted all he could get. He was blackmailing you."

Dr. Harry Rigmire thought his own, private thoughts. Perhaps they had nothing to do with his next words.

"You accuse me of his murder, too?"

Johnny Kendall said, "I don't know the details. Inspector Clay doesn't welcome amateur sleuths on his cases! I don't know how you found out Elroy was staked-out above Sherwin's apartment. Maybe that's where you were to deliver the first installment he demanded!

"Anyway, you went there with a gun. You made him address that envelope at the point of the gun. You got his fingerprints onto the envelope flap.

"And you left the *Anti-Alcohol* there. Because of course Madeleine gave the vial to you! She'd never have kept that discovery from you, certainly.

"And finally," said Johnny Kendall, "it's perfectly obvious you wrote that diary. And why."

Dr. Rigmire's eyebrows went up.

He smiled.

"Oh, now. Come. It wasn't even a physical possibility for me—with one hand—to write that diary. In that time."

"It would have been awkward, but quite possible," said Johnny Kendall. "I think you used both hands, though. And besides, part of that diary was prepared days ago. You had it in mind—if not in notes—it was merely a copying job."

"What part?" said Dr. Rigmire.

Johnny Kendall told him:

"Part of it in the middle—the third section—all of that had nothing to do with the lodge. Or with Crestpeak or Sheriff Ellsworth, either. It was the part about the police rushing around in their high-powered cars, doctor. It was a different scene entirely—and a different scheme of murder, too. A scheme to outwit the Altamont police by means of a faked garage hold-up that never quite came off.

"Madeleine—" said Johnny Kendall—"saw a prowler in the shrubbery Monday night, before any of this began. I am convinced she saw a murderer, lying in wait to stage just such a bit of pretended banditry as the diary describes. Cousin Joe and your wife would have been slain then and there. Only your daughter went to your study, she saw someone in the shrubbery, and you couldn't kill your two victims after she raised the alarm. You had to pretend you'd overheard, and that you rushed out to look for that prowler.

"That," said Johnny Kendall, "was your plan, a

cold-blooded one you'd worked out methodically, and very probably had argued out with yourself in written notes.

"So when it came to preparing the diary—because time *was* short—you simply picked up that idea, and dropped it into the middle of the thing."

Dr. Rigmire asked: "But why the diary at all?"

"You had to get Babette Hazelle out of jail."

"You credit me," said the medico, "with that much generosity?"

Johnny Kendall didn't.

"You were perfectly willing for the criminal to be Doc Dwyer's *unknown woman*. But she mustn't be known. She mustn't be brought to trial. You didn't want a trial, with the publicity, with the press and the defense attorneys poking into your affairs. That was one thing."

Johnny Kendall paused.

"The other thing—there was still your wife. *She* couldn't live to turn Uncle Walter's wealth over to Poonghee Sherwin. The 'assassin' had to strike again, and next time, with Beryl Rigmire 'accidentally' in the line of fire.

"So, Babette Hazelle wouldn't do. You needed the fantasy of an insane killer who would make yet another attempt on your life. You prepared the diary for that reason, and you did your best to sell that interpretation of it to the police.

"You relied," Johnny Kendall said, "on your reputation to cover up a darned shaky knowledge of psychiatry! Do you remember telling me nobody could make sense of the doodlings a madman left on an asylum wall?

"Well, come to think of it, interpreting insane persons' drawings is one thing psychiatrists can do! I remember seeing an article about that in one of the picture magazines—now that I think of it."

Dr. Harry Rigmire stared away, silent.

Johnny Kendall said:

"Well, anyway. The diary was prepared to make it credible that there *was* an insane assassin on your trail. And what grew out of that, grew out of the need for secrecy.

"First, a method of obtaining a typewriter so *that* couldn't be traced to you.

"Second, a place where you could sit down and pound out your copy, which I don't doubt you'd already put into longhand notes during the past 48 hours—so the typing itself amounted to just a mechanical chore.

"Elroy's stake-out over Sherwin's apartment—" said Johnny Kendall "—answered both requirements. You could get the Corona without Garrant so much as laying an eye on you. And by using Sherwin's name—by moving his card from the 2-B slot to the 2-C doorbell button downstairs—you planted a fresh confusion for Inspector Clay.

"For suppose he followed this far? It would point to Sherwin, wouldn't it? But why should Sherwin have bought the typewriter in his own name, and then had it delivered to the wrong apartment?

"He wouldn't, of course!

"And you knew the police couldn't get around that difficulty. The whole point being, you didn't want to implicate Sherwin too deeply. It *had* to be an insane outsider who would kill your wife next—the last thing Sherwin could think of doing!

"But," Johnny Kendall said, "that's Clay's worry. I'm not so much interested in what happened in Altamont. I'm interested in a murder that happened right here."

The doctor considered. "What do you expect me to do? Blurt out a damning confession for your benefit?"

The younger man shook his head.

"I guess you have," he said. "Already. Madeleine went to you, of course, with what she overheard. When you learned photographs had been taken that undoubtedly included your woodpile, you rushed out here to set fire to the place."

Dr. Harry Rigmire said:

"Nonsense. You're wasting your talents on the mountain air, young man."

He reached inside his coat.

Johnny Kendall came a step closer, quickly.

"No—" said the older man "—I'm not fool enough to pull a gun on you. Just a cigar. Will you have one?"

Johnny Kendall shook his head over the proffered cigar case.

The physician helped himself. He pressed the cigar's end gently . . . between thumb and forefinger of his right hand.

"I grant you," said he, "it *could* have happened. Just as you say."

A pause.

"But let a competent lawyer at this photomontage of yours! Let such a lawyer separate the seed from the chaff!"

Another, longer, smiling pause.

"Think back, Kendall. Of all you've said—how much is hearsay and opinion and conclusion? All you can testify to is what you've actually witnessed, you know.

"Why," said Dr. Harry Rigmire, from behind an uptilted cigar now, "it's a 1000-to-1 I'll walk out of the courtroom a free man."

Johnny Kendall considered.

"You may do that," said he.

Dr. Rigmire stared.

"You take a licking very coolly, don't you?"

Johnny Kendall smiled, shrugged, said: "I'm consoled by what a very respectable philosopher told me once."

"Indeed?"

"Yes. He remarked with quite a lot of feeling that men forge the weapons for their own destruction."

Dr. Harry Rigmire stared hard at the younger man.

Johnny Kendall nodded.

"I see it working out that way," he said. "One thing,

you've lost Geneva Carr to Earl Sawyer. I suppose it hurts your pride more than your heart, and with you that'd hurt more. And I'm not sure Mrs. Rigmire *can* claim that money now. But if she does get it, by the time *you* walk out of the courtroom, it'll be gone—by that time, Poonghee Sherwin will be sitting pretty in his underground fane.

"So what have you got to show for it, after all?"

He grinned wryly.

"It seems to me," said Johnny Kendall, "you take a licking pretty coolly yourself."

Dr. Harry Rigmire's face was expressionless. His face was utterly blank.

He picked up the cigar case and tucked it inside his coat.

His hand jerked out of the coat.

"Well, Kendall—!" he said, coming to his feet. His hand pointed. The gun was a short-barreled Bankers' Special; so short that the .38 muzzle was only fractionally in front of the ejector rod.

The door flew wide open.

Pop Capp stood there.

Pop was excited. His face was very nearly the color of his celluloid collar.

But his pyrostained fingers were entirely steady around the butt of his big, blued, Frontier model six-shooter.

"Now, Doc, you be careful!" said Pop Capp. "This is a filed gun, and it goes off easy. And it makes a considerably bigger hole than the gun you got, too."

He was right.

The .38, which had been a formidable weapon in its own right a moment ago, had now dwindled to pop-gun proportions compared to the heroic bore of the ancient Peacemaker.

It is given to few men to look into the muzzle of an old-style single action six-shooter without quailing; particularly when they are obliged to look over a shoulder to see one that is very nearly behind them.

It wasn't given to Dr. Harry Rigmire.

Stark-faced, his eyes the dull color of the grease smudge on cheekbone and turban, he let fall the Bankers' Special.

"After you pick that up, Johnny—" said Pop Capp— "I brought somebody along."

Johnny Kendall stared.

"Babette!"

XXIX

H<small>E WAS AMAZED. HE ASKED, "YOU MEAN JIM WAL-</small>lach and Frank Ellsworth figured out from those pictures—?"

Pop Capp said, "It wasn't that exactly. Wallach sent his anonymous threatening note to the police laboratory in Altamont. They found thumbprints inside the envelope flap.

"And," said Pop, "there seems to be a State law all bank cashiers have their prints on record."

"Great God!"

"It took Wallach awhile to make Wesley Clement admit it," said Babette Hazelle, "but it also seems I'd better keep my window shades pulled *all* the way down, even at three o'clock in the morning."

"Wesley Clement!"

Pop Capp said it was a thing. "You wouldn't expect the cashier of the Crestpeak State to own up to playing Peeping Tom with his opera glasses—even if what he saw proved Babette was fourteen miles from here when the murder happened!"

"He saw her—?"

"Twice that night," Pop said. "The first time about 10 P.M., which was when she took off that rayon dress that had the blood on it. And then again, at 3 A.M., when she went home with your negatives."

"Well," said Johnny Kendall, "it's good news—but I can't see why it took you so long to get here with it."

"Doc Dwyer was out on a case, and I waited for him up to the last minute," said Pop.

"But," Babette added, "that's not the main reason. Pop had a blow-out down the road. We thought we could walk faster than we could fix that."

And then she said something which was destined to remain in Pop Capp's memory, at least, longer than any other detail of the case. If he had only acted on her advice!

As he said to Johnny Kendall when Johnny Kendall was in Crestpeak the other day, on furlough from photographic duties with the Air Corps.

"You remember, Johnny, what she told me that night?"

Johnny remembered it very well.

"Pop," Babette said earnestly, "you'd just better get yourself four new tires on that jaloppy!"

www.ingramcontent.com/pod-product-compliance
Lightning Source LLC
Chambersburg PA
CBHW020225260626
47156CB00002B/536